ADDICTED

Charlotte Stein

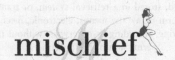

mischief

This novel is entirely a work of fiction.
The names, characters and incidents portrayed in it are
the work of the author's imagination. Any resemblance to
actual persons, living or dead, events or localities is
entirely coincidental.

Mischief
An imprint of HarperCollins*Publishers*
77–85 Fulham Palace Road,
Hammersmith, London W6 8JB

www.mischiefbooks.com

A Paperback Original 2013

First published in Great Britain in ebook format by
HarperCollins*Publishers* 2013

Copyright © Charlotte Stein 2013

Charlotte Stein asserts the moral right to
be identified as the author of this work

A catalogue record for this book is
available from the British Library

ISBN-13: 978 0 00 753332 9

Automatically produced by Atomik ePublisher from Easypress

Chapter One

The Master, by Kit Connor

I know how wicked I must look, all bound like this. He hasn't even used something decent like a length of rope or a nice scarf. He's used fat strips of red ribbon, and everywhere he's wrapped them I can feel their thick edges digging into my flesh. Can feel them turning me into something obscene – breasts pushed up and out by the presence of them laced beneath, eyes sightless behind scarlet silk.

Yet no matter how lewd I look – how ready to be used – he doesn't make a move towards me. I can hear his heavy footsteps against the glossy wooden floors of this expensive apartment, and occasionally there'll be another hint of him: the faint tang of his cologne.

But nothing substantial.

I don't get anything substantial until I hear the whisper of his breath, and have to wonder if that sound is slightly heavier than it would usually be. Do I look good enough to make my Master pant with anticipation, perhaps?

I doubt it, but find myself hoping anyway. I always hope, no matter how unlikely it is that he would show me the smallest sign of his own pleasure. He is like granite, my Master, he is a rock I cannot penetrate, and yet he moves me to do things I never thought I was capable of.

'Take your clothes off,' he had said to me, and I did it. I didn't even ask him to close the curtains over the broad glass-covered cityscape that I know lies behind him and in front of my bound form. We're high up here in this island of luxury – London is just a dot – but it's possible that someone could catch sight of me. Someone might look out of their high-rise window and see me across the city – a faint blur of naked skin, striped with red.

Though, alarmingly, the thought doesn't dampen my ardour. It enflames it instead. It makes me slick between my legs, to the point where I'm almost uncomfortable.

I think he knows it. He never seems surprised to find me wet and wanting, and he's even less surprised now when I break, quite suddenly.

Which seems unfair, because *I'm* surprised. I even shudder to hear myself say:

'Please touch me.'

Though I confess, it's the good kind of shudder. My sex swells, my body thrums, I *ache* to think of him in me. God, a hand on my breast would be so good right now – maybe rubbing one of my nipples ever so lightly, the way he so often does when I'm writhing and past the point of no return. That teasing, twisted look on his devil's face, as he works one stiff little point back and forth, back and forth.

Lord, I can't *stand* it. I can't, I can't – and then he goes and says:

'If you're a good girl, perhaps I will.'

And I can stand that even less. I want to scream at him that I'm not good, that I'll never be good, but the truth is

– he sees to the core of me. He knows the layer of restraint I've built up around myself; he's unearthed every hallmark of a buttoned-up, too-perfect princess.

And he won't be satisfied until he's stripped it all away.

I can almost hear him now, contemplating how best to ruin me. In fact, I'm sure the red ribbon blindfold has become somehow see-through, because I can nearly make him out in front of me. That firm, slanting jaw like something out of a magazine that doesn't exist – *Moody Men Monthly*, perhaps – and those eyes, both steely and shot through with tease.

He'll be wearing just his pristine shirt, by this point – suit jacket discarded – and, as he examines me, his left hand will toy with the cuff beneath his right.

Because it gives the proper look, I think. The look of a man of clear means and sharp desires, who never has to ask for a single thing in life because oh, people just *give it*. He points, he demands, he simply stands there with that one crisp cuff beneath his fingertips, and people *give it*.

Like me right now.

'Lean forward,' he says, and I do it. I lean forward as far as I can go without falling off the bed, thigh muscles straining, body protesting. I know I won't be able to last long like this – knelt and bent until I've made a rigid Z shape, for his pleasure – but I know just as deeply that he's going to make me stay like this for a long, long time.

And maybe, in the middle of me holding this position, he's going to reach up and get a fistful of my hair, and tug me until I feel something solid rub over my cheek.

Of course I know what it is. What sort of fool wouldn't? I didn't hear the rasp of a zipper, but that doesn't mean anything with him. I'm convinced he could get out of his clothes just by willing it to happen hard enough. Lord knows, it took nothing to get me out of mine.

It didn't even take anything to get me bound like this, straining, as his erection slides everywhere but the place I want it most. But he doesn't try to force me into taking him.

Instead he teases, and torments, and keeps me still with that hand in my hair, until *I'm* somehow the one who goes for him. I just part my lips and follow his slow thrusts, searching blindly for the thick head of his manhood.

And when I finally get a taste of him – just a little lick of something so good and solid – it feels like victory. I can ignore the mocking laugh he gets up, the moment I lose him again. I don't have to feel like a failure, or like something made weak.

Because that one little slip means *he* failed, not me. He was made weak enough to allow my mouth on him, my tongue on him, and that same feeling of sudden triumph surges through me the moment he lets it happen again.

His hand is so tight in my hair, so very tight, but somehow I manage to suck him into my mouth. And I do it so greedily, tongue lashing the underside of his thrilling rigidity, mouth wet and tight around his length.

For the first time, I long for my hands. He's just so big, that's the thing, and there's so much of him I can't reach no matter how greedy I'm being. Of course, I go to take him all – pushing hard against my gag reflex, making myself as relaxed as I possibly can to feel him pushing and shoving against the back of my throat – but I've never been good at it.

I have to pull back, and God, I get a startling thrill when he won't let me. He holds me there, mouth full of him, hand suddenly a fraction too tight in my hair.

'No,' he says. 'No, take it. Take it.'

And I don't even know what happens to me, once he

does so. I go tense, and then I go hot, and then I can't help moaning around a mouthful of him. I'm not choking – not exactly – but it feels like I'm about to at any second, and something about that is just …

Electric.

It's shameful, it's awful, but I can't deny it. If I wasn't so stuffed full of him I'd beg him for more, more – do it harder, be rougher. But the best thing about my Master is that he never crosses that point. He always knows how far to take me and no further, and yet still there are moments like this.

Moments when I forget my own name, and the ache between my legs spreads down through my thighs and up through my belly. I'm on the verge of orgasm, I think, but that seems utterly crazy without so much as a hand on me. I mean, I sometimes come the moment he touches me … but that's different.

This is … unnerving. I stir restlessly, burning muscles briefly forgotten, and the second I do he seems to know what it means. He laughs again, dark and throaty, then decides that what I need is an extra dose of torment.

Or, better put – he runs one finger over the curve of my shoulder, and down my arm.

I could scream. It's hardly a touch at all, and the meanness of it makes me react in a way I wouldn't usually. Usually I wait for his commands, but now I can't, I can't. For just a second I lose control, and squeeze my thighs together to get that good bloom of pleasure going.

But he doesn't do what I expect in response. Typically, if I give in and get greedy, he'll move away. Deny me even the slightest thing – like, say, the maddening taste of him.

This time, however, he doesn't let go of me. He doesn't step away, and leave me in a trembling, tortured mess on

5

the bed. He rocks into my mouth faster, instead, and then just as I think I've got away with it he tells me in a rough, filthy-sounding voice:

'Get those legs apart.'

I could cry. I think I do cry. My sex feels so tender, so swollen, that even shuffling around on the bed and spreading my thighs apart makes it twang with arousal. I'm so close to coming that someone could breathe on me and it would happen, but for now I have to make do with this:

Him thrusting jaggedly into my mouth. His hand in my hair, controlling the depth and length of each suck. And then, oh, God, then even worse than all of this – him telling me terrible things like *I'm never going to let you come. I'm going to leave you here, on this bed, bound and beautiful for my pleasure. And every day I'm going to come in here and use your mouth until I spurt, and you're going to love it.*

It's that last thought that settles in my mind and won't let go. Just the idea of him being this person who actually *can* will things to happen. Who can make me crazy at the mere thought of something, who can make me give in even when I'm sure I don't want to.

It lodges in the back of me somewhere, that thought. It makes my knees weak and my body lose all of that careful rigidity I've built up in this awkward position – and for a second I can't hold it. I almost collapse face-first into his groin, despite the hold he's got on me.

But it's OK, because he knows that too. He knows it and, without saying a word about my weakness, he rolls me over onto my back. He carries on, as though getting me into this new position was all his idea and has absolutely nothing to do with me reaching my limit.

Oh, I love him. I love him I love him I love him.

'Yes,' he says, and then I feel his hands between my legs. So sudden I can't process it, at first – or at least I can't until he strokes over my clit. After which my whole body loses the liquidity it had just fallen into, and stiffens quickly and easily.

'Yes, now,' he says, and I have maybe a second to wonder what he means, before great jerking jolts of pleasure go through me. They swell up from the clit he's barely touched, taking me out and through and all the way back again.

Though it doesn't stop there. The moment I feel the patter of him on my upturned face – the moment I hear him grunting like an animal – the pleasure washes through me again, a double wave of bliss that seems to barely have anything to do with the finger he's still got on my sex.

Though I have to say, the feel of him worrying it – just a little, a slick back and forth – is a glorious extra. It makes my legs jerk out straight and then sounds spill out of my mouth – long, rattling, dirty sorts of things.

Followed by words I don't mean to say.

'Uhhh, you're making me come,' I tell him, as though somehow he won't know. Like it's a thing that needs to be spelled out, in the world of me and my strange Master.

Which it may well be. He sure seems to appreciate it, after all – and he never appreciates anything. He's always aloof, always impervious to any pressure, but in this burning hot moment he puts a soothing hand in my hair, instead of a rough one. He strokes me, and says amazing things like 'Yes, yes, that's my girl.'

And I suppose I am – his girl, I mean. Though to know how I got there, you'd have to go back to the beginning.

Chapter Two

The first thing I hear after I've finished reading is my best friend's laughter. And the second thing I hear is more laughter – this time with actual tears streaming down her cheeks to accompany it. Apparently, my erotic masterpiece is amusing to her. More than amusing, in fact. After a second she holds a hand up, like she's begging me to stop the mirth.

It takes her a while to realise.

'Oh,' she says, as she wipes away the tears. 'Oh, you were serious? This is a serious start to a serious novel?'

I kind of wish it wasn't, now. But I plunge on, regardless. I mean, I read it with the intention of getting some feedback. It's probably best if I just brace myself and hear it.

'I know it needs work.'

'Oh, honey, I'm sorry,' she says, and I can tell she really is. She's a good friend, Lori. She's not the type to laugh because she's a horrid jealous cow – though really, what does she have to be jealous of? She's blonde, I'm not. She's tall, I'm not. She's interesting.

I am not.

Which is probably why I'm writing ridiculous stories about kinky things I'd never dare do. *She'd* probably dare do them,

9

when I really think about it. If she stopped finding them hilarious for five seconds.

'It just wasn't what I expected, that's all. I mean, the blindfold ... the businessman ... I didn't think you were capable of writing something like that.'

I flame red, then, thinking of the words I actually dared to speak aloud. How did I do that, again? Typically I can't even tell a sex partner that I'd like to kiss and cuddle, now. So this seems ... suddenly impossible. I've somehow made it impossible, after actually doing it.

'It was so *graphic*.'

Oh, God, it is. It was. What's wrong with me?

'And a little ...' She pauses, wincing. But it's OK, because I'm wincing right along with her. '... unrealistic.'

She clearly doesn't know that a word like that is a lifeline to me. She looks as though she's just murdered my grand-mother, but the second she says it this weird relief slides through my body. *Unrealistic* – I can handle that. Hell, she's probably right.

After all, what do I know about sex? Nothing. Less than nothing. Every sexual encounter I've ever had has occurred beneath the sheets, under a double layer of darkness. Once I started kissing some guy's elbow, thinking I'd found his cock. And as for the pleasure I've just described to her, in my twisted tale of kinky delights ...

Well, I guess that's disingenuous of me, at best. I should have written:

Sex for her was sort of like being vaccinated, by a big pink finger.

'You're not mad, are you?'

'No.'

'Because, you know, it's just ... well. People don't really

do those sorts of things, do they? In real life, sex has consequences. And there are all these issues, obviously ... especially for women.'

She's got a point. So why do I kind of wish she didn't? I remember being this gawky teenage girl, once, who truly believed in passion and pleasure and crazy thrills. There were no double duvets and fat finger vaccinations in her future, no way, no how. She was going to take sex by storm, and experience delights the likes of which the world had never seen.

Where did she go, exactly? How did I end up here, with these papers in my hand and the certainty that Lori is correct? People don't really blindfold each other, down here in mundane reality. And if they *did* manage to do a thing like that, it would probably end really badly. Someone would stumble into a chair, and accidentally fracture their jaw. Or maybe my kinky businessman would turn out to be a total asshole, who filmed everything on his camera-phone then put it all up on YouTube.

Are those the kinds of consequences she's talking about? Because I can absolutely see myself being on YouTube; for wanting something as simple as excitement. In fact, I can imagine worse, when I really put my mind to it.

Maybe he'll sell me to slave traders, and I'll end up in a sex factory – for ever being vaccinated, for the amusement of strangers.

'Here,' she says, and I know what's going to happen before she's even finished fishing through her wallet. She's finding a card for me, with the name of some expert on it. She did the same thing last year, when I told her I was afraid of spiders – she sent me to a wellness specialist, who made me touch a spider.

Which doesn't bode well for this particular scenario.

I can't imagine myself fingering a penis, to get over my need for more exciting sex. If anything, the penis fingering is only going to make me crazier – though of course I don't say that. Mainly because it's insane, but also because I suspect she's going to offer me something far more daunting.

'You want realism? You should try this on for size,' she says, then hands me a square of yellow construction paper with a terrible-sounding title emblazoned across its front. *Sexual Healing*, it says. As though Marvin Gaye is going to help lower my expectations and make me all normal again. 'It's a kind of therapy group for people with sexual … issues.'

Oh, God, there's that word again. *Issues*. And if I'm not mistaken, she seems to think that I have them. This isn't just a friendly word of advice to help me be more than a librarian.

This really *is* her way of making me touch a spider – only the other way around. She wants me to sit in a cold, probably clinical room, with people who think sex is a hideous nightmare. I'm going to come away even more depressed about the whole thing, and probably never do it again.

Is that the aim here? To make me never do it again?

'Lori, I really don't think I need to visit a sex issues group,' I try, but I already know it's too late. Her eyebrow is raised in that particular pointed way – the one that makes her look like a schoolteacher, who always knows what's best for me. And once it's up there, I simply can't finagle my way out.

The weight of her one eyebrow is like seven bags of sand, tied too tight around my neck. I'm being dragged down to God knows where, and there's really nothing I can do. I simply have to take the card, and hope for the best.

Even if the best is me signing up for a life in a nunnery.

* * *

The meeting isn't held where I thought it would be, in some sterile semi-hospital, set in the middle of endless green grounds. It's on Becker Street, right in the heart of the city. The front of it reminds me of an old abandoned warehouse, or maybe a crumbling town hall, and it's sandwiched between a barely surviving video store and a pizza place.

The flickering pink neon from the latter's window gives the dark, narrow building a tawdry air – and it's worse inside. Kind of homey, in one way. But worn and withered, in another. The big heating pipes that run along the hallway remind me of school, as does the wrought-iron banister that lines the staircase – the one that leads to God only knows where. When I dare to duck my head and look up those stone steps, all I can see is the fuzzy, faded darkness that all old buildings seem to have.

And just past the stairs to hell is a noticeboard, which brings me no more comfort. The signs tacked to the cork surface are gaudy, even jaunty, but the things written on them are not. *Anger Management*, the first one says. Followed by *Violent Outbursts, Night Terrors*, and my personal favourite: *Inexplicable Rages*.

As opposed to the totally explicable ones, I suppose, where the situation warranted you throwing a chair across a room before tearing out all of your own hair.

What exactly have I gotten myself into here? I don't have night terrors or angry outbursts – and, more importantly, I don't have sex issues either. What am I supposed to say, if everyone starts going into their deepest, darkest fears and problems? Lori made it sound quite light and fun, but this isn't a light and fun sort of place.

This is the sort of place where I'm going to be exposed as a horrible fraud, who preys on the issues of others. It will

13

come to my turn and I'll have to say the only thing I can: *One time Martin McAllister accidentally slipped his cock in my bum a bit, when aiming for my vagina. And then he expected me to be mortified, only I wasn't!*

God help me, I wasn't.

And then maybe I'll cry a little, or wring my hands, just to make the whole thing more convincing. Though I can already tell it's not going to be. My sensible half is laughing at my ridiculous attempts at sexual verisimilitude, and even if she wasn't I'd be aware of how silly I am. I have to go, now, before others find me out. I have to Google sex and authenticity instead of making any attempts at actual research – after all, that's what most authors do, isn't it? Scour Wikipedia for a helping hand?

But of course it's already too late. I can see some kindly aunt-type standing by the door to the main hall, and as I do my best to slink past her, she hooks my arm. She actually hooks my arm, like she just knew I was trying to make my escape.

And once I've looked her in the eye, I know I'm not going anywhere. There's just nothing I can convincingly say to this woman, to make a clean getaway. She has the friendly, open face of some beloved relative I don't actually have, and, when she speaks, things only get worse for me.

She has a Scottish accent. A kindly, whisky-biscuit Scottish accent. And she uses that accent to say the following:

'Are you a little bit nervous, petal? Don't be. Come on in, and have a cake.'

Which is quite possibly the most welcoming set of words I've ever heard. It started with an acknowledgement of my main weakness – nerves – before launching into the kind of epithet I've always wanted. And to finish, she offered me a cake.

A *cake*.

She gave it to me with both barrels, and doesn't even know it.

'Well, maybe I can ... sort of ... I don't know ...' I hear myself saying, as she leads me into a hall that time forgot. Honestly, for a second I expect my old headmaster to come bouncing over the trampoline-like wooden floors towards me – which only makes things worse.

I can't lie in front of my old headmaster. I can't even lie in front of this lady. She asks me what my name is, and instead of offering the fake one I thought up for this very occasion, I go with the real deal. *Kit*, I say, and then she writes it on the sticker in her hand and plasters it to my right boob.

Now I have to be me, for all eternity.

'You just take a seat when you're ready, Kit,' she says, but the sight of that prison-like circle of plastic chairs makes me dizzy. I try the fold-out table of orange squash and home-baked treats, instead, only to find I've forgotten how to eat. My hand shakes as I raise a square of ill-gotten ginger cake to my mouth, and I end up putting it back down.

But that just makes me look like some nervous first-timer. A willowy woman in seventeen layers of lovely clothes pats me on the back, and tells me everything will be fine. 'Just share your inner self,' she says, as though my inner self could be so easily persuaded. I can't even tell someone on the subway that they're standing on my foot, let alone this.

Because, oh, *this* is something else.

The guy in the tweed with the nice professor's face – he can't stop masturbating. He masturbates so often that I find myself doing the maths in my head, but once I have I'm no less in awe. His weekly total is more than my yearly one. In fact, if I divide the four and carry the one, it's more than

I've ever masturbated in my entire life. I don't even know how he's functioning, in all honesty. I don't even know how someone can physically crave something that much ... something so small and ordinary and *nothing*. God, when I do it – it's nothing.

But when he describes it ...

'It's a rush,' he says. As though it's some new drug I wasn't aware of. And then even more thrilling: 'It's a rush to think I might get caught. I do it in my office, sometimes, with the door unlocked, half hoping someone will walk in.'

And once he's done, all I can think of is my old university professor, Dr McCaffrey. Dr McCaffrey, with those leather patches on his elbows and his pipe and his neatly parted hair. And most of all those steel-grey eyes of his, surveying the study hall with a kind of disaffection.

Did he have a secret life like this, behind the cold façade? Did he imagine keeping students behind after lectures – students more lovely than me, obviously – before offering them something strictly prohibited in the university handbook?

Bend over, he says in my head, and then he raises that pointer of his, about a second before I snap back to reality.

God, Lori's right. My attitude to sex *is* weird. They're talking about their problems, and I'm in the middle of some crazy fantasy featuring a teacher I once had. I'm imagining what it's like to be this consumed by sex, to be this nuts about it. The woman on my right has a ritual, for fuck's sake. An actual *ritual*.

She goes to the same bar every Saturday night, and picks up a dark-haired man – preferably with a moustache. And then she takes him back to her apartment, puts a collar on him and makes him stumble around her living room like a dog.

My Saturday-night ritual consists of me deciding whether

to wear pyjamas or a nightie to bed. Is a jam sandwich a good idea, after ten-thirty? Or will I wake up feeling nauseated and too thirsty? Chances are I'll be thirsty. And then I'll drink half a pint of lemonade and need to pee at six in the morning – it's a whole big thing, and far too much hassle.

Better that I don't have the jam sandwich.

Yeah, that's right. She has trouble fighting her urge to have wild and anonymous sex. I have trouble deciding about preserves and buttered bread. I'm ashamed of my attitude to late-night snacks. If I needed any further proof that I shouldn't be here ... that I should feel guilty about peeping in on their private feelings ... this would be it.

I mean, these people are really hurting, about actual things. They're all freaked out by their obsessions and unsure of what to do next – all of them are. Every last one of them, down to the girl who can't even bring herself to say the word 'vagina' and the man who's never so much as shaken a woman's hand.

I don't belong here.

And neither does that guy on the other side of the circle.

I don't know how I missed him, at first. He's completely unmissable, in every way possible. He's like a sore thumb in a room full of perfectly healthy fingers, though I really don't think I can be blamed for overlooking him. I was just so engrossed in other people's sad tales and my own rampaging guilt that I didn't pay any attention to the one other person in the room who isn't real. Maybe I thought he was a mirror on the other side of the circle, reflecting me.

Because it's obvious he is. He isn't slumped in his chair, defeated, or full with celebration of some small victory over sex. He doesn't look the least bit sad or ashamed about anything. His arms are folded jauntily over his chest, and I immediately notice two things because of this:

First, his arms and his general chest area are absolutely enormous. They're so enormous that they briefly blot out all light in the universe, and cause a cataclysm the likes of which the world has never known.

And:

Those earth-destroying arms are covered in tattoos.

Though maybe all of that is just a slight exaggeration. He's so incredible-looking I briefly hallucinate, and imagine him pounding downtown Los Angeles with his immense fists. He's already taken root in my brain, and I don't even know how. His face just exerts some kind of gravitational pull, and the moment I make the mistake of looking I'm caught for ever in his orbit.

I can't explain it. Usually I barely register men at all, and I certainly don't find myself engrossed in the way they look. Guys that women call attractive – footballers and rugby players and other rugged examples of extreme manhood – I barely pay attention to. I'd kind of accepted that my responses were mostly dead, in terms of actual men in real life.

But this guy … oh, this guy. I don't even know what it is about him, but the moment his sultry blue gaze locks with mine something happens inside me. That dead thing rises from the grave and starts stumbling around, looking for loins. I'm lost, I think, I'm totally lost. I can't even stop staring at him, despite all of my best efforts.

I glance at the pictures some kids have drawn on the opposite wall. I pretend my fingernails are suddenly as fascinating as the riddle of the Incas – but it's all in vain. I end up taking in everything about him, whether I want to or not. I even take in the parts that are completely unremarkable, like his shortish dark hair, unstyled and lazy-looking. Or that tattered

T-shirt he's wearing, pulled taut across his unbearably broad chest, and those jeans that seem similarly thin and ready to expose him at any moment. His thighs look like ham hocks beneath the material, thick and juicy, but that's not what draws my eyes the most out of everything he's wearing.

His flip-flops do. His ridiculous flip-flops – so casual in a room of neatly tied and laced shoes. Everyone else is trying like mad to contain themselves, to be respectable and normal and totally OK.

Whereas he clearly doesn't care. He's half-smiling before he's even started talking, with a mouth so wicked I'm afraid seeing it might constitute a sin. His lower lip is as plump as an overripe fruit, and, when he thinks no one's looking, he licks it. He licks it in a way that makes my body respond – like some secret sex sign I didn't even know existed.

Suck me right here, that sign says, and the worst of it is … I want to. I'd crawl across deserts to take that lower lip in my mouth. I'd renounce my life of jam sandwiches and terrible sitcoms for one kiss from a pout like that.

Because it is kind of a pout. His face is this insane mixture of rough masculinity and sensuous something-else, and the battle between the two is so engaging you just have to look. He's covered in stubble, of course, and his strong nose is just a touch too big for his face. His eyebrows are thick, dark – almost oppressive, in fact.

But then they're paired with the longest, blackest, loveliest eyelashes I've ever seen on a man. He shuts his eyes briefly and they fan over his cheeks like something a geisha girl would carry. And then he opens them, and that's no better either. I don't know if the blue is enhanced by the dark rings around them, or if his gaze is just naturally like this – naturally heavy, naturally smoke-screened, naturally hypnotic.

But either way I don't suppose it matters.

He knows I'm looking, now. That little half-smile has quirked up a quarter of an inch, to see me falling all over myself – because he's definitely that kind of man, I can tell. He's the kind who thinks every girl is head over heels in love with him, to the point where he has to be a jerk just to get them to look the other way. The kind that shoulders past lesser people in bars, and strolls around town centres with his top off. I bet he goes on holiday with Club 18-30, even though he's clearly over that, and when he returns he talks to everyone about larging it and getting his end away.

Yeah, I've got his number.

Until he speaks, and then I don't know what I've got.

'Yeah, so I'm Dillon. Dillon Holt,' he says, like he's introducing himself at a barbecue. You got any hotdogs, dude? I think, deliriously, before he plunges into the opposite world everyone else is in. There's not a hint of discomfort in his voice, when he says: 'I'd say I've slept with quite a substantial number of women – maybe a hundred?'

I think I can see him counting, in his head.

'Maybe more like two hundred, huh?'

And to make matters worse, his accent isn't some buttoned-up English thing, layered with a thousand years of repression. He's American, I think, and his voice has that breezy, open, friendly quality to it that draws you in immediately. It makes you feel comfortable, even though you probably shouldn't be.

I should still be guilty, and ashamed of myself.

But he makes short work of that.

'Big girls, little girls, dark-haired, blonde, burgundy ... girls with weird bits, girls who don't know how to dress – I'm not fussy. I'll take all comers.'

Oh, God, he's not fussy. He'll take all comers! Which

probably shouldn't seem like a good thing, here. And a second later, he seems to twig to that.

He clears his throat, and starts again.

'I mean ... uh ... I used to take all comers, until I realised that was really bad and ... uh ... unhealthy for me, as a person, and also it ... you know. Negatively affects those around me in terrible, terrible ways.'

Is he reading this out of a handbook? I kind of feel like he's reading this out of handbook. He picked it up on his way in, and is now awkwardly fudging his way through the spiel he thinks he ought to give.

'I've gotten myself into some really bad situations – on planes, on trains, in automobiles. And this one time, on a beach. Though in my defence, that last one wasn't really my fault. I missed the sign that said, "You're now wandering off the nudist part," and after that I was just some guy on a beach with my nadgers out.'

Oh, Lord, I love the way he says nadgers. I love the way he says planes, trains and automobiles, like the pornographic version of a much-loved John Candy movie. It makes me realise that he's not my reflection at all. He's what my reflection *would* be, if I was without shame or any kind of nervousness. If I didn't feel guilty about anything, and instead just reeled off the truth.

Which he continues to, in great and varied detail.

'I've been arrested a couple of times for things like that – in changing rooms, and so on and so forth. I guess I'm just really sort of into being naked, you know? And that ... uh ... has gotten me into trouble a few times. My ex-girlfriend's mom once caught me in her greenhouse without any clothes on – maybe 'cause I was kind of communing with nature, or something else that probably isn't true. And then I, ahem, communed with her and her daughter.' He pauses, and I know – I *know* – he's trying not to laugh. About a second before he adds: 'And their friend Alan.'

Alan. Did he say *Alan*? Oh, Jesus, I think he did. I think he'd be raising both eyebrows and grinning devilishly, now, if he thought he could get away with it.

But everyone is nodding so sympathetically, and the Scottish woman is telling him that she's using crystals to de-cloud his sexual aura, so really he can't do anything of the sort. He can't do anything but continue into what I can only describe as bragging, now. He's bloody bragging, I swear to God.

'And then there's the reason why I'm here – I went over to see a couple of friends of mine, a couple of girls. Not girls I was screwing around with, or anything. They just said, "Oh, come around, Dillon,' so I did. I came around thinking I'd maybe get a sandwich – and God knows I can never say no to a sandwich. I'd probably go to Hitler's house if I thought I'd get some pastrami between two slices of bread, so you know. It's not like I can be blamed, right?'

It's OK, Dillon. I totally understand your predicament. I'd be round Hitler's house with you, munching on a slice of wholemeal slathered in strawberry conserve.

'I mean, how was I to know one of them was going to take her top off? She just did it right out of the blue, halfway through the cheese and pickle she'd made me. I've literally got it hanging out of my mouth, and her friend's in the middle of totally ordinary conversation about some British sport I don't understand – then bam. Naked time.'

I get the impression that naked time kind of happens to him a lot. Maybe because his thousand-yard stare of utter sex just melts the clothes right off women's bodies.

Though, to his credit, he actually doesn't seem smug about any of this. If I was going to identify his expression, right now, I'd probably call it bemused and/or amazed. As though sex is some facehugger that sneaks up on him in the night. Vaginas just attach themselves to his face, before he knows where he is.

'And then the other friend takes her top off, too. I'm just sat there eating my sandwich, with a naked girl on either side of me. I mean, what am I supposed to do here?'

Not sound like you're actually asking, I think, but of course I can't say that.

Everyone's completely engrossed by what he's saying – even the girl who hates the word 'vagina'. In fact, she looks almost as giddy as I feel. She's vicariously living through Dillon Holt, and I don't blame her in the slightest. In fact, I feel slightly better about my own desperate need to hear more.

'So I kiss one,' he says, and, oh, I can almost see it. I bet she was tall and blonde, like Lori, and in my head, when he presses his mouth to hers, she dissolves under the pressure. Her lips part to invite him onward, to get more of that softness pressing and working against her – and then maybe after a while some of that slippery, sinful tongue. I bet he's forceful, when he gets going. I bet he's lewd about it, thrusting in a way that mimics the rhythm he'd use later on … and ohhhh God.

All of this from imagining a kiss?

Clearly I'm going to pass out, if he goes any further.

'And she gets all squirmy, the way a girl gets when she's really excited, you know?'

Oh, Lord, he's going further. And he's talking about the way girls get, as though he's really, really experienced in that field. He's a Professor of Lady Arousal, and now he's going to rub that fact right in my face.

The last guy I dated thought clitoris was an island off the coast of Greece.

'Then the other girl starts getting kind of irritated that I'm paying the first one the most attention, and she wants a kiss too. I couldn't very well say *no*. So I give her one – only she's not satisfied with the usual, polite, cheese-sandwich-and-a-cup-of-tea sort of peck. Yeah, she's kind of wanting the same thing, only lower down. And by this point, I really want to go lower down. I'll say it right now – I *love* eating pussy. I could eat pussy all day every day until the end of time, just to get a girl all flushed the way she gets, and hear those little soft, desperate moans or maybe even the loud, aggressive ones ... I don't mind. Pull my hair, call me names, sit on my face, I'll take it and come back for more, I swear I –'

He cuts himself off here, but it's fairly obvious why. It's kind of like seeing someone wave a beer around at a meeting of alcoholics anonymous. Or a meeting of people who can't drink, because drink makes them insanely nervous. The group is split between those who've gorged themselves to breaking point, and those who are starving in the desert.

And I don't know who it's worse for.

Me, I think, me, though I can't say why. Because he's so casual about it? Because it's so easy for him? He makes sex sound like all the tales I've always wanted to tell, instead of the reality it usually is. *This* is the reality, I know – people who want to heal and transcend and eventually become ...

What he is.

Happy.

Lord, he's *so* happy.

'But obviously I realise the detrimental effect this unhealthy pussy-eating obsession has on my psyche.'

He doesn't realise that at all, and we know it. Even the Scottish lady knows it. She's just as caught up in his tale as everyone else, cheeks pink and eyes bright with that one idea he represents. That one great, good idea that she actually promotes: sex should be something exciting and positive and good.

'Well, I don't know about that, Dillon,' she says, and when she does her voice flutters, the way I imagine mine would if I was talking to someone like him. And she's toying with the crystal on the chain around her neck in this very specific sort of manner, too – a very amusing manner. I want to giggle hysterically, but I rein it in just in time to hear him say this:

'OK, maybe the love of oral sex isn't so bad. But jumping out of a second-floor window when one of the girls' husbands comes home – just in time to see his wife riding me like a bronco while her friend smothers me on the other end ... yeah, that's probably not that cool. You should have seen my knees, man! Skinned them all the way to the bone. Had to walk into the emergency room wearing a cardboard box; so it really wasn't a surprise when the nurse who patched me up sent me here.'

I love the fact that he's so concerned about his knees. And that he jumped out of a window, naked. I know probably I shouldn't, but I do just the same. In fact I think I look as moony as the Scottish lady does, if his amused expression is anything to go by. He's levelling it right at me, those blue eyes suddenly as sparky as someone's finger in a socket.

And he doesn't leave off – not even after she's turned her attention my way.

'We have another new member of the group today,' she says, and like an idiot I glance around, searching for this other person. Maybe they're even more handsome and beguiling than Dillon Holt, and I can focus all of my faint-heartedness on them instead.

Only then I realise. I realise about a second before she says my name.

'Kit.'

I wish I'd given her a fake one. I could have got an extra thirty seconds' respite out of her calling for a Cassandra who doesn't actually exist.

'Oh. Yeah,' I say, but those two non-words don't buy me any time. I have to decide now what I'm going to go with: shy incompetent or wild party girl?

Judging by his expression, he expects the former.

Which is probably why I go with the latter. I paint a vague picture of Kit the lonely one-night-stand addict, hopping nightly from bar to bar in the hopes of making some connection. And though it kind of sounds like hokum, while I'm saying it, that last word leaves me feeling ... I don't know. Unsettled?

I find myself thinking back over my life, sifting through various relationships and friendships ... things that should have stood me in better stead than trawling night spots for tail. But really, when I consider it ... when have I ever connected with anyone?

I haven't. And that slight sinking of his oh-so-amused expression confirms that much. He can see it in me, I think. He can tell that I'm being honest, in some tiny way – that I've just exposed a part of myself I didn't want to give.

And now he's sad for me.

Christ.

'I can't really say any more,' I say, to the circle. At which, they all nod sympathetically and give me reassuring pats on the back, and the kindly Scottish aunt says, 'Well, why don't we move on to some healing, wholesome one-on-one time?'

I'm almost relieved, in the few precious moments before I realise what that means. In fact, I make it all the way over to the squash and cake table, before it comes to me. I've got a cookie in my hand and I'm thinking, Hey, at least I've got some kind of epiphany out of this. Maybe I can ask Tom from the library out, the next time he rubs against me between the stacks. That'll be some kind of connection, all right. Or at least it'll prove I'm open to connections.

And then I see him, out of the corner of my eye. I see Dillon Holt, strolling towards me, in a way that makes me want to glance over my shoulder. You know, just in case there's a sexier, wilder sort of chick behind me, and she's actually the one he's aiming for.

This imaginary woman has to be the one he's aiming for. Right?

Only I don't think I'm right at all. The kindly Scottish aunt said 'one-on-one time', and this obviously does not mean what it did in my head thirty seconds ago. My head thought she was suggesting we have a deep, meaningful discussion with a slice of ginger cake, but I can see now that I was wrong.

'That's right,' she calls out, over the mostly paired-up room. 'Hold your partner in your arms, and show them that you're there for them.'

And then it clicks in my mind. Dillon is coming over here because I'm the person he wants to hug. He was touched by my lack of any kind of connection with fellow human beings, and is reaching out in his own lunkish way. He wants to show me it's OK – but unfortunately, he wants to show me it's OK by *putting his massive arms around me*.

I can't have that. There's a toilet somewhere beyond the double doors into this hall, and I need to feign interest in that place immediately. But how best to do it? If I raise my hand and ask for a bathroom pass, I'm going to look like the biggest fool on the planet. And if I don't ask, then it's not going to be clear what I'm doing. When he gets over here I won't be able to politely excuse myself, and I'll just have to walk away.

He'll think I'm an ass. He's going to think I'm an ass. And by the time I'm finished panicking over what an ass I am, it's far too late. He's already upon me – and, Jesus, he's even bigger than he'd seemed across the circle. He has to be at least six foot two, if not more. His shoulders are so immense I can't see the ends of them, once my eyeline is level with his chest.

You can't even call what he does standing. It's more like *looming*. I'm being loomed over by the most handsome man I've ever seen in real life, and once he's there I don't have a chance of escaping. It would take me seven years just to run from his left bicep to the tips of his fingers – though running isn't even an option. The moment I think of it – like a desperate light bulb going off in my panicky head – he leans down and enfolds me in those enormous arms.

He *enfolds* me. I didn't even know I could *be* enfolded. I'm not sure what to do, once it's happening. My own arms go really stiff and sort of stick out on either side of his body, and I forget to turn my head when his chest angles down – which just leads to a kind of awkward face-mashing against his left pectoral muscle.

Though, in my defence, I'm not used to men having something in that place. Typically it's just skin and chest hair, or maybe gigantic pillows of extra sweaters. Some of the guys I've dated weren't really keen on hugging full stop, so there's no helpful comparison there.

This guy hugs like his life depends on it. He hugs me so warmly that something embarrassing starts happening in my general eye area – something that stings a bit and mortifies me to my very soul. Apparently I'm so starved of affection I tear up when a random bloke squeezes me a bit.

I'm like a tube of toothpaste that's never been used. My destiny in life – to have people compress me – has not been fulfilled.

Until now.

He has a hand on my back, and he's kind of rubbing it up and down. Not in a sexual manner, you understand. Just in a nice, soothing, warm sort of way. He's so full of heat that he's got a ton of it to spare, and he just hands it around to random strangers, whenever the mood takes him. He can afford to, after all.

Women hurl themselves at him while he's eating a cheese sandwich. He's not going to nearly cry because he's being hugged – but I think he understands that I might.

'Yeah, that's nice, right?' he says, and I just sort of nod helplessly. I don't want to; because if it turns out that he is an arrogant ass then this is only going to make him worse.

But I just can't do anything else. He feels *incredible*. And he smells much, much better than I thought he would, when he was sat all the way over there like some half side of beef. I thought he'd have a musky tang, but mostly he's made up of shampoo and fabric softener. He's like a big pile of laundry, fresh out of the drier – and I don't mind admitting that I kind of want to bury my face in him.

In fact, I'm almost comfortable enough to do that, by this point. My limbs have gone all loose and lax, and I'm pretty close to returning the favour. All I have to do is make a loop around his broad back, then squeeze gently.

Seems simple.

And then he whispers one word, in my ear. One shocking word that makes my hair almost stand on end.

'Faker,' he says.

Chapter Three

I know he's behind me. It's like his presence is pressing against the fabric of the universe, and I'm forced to notice it whether I want to or not. Plus … you know. I can also actually *see* him in the flat-black gaze of the shop windows across the street. He's about ten paces back, hands stuffed deep into the pockets of the hoodie he's put on.

I'll admit: I kind of expected him to brave the elements in just that ridiculous T-shirt. But it makes him more human to see him with some layers on. He's not some sexual superhero, swinging through the November-washed streets in just his undercrackers.

Even he has a line of normalcy drawn in the sand of his insides.

It's just that this line includes following me – because come on, now. He totally is. I stop when I get to the window of a newsagent's and pretend to be examining a sign for someone's missing cat, just to see if he'll stop too. And when he does, it couldn't be more obvious that he's only doing so because I did. He has to feign interest in the contents of a store that sells orthopaedic trusses, for God's sake.

I almost want to shout back at him that he'd look great in a girdle.

31

But I refrain. Jokey comments about his gut-restraining needs will only encourage him – and after I did so well to evade him back at the hall. Out here, I'm never going to get away with declaring loudly that I need a wee. There's no one here to frown at him for stopping me visiting the toilet.

He had to let me go, then. He doesn't have to let me go now.

Unless this isn't actually a thing – which could be the case. Maybe I'm just imagining him all hot on my trail, ready to take me down for the terrible crime of sex-addiction fakery.

'Hey, Kit – wait up!'

Or maybe not.

I try walking faster, but to no avail. You can't block out sound by moving your feet more rapidly – and even you could, he'll soon be close enough for me to read his lips. Two of his strides make up seventeen of mine, and he makes short work of the distance between us. In fact, I'm starting to wonder if his speed and persistence mean something else.

Maybe he *kills* people for faking sex addiction. He's the fabled Fake Sex Addiction Killer, and I'm about to be horribly offed in the doorway of a Burger King.

'This is a *really* long way around to the bathroom,' he says, which at least reassures me on the murdering front. If not the *anything else* front. He's going to want to have a discussion, now, about that one word he whispered, and I am not at all prepared for it.

I didn't bring my conversational shotgun.

'Are the facilities not seven streets down? Oh, that's pretty foolish of me. Well – I'm here now. Might as well keep going. Goodnight, Dillon!'

I say 'Goodnight, Dillon' far too hysterically. Even I know that, and I'm the person who never realises when I'm being

32

hysterical. I just discover that *Masterchef* didn't record and then hurl the remote control through the television.

'Hey – you remembered my name.'

I don't look at him when he speaks. Sensing the weight of those beautiful eyes on the side of my face is enough. I feel like I'm basking in the light and heat of some sun from a distant galaxy, where everything is beautiful and nothing hurts.

'I think anyone would remember your name.'

'Huh. Really? Why's that, then?'

Because you delivered a ten-page essay to the class: Why I Like Oral Sex, *by Dillon Holt. Because you look like the picture they put under the word 'memorable' in the dictionary. Because of a million things, a billion things, all of which cannot be said by someone like me.*

'Because you went to a sexual healing group to *brag*,' I say, finally – though I immediately regret it. It's the only answer I had in my head that doesn't feel true, and now I've slathered it all over him. He's going to nail me for it, I know.

And he does. He just does it with more gentleness than I expect. He actually sounds as light as air and like he's half-laughing when he says:

'Is that better or worse than going to a sexual healing group with a fake sex addiction?'

'I didn't fake anything.'

'Oh, honey. Come on. Nuns could have told you that you were faking. I've heard more convincing tales of sexual excess from my elderly grandfather.'

Christ, I *knew* I shouldn't have said that thing about the leather miniskirt. I bet true sexual adventurers haven't worn leather miniskirts since 1982. And besides ... he's got to know what that would look like on me. I couldn't land a fish in something that showed my thighs – never mind a man.

It's no wonder he's sceptical.

Though, lucky for me, he doesn't continue this line of questioning. I'm already cracking under the pressure, and he's barely begun his cross-examination. Thank God he changes the subject, to something even worse.

'Did it really seem like I was bragging?'

I have to look at him then. That note of sincerity in his voice kind of makes me do it – but his expression doesn't contradict what he's saying. He's almost wincing, with one thumbnail caught between his teeth. As though he truly didn't realise how he was coming across. He just said what he was feeling – in the exact way he does now, while I'm all naked and unprepared.

'Guess it did, huh?' He shakes his head. 'Really didn't mean it that way. Just never revealed stuff like that before … kind of felt like I was talking about someone else's life. But nope – that's me. The guy who ran to a hospital wearing a cardboard box.'

He sounds rueful, now, and it makes me wonder: was he really aiming his amusement at the whole idea of sexual healing? Or was he laughing at himself, for being such a fool?

'But enough about me. What about you? What made you fake being a sex addict?'

Shame, I think, but I can't say that.

So it shocks me when he does it instead.

'You embarrassed about how you really are?'

'No.'

Yes.

'You don't have to be – there's no crime in being a little shy. Is that why you went there in the first place? To maybe get you out of your own shell for a while?'

For a second I'm too stunned to speak. How does he get something like that? It isn't even the actual reason, and yet somehow it feels more real than anything I tell him next. I make my voice strong and firm, and I go with the party line. But inside I'm still that fumbling fool who couldn't even hug a man properly.

'I'm doing research for the book,' I say, and he buys it. Why wouldn't he? I bought it, and I'm the one living this life. I believed it right up until the moment he called me out, and if possible I'm going to keep doing so.

I'm not timid and tentative and unable to look him in the eye.

I'm Kit Connor, sultry sex bomb. Who flushes red when he says:

'A dirty book?'

'Yes.'

'About insane braggarts like me?'

'No,' I say, but there's another version of that answer in my head.

Yes. Yes. I could devote an entire book to you. I could tell tales of your eyes for ever, and never stop writing lines about the laundry-sweet scent of your amazing skin. You, Dillon Holt, are all the things I've always wanted as inspiration, and never quite found in anything but fantasy land.

Thank God I don't go with it. My head sounds like a drooling moron.

'You've gone all quiet.'

Because I'm busy being mortified over things I didn't actually say aloud. That's how big my capacity for embarrassment is: I go all red over non-existent gushing about hot guys.

'I'm just thinking.'

'About what?'

Oh, now I'm in trouble. Why did I lead him down this path? Now I've got to come up with an actual reason for my sudden lapse into silence.

'About why you were really there. You know, if it wasn't about you being an insane braggart. Which I don't believe it was, by the way.'

There. Perfect.

Or it would have been, if he didn't take my words as his cue to start walking backwards right in front of me. Now I'm all boxed in, and even worse – I have to look at his gorgeous face, while I attempt to lie. This just isn't going to go well for me. Everywhere I look, there's more of him. He's kind of hunching his shoulders against the cold, and they're *still* taking up my entire world.

And now he's saying things. Revealing, warm sorts of things.

'I guess I just wanted to find out why I feel this way.'

Oh, Lord. He's talking about feelings. He's looking at me with those eyes and talking about feelings. Shouldn't a guy like him be mashing a beer can to his head while mooning the Prime Minister? I'm sure that should be his MO.

But apparently it's not.

'And how do you feel?' I ask, still expecting something stupid. *I feel like lighting my own farts*, he'll say, and then he'll snort and probably run off to find some guy to punch. I'll see him on an episode of *Street Cops* two months from now, and never regret jumping over a hedge to escape him.

Though all of that nonsense just makes it more of a shock when he answers:

'Empty.'

Man, does he ever have a way with his single words. That whispered 'Faker' made my pulse race; now my heart sinks all the way through my body and right out onto the street. I can't speak for the longest time, and when I finally do it's not about anything useful. It's all general and blasé, despite the very specific echo I've got inside of me.

'Hate to break it to you, but I think everyone feels that way,' I say, while the echo tells the truth: *Especially me,* it says. *I'm so hollow you could fill me with helium and float me up to Mars.*

Which is a depressing thought, when you really think about it. I'm almost glad when he flicks the switch from serious to silly again – despite the topic he raises.

'Even fakers?'

'Are you seriously bringing that up again? I just wanted to … learn about sex things. I just wanted to make my work more … real.'

He nods, sagely.

'Ah, yes. Sex things. I believe that is the technical term.'

'Shut up,' I say, and come dangerously close to batting him playfully when I do.

'Why, when we're so close to a breakthrough, professor? I really wanted to discuss my pee-pee and your yoohoo.'

I give him a withering look.

'I don't call them that.'

'Are you sure? Maybe *you* can't say "vagina" either.'

'I can absolutely say … that word.'

He hoots with laughter to hear me evade it, but there's nothing I can do. Somehow the word just won't come out in his presence, no matter how much I want to prove him wrong.

'Yeah, it definitely seems that way.'

'Hey – I'm trying to write a book. Not talk dirty to you.'

'Does the *book* have a vagina in it?'

'Of course it does.'

'Are you sure?'

'Well … maybe I don't exactly call it *that*. I mean, it's not a particularly sexy word.'

I realise a second too late that it's the wrong thing to say. I've added a Y to the end of sex, and now my writing is no longer the biology textbook I know he was thinking about. He called me Professor, and talked about technical terms – but I've lost all that now.

'Oh-ho-ho,' he says, as my dignity disappears down the drain. 'So I guess it's not just a dry treatise on the benefits of having one?'

Is it weird that I like him using the word 'treatise'? Because I totally do. I like how heavy and solid he seems, while all of this too-fast talk rattles out of his mouth. I can't even keep up with most of it, despite the immense effort I'm putting in.

'Having one of what?'

See? That's real effort, there. I'm terrified of the answer, but I'm still asking the question.

'A *vagina*. Were you really that mystified there, or are you actually not sure?'

'Sure about *what*?'

Goddamn, he needs to finish his sentences.

'About the benefits of having a vagina.'

'Look – I know the benefits, OK?'

I totally don't. Currently it feels like an angry animal that wants to eat him, between my legs. That can't be a benefit, can it?

'You sure?'

'Yes.'

'Because I can help you out in that area, if you were a little shaky on the many and varied advantages to having a yoohoo.'

38

He's like a used-car salesman. Who sells lady bits.

'I don't need your help anywhere near my area, thanks.'

'Ooh, baby, stop, that almost sounded like a proposition.'

'What? It did not.'

'You're getting me so hot, I swear.'

Of course, I realise here that he's teasing me. So it's quite alarming to feel a kick somewhere lowdown, in that long-dormant area between my legs. He just fakes excitement, and apparently I go nuts. The angry beast rears its head, and starts searching for manflesh.

'I didn't ... I didn't even say anything, I –'

'I'm just messing with you, Kitty-cat. When I said "area", I meant the book. I meant I could help you with your *book*.'

Is he being serious now? It's so hard to tell with those madly expressive eyebrows of his. And that mouth – it's always twisted into the cheekiest little smirk. He'd never be able to deliver someone's eulogy. Everyone would think he was amused by some guy's tragic death.

'I really don't need help.'

Only I do, oh, God, I do, I know I do. I couldn't say 'vagina' in front of someone so handsome, and now I've just shooed him away from my 'area'. He didn't even *mean* 'area' in that manner. He meant something else, and my nineteenth-century brain just got itself all into a tizz. I'm still in a tizz right at this moment. My heart is thumping and thumping, as though we just wrestled for the world heavyweight title.

In fact, it feels like we really *did* wrestle for the world heavyweight title. I'm all sweaty and prickly, and my face won't go a normal colour no matter how hard I try.

And then it occurs to me, in a scary rush: *is this what flirting is?* No, God, no – it can't be. This isn't flirting. Flirting should feel light and breezy, like a Cary Grant film about fast-talking news reporters. I should be jauntily walking away now, while he shakes his head ruefully. That darned Kit!

Oh, how I wish I could be that darned Kit.

Instead of someone he gets to say this to:

'I think you need help.'

'Yeah? With what?'

I don't know why I keep asking these questions. It just leaves me so open.

'Sex.'

This is *definitely* flirting. I've no idea why it has to feel so nightmarish, however. He says one word, and bombs go off inside my body. I don't even know how he does it. He just opens his mouth, and previously innocuous terms become so sinful. So alien and the opposite of everything they were before. Martin McAllister once said 'sex' to me, and I think I answered, 'If we must.'

But when Dillon says it, the word just slides out of his mouth, ripe with the promise of a million things I've never known. Yes, I think. Do sex to me.

And then I'm just mortified over something I didn't say all over again. This guy … this guy is *never* going to do sex to me. He'd probably sooner fuck a postbox, and here I am mooning over him like a teenager with a crush.

It's awful. It makes me say things like this:

'Because you're such an expert in the field.'

Just to make certain he doesn't cotton on. Sarcasm is bound to make it seem like I don't fancy him, surely? Guys usually hate it when I say things like that to them.

So why doesn't *he* hate it? He's not normal.

'I know more than you. I bet you're not even sure how it starts out,' he says, in a manner that's just as warm and friendly as it was before. I think my sarcasm just bounces right off him – probably because of his immense chest.

'I do so.'

'Show me then.'

'Show you what?'

'Show me how you start things up.'

This is a trap, and I absolutely know it. But I also know that I no longer care.

'Well, I'd probably ... I'd probably ... look deeply into ... someone's eyes.'

He chuffs and rolls his own, as though he really is my teacher, trying to give me a lesson. *Could do better,* that expression says, and then he corrects me.

'That's not how you get things going. Here – it's like this. First, I slide a hand around your waist,' he says, which sounds so innocent on its own. He could be teaching me a dance step, in a class full of cookies and kids and marshmallows ... if it were not for the *actual hand that he slides around my waist*.

This isn't just a tutorial. He's going for a full-blown demonstration, with things like fingers on my hips, and ohhhh his touch is so warm and firm and good and fuck fuck fuck. Why didn't I stop this when he first started talking? I'm like Admiral Ackbar, yelling 'It's a trap!' two hours too late.

'And then, while you're busy staring at my hand like it sprouted out of my forehead, I just ... leee-ee-eeaan down ...'

Oh, my God, he's actually leaning down. No, he's *really really leaning down* – like the way people do when they're going to kiss someone. And no matter how much I bend my back, I can't quite get away from him. I'd have to be a championship limbo artist to evade his face and his mouth and are his eyes actually closing?

They are.

'Dillon,' I say, then again with more panic and less ability to breathe, 'Dillon, Dillon, don't lean down. Don't, don't – stop leaning, stop leaning, please for the love of God stop leaning in, are you leaning in, oh no!'

Yes. I actually use the phrase 'oh no'.

My deepest apologies to my vagina, who expected a kiss, and instead gets this:

'How do you make *leaning* sound like a dirty word?'

'It's a gift,' I say, and I must applaud myself for doing so. The sentence comes out so bright and chipper, even though I'm delivering it three inches from his glorious mouth. In fact, this entire conversation is now happening with me dipped down in his arms, like the dance partner I almost was.

'It really is,' he says, while I try not to enjoy the feel of his hand in the middle of my back. Or the heat of his breath against my lips. Or the hint of his body pressed against mine. 'I think you actually gave it an extra syllable.'

'Can you let me up now?'

'Do you really want to be up?'

I hate the way he asks me. It makes it almost impossible to say yes – though I do my damnedest to. I make my mouth move, and some sounds come out. If you turn your head on one side, they could almost be an affirmative.

Plus, I do actually push against him.

If pushing means flapping my hands ineffectually against the solid mass of his stupidly big body. It's really not a surprise when he eventually laughs and lets me go.

'All right, all right,' he says – probably because I was making a noise like a child who's got stuck. He even spreads his hands apart in a gesture designed to soothe, while I attempt to straighten my clothes.

Of course, my clothes don't actually need straightening.

It's not like he yanked my shirt over my head and then gave me a wedgie. It just sort of feels that way. It feels like I have to do something to put myself back together – I need time to think and process, before he says anything else.

Without it, I'm likely to say yes to anything.

'I tell you what.'

Like this. I'm going to say yes to this. I can feel it.

'You really want help with your book?'

No. No, I definitely don't. And no amount of sweeping me off my feet is going to change that. I don't care how handsome you are, or how much I internally swooned when you dipped me. That was just the logical reaction to something I've never experienced before. You caught me off guard by being different to every other guy I've ever known.

Have mercy. Please have mercy.

'I live at 453 Maitland Avenue, apartment 6C. Come by tomorrow, and we'll talk.' He nods, satisfied. 'Yeah. I think we could have a great, loooong talk.'

And what do I say?

I say OK.

Chapter Four

His apartment isn't really an apartment at all. It's more like a converted floor of a warehouse that didn't actually get converted. The floors are that grey, untreated wood that you often see in seventeenth-century sweatshops, and he hasn't bothered to make things like 'rooms'. There's a badly hung curtain between his bedroom and his rudimentary living area – and when I say rudimentary, I absolutely mean rudimentary.

Cavemen had more mod cons than this. He invites me to sit on a garden chair, and I'm actually grateful for that. Because the only other seat in this 'living room' is a crate that used to hold melons. His television is sat atop another television, which I'm assuming doesn't work. Unless his attention span is so bad that channel changing just wasn't cutting it any more. Maybe his remote control doesn't move fast enough – who knows?

I don't.

I'm too busy studying every bizarre detail of his mad home, so that I don't have to look directly at him. Because when he answers the door, he doesn't do it like a normal person. I can't give him the bottle of wine I brought, and inquire after his mother.

It's impossible to do those things, when your host is completely naked.

And all right, he's not completely naked. He is, in fact, wearing a towel. But when I say wearing a towel, I mean it in the loosest sense of the term. He hasn't even folded it around his body then made one of those nice little tucks at one corner.

He's just kind of … *holding* it over his bits. And the hold itself is very tenuous. He's practically doing it with his pinky finger, and the drape that's causing is very narrow. Before I've had chance to stop myself, I've glanced down and seen just about everything he's got. I can practically make out the insides of his thighs, which has to be some sort of optical illusion.

If I can see the insides of his thighs, I should be getting an eyeful of his cock – but thankfully I'm not. I'm just seeing everything else instead. The arrows of muscle either side of his groin, the hair that leads all the way down to there … and his tattoos, oh, God, his tattoos. They don't end with the coils on his arms. He's got a dragon crawling over his left side, like something leading the way to places I definitely want to go. Its open mouth is about a millimetre from his left pec, and that pec looks eight hundred times better than it did when he was clothed. His T-shirt lied: he isn't just hunky.

He's good enough to turn me into a drooling, gibbering mess. I'm thankful that he offers me a seat, because if he hadn't I would have definitely ended up on the floor.

And I think he knows it. Of course he knows it. You can't have a body like that and not know it. He just swaggers around with it all hanging out, and expects me to look.

But he's not going to get me that easily. I sit on his garden chair with my knees together, staring straight ahead at the curtain with ducks on it. And no matter how many times he passes me by, waffling on about how he's just going to get dressed and do I want a cup of coffee and so and so forth, I don't turn my head.

I can see him in the periphery of my vision, all gleaming and slippery from the shower, skin like honey in the low light that's slanting through his makeshift room partition, and I resist I resist I resist.

Until he turns and heads back to his bathroom, flashing his completely bare ass as he goes. I totally don't know how to resist then. The glimpse of him is so shocking that I have to turn, to get the full impact – and it is an impact. His ass is like a meteor, smashing down on my defenceless body.

I've never seen another quite like it. It's so round and firm and full. And it has these hollows on either side of the cheeks that flex and fill out every time he takes a step. For a second I'm actually hypnotised by them. I'm hanging off my chair trying to follow them, and then he disappears into the bathroom and I actually curse in frustration.

He definitely does it on purpose. I see his expression before he lets the door swing shut and it's pure victory – though I don't hate him as much as I should for that.

He's victorious because *I* looked. He actually cares that I did.

Is it OK if I kind of like that?

'So, uh … this book you're writing …' he calls through the door.

'Yeah?'

'What exactly do you think it's missing?'

'Realism,' I say, but that's not what I'm thinking. Passion, my mind whispers, and I know that's true, too. *There's nothing I've ever put in a book, that's half as good as you.*

'You think realism's so important for a sexy book?'

'I think that it's hard to be excited, when you don't really believe in something. When it seems unlikely that it would ever actually happen, in real life.'

'And what kind of things do you think wouldn't happen in real life?' he asks, and I'm alarmed to find myself stumped. Was it the blindfolds and the talk of Masters that Lori didn't buy? Or was it something else? When I look back on it now, the story seems so artificial. So full of things that I've never experienced.

But I don't think that's about realism, exactly.

It's more about me, and all the things I'll never be.

'I don't know. Some of the kinkier stuff, maybe?'

As soon as I've said it, I know it's the wrong thing. And I was so proud of myself for hitting on an answer that didn't sound quite so depressing! But of course, he homes in on it like a laser. I can almost hear him laughing, through the door.

'Kinky stuff, huh?'

'Well ...'

'That what you like to write about?'

'Not exactly, I –'

'Do you dream about being taken by a guy wearing a leather mask?'

'That's, uh ...'

'Or maybe you're the one doing the taking, am I right? You got a secret dominant side, little mouse? You gonna tie me up and torture me with a hot poker?'

'I hadn't really thought about doing anything to you. At all. You know, in case you were worried about that. Which you don't have to be, because I'm purely interested in ... uh ... in growing. As a writer. See – I even brought my little Dictaphone and my notepad and ... and ...'

48

And dear *God* I wish I could stop talking. He emerges from the bathroom – thankfully in a T-shirt and shorts – with an almost bursting look of amusement on his face. As though I'm just adorable, in the worst possible way. He even gives my hair a cute little pat as he passes me on his way to the kitchen.

And then he says this:

'Hey, calm down, OK? My penis isn't going to suddenly lunge at your face.'

Which makes no sense at all. I wasn't thinking that. I was thinking he was scared of *my* vagina suddenly lunging at *his* face. Lord, how can someone be so open and so mysterious at the same time?

Even if I sort of suspect that he's not being mysterious at all.

'Did you say you wanted a coffee?'

I should say yes here, I know – normal people have a coffee. But then, normal people also know what to do when a guy hugs them, so in for a penny, in for a pound. He might as well see me for what I am, right now.

'I don't drink it.'

'Really? Great. Now I don't have to pretend I'm not a child who only drinks soda.'

It's the first time I've really laughed in his presence, but I just can't help it. I'm startled by his response – so close to how I feel, about that very thing. I've just never really said the idea out loud. I've always been embarrassed by my lack of sophistication.

But of course, he doesn't care about stuff like that.

He just swaggers back in, and hands me my fizzy pop.

'I got beer too if you want it.' He knocks the cap off his bottle on the edge of a table, then takes a casual swig before finishing the thought. 'Maybe later though, huh?'

'Why? What's going to happen later?'

Christ. Yet again my brain speaks before my mind has chance to get into gear. He sits himself down on the box, and kind of leans back on another two boxes that sit nearly behind it – like an armchair, I think, only rubbish. And then he grins at me, lazily.

'Ohh, you have no idea what I've got planned. Bad things. Outrageous things. You'll be talking to your therapist about them in ten years' time.'

'You're fucking with me.'

'Yeah, I totally am. Take it easy, Kitty-cat – I'm not some sex demon.'

What a fucking liar.

'I tell you what,' he says. 'Here's how I think things are really going to go. Ready? You braced yourself?'

I have.

'I'm going to talk about some stuff until you can't take it anymore, then you're probably going to throw a chair at me and run right out of the apartment. Am I close?'

'No,' I say. 'I was actually thinking of using the fire extinguisher.'

'Oh, I like that deadpan, Kit. I like that a lot. How did you know my weakness?'

'Your weakness is a woman using deadpan humour?'

'My weakness is brunettes with bee-stung lips and big round asses. The humour's just a bonus.'

'So … you … fancy … yourself?'

'Huh?'

'Well, you're a brunette with bee-stung lips and a big round ass. In fact, your ass is so big and round you could put it in the sky and mistake it for the moon.'

I've gone too far. I see that now. Flirting is just too

50

dangerous for someone like me. I have no off switch on my mouth, and once it gets going it doesn't know when to stop. Now I've not only told him that he reminds me of a hot woman – probably Angelina Jolie, if I'm interpreting his comments correctly – but I've admitted I looked at his ass.

And that it did shine its glorious light upon me.

It's no wonder I'm holding my breath. But then he laughs, and I get to let it out. He really, *really* laughs. I'm starting to worry about how much he's laughing. Is this the hysterics before the sudden axe murdering?

'Is that a good thing?' he says, finally. 'I don't know if that's a good thing.'

I can't leave him hanging. *No one* would.

'It's a good thing. Your ass is ... very pleasant.'

'Well ... thank you. But, no. I wasn't talking about myself. I was talking about –'

'Angelina Jolie?'

'Yeah – I hear she's a real deadpan hoot,' he says, sarcasm so thick I almost gag on it. I have to swallow quickly and compose myself, because then he comes out with this: 'I'm talking about you, you idiot. You have *seen* you, right?'

And after he has, my world turns upside down.

'Of course I have. I saw myself last Wednesday. My hair was doing this woo-woo thing,' I say, but only because I'm panicking. My palms have gone all sweaty and my mouth has dried to a crisp. It's like my saliva has disappeared down into my hands.

And all because he said I had nice lips.

'Can you give me a demonstration of this woo-woo?'

'Well, my fringe was kind of going out here like – Christ, what am I doing? Don't ask me to do stupid things.'

'Why?'

'Because I *might do them*.'

Ohhh, Lord. I did not mean to say *that*. Now he's got this weird, heavy expression on his face, and the pressure of it is fairly intense. His eyelids go all low over those smoky eyes, and I can almost feel what he's considering.

He's considering all the things he could ask me.

And all the things I'd definitely do.

'OK, so ... anyway. Let's get back to why I'm here,' I say, just to clear the air and restore normality. After all, I'm likely imagining the whole *asking me to do stuff* thing. That's probably just his default setting: hot staring.

'Is it seducing me? Because you're doing a great job of that.'

Or not. Oh God, this isn't his default setting at all.

'Sorry – go ahead. First question,' he says – possibly because he can see how stunned I am right now. I think my mouth has fallen open, and my face feels like it's on fire. My whole *body* feels like it's on fire.

There's a new pulse that's just started up at the centre of myself, and it's beating hard enough to show through my suit.

'Um ... OK.'

I get my notepad and flick it open, grateful to myself for having the foresight to jot down some mild queries. So it's unfortunate, really, that they're all now nearly impossible to say. I stare at the first few in dismay: *Have you ever tied anyone up? Do you ever take a woman to the top of a glass building and blindfold her with red ribbons? Am I insane and too steeped in fantasy land, wanting to write about those things?*

I can't ask him stuff like that, after he's said 'seducing'.

'Well ... uh ... maybe you could just tell me ... something. Like in the group. You tell me a story, and I'll ... take notes.'

'A story, huh?'

'Yeah.'

He pauses, as though he's truly considering. Though he doesn't pause like a normal person, of course. Now he seems to be smiling without moving his lips, and his eyes are full of this devilish sort of delight. He's going to really sock it to me – that much is clear.

'OK. How about this? There once was a man from Nantucket ...'

I come close to throwing my pad at him.

'I was really expecting something then.'

'I know. You're practically pushing your pen tip through the paper.' I glance down, and sure enough, there's a blob of ink the size of a tomato, soaking through the top layer to seven other layers beneath. I'm a nervous wreck. 'What exactly are you going to note down, anyway?'

Maybe he's a nervous wreck too.

But if so, I wish he'd show it.

'Just any relevant details.'

He makes a worried, this-food-is-going-to-taste-bad face.

'Like ... what? Girth, thrusts per second ... are you measuring me for a sex suit?'

'Yeah, and then I'm going to shoot you into sex space.'

'Awesome.'

'I'm just looking for some authentic experiences, that's all.'

'And what if my experiences don't seem authentic?'

Alarms bells ring, at this point. But apparently, they're the kind of alarm bells that make you want to move towards the danger, instead of running away. They've been wired wrong, and now I'm stumbling towards his so-wild-they're-unreal stories without a thought for my own safety.

'Well, that's the point, isn't it? If you've done it, then it's believable – whether I'm convinced or not.'

'So it's sort of like I'm giving you permission.'

'To do what?'

For some reason I think of a swimming pool filled with writing bodies instead of water, and me poised on some impossibly high diving board. *Go on and jump*, he says. But how can I, when I don't know if anyone will catch me?

They seem pretty preoccupied by each other's groins.

'To write what you want to write.'

Oh, what a lovely concept. What a lovely, lovely concept. I don't tell him how much it makes my heart sing, however. He'd only get the wrong idea.

'I suppose.'

'OK. So I'll start at the beginning, then.'

'The beginning?'

'Yeah. The beginning of my escapades.'

My mind immediately sends me an image of a gaudy comic book, with the words *The Madcap Adventures of Dillon* on the front. At which point, I have to accept that I'm not going to get anything down to earth out of this. He probably doesn't even know what down to earth is. He only knows wild, and electric.

Yet somehow I hardly care.

'The beginning, then,' I say, because apparently I've already jumped.

I'm halfway to the writing water already.

Chapter Five

'I didn't know her first name. She was always Mrs Goldman, to the staff. Hell, I think she was Mrs Goldman to everyone. Her husband probably called her that in bed. I know I wanted to call her that in bed. It was bad enough that I was seventeen and still a virgin – I lived in permanent boner-land anyway. But trying to trim the hedges round her pool while she lay there on a sun lounger, half-naked, all oiled and shit ...

'It was pretty torturous. She had the kind of breasts you don't see any more. Eighties breasts. Really round and real, always trying to burst out of tiny bikini tops. And eighties legs, too – strong, thick thighs that sort of slid against each other when she moved. She glowed, you know? Her skin was always like satin. Some days I'd go inside to the bathroom just so I could, you know, take care of myself ... which I'm pretty sure she knew.

'How could she not? That summer was so hot you couldn't wear anything but shorts, and I knew my dick was always straining through the material. Weird thing was, though – that only turned me on more.

'She told me once that I had a blow job mouth, and I guess that's true. I *do* love to suck on things.'

He gazes off innocently at some innocuous spot, everything about him so casual, so calm about this. He's propping his chin on one hand, his bottle lying lazy in the other – while my mind frantically fumbles towards thoughts of that thing he said, about *Alan*.

It doesn't get very far, however. It went sort of blank right around the idea of him looking at himself naked. The image he paints is so vivid that I can't see anything but it for a second – like the photo-flash of something, seared on the insides of my retinas. There's the outline of his body, thinner than he is now but somehow just as compelling. And his skin ... oh, God, what must his skin have been like at that age? I imagine it the way he described hers: as glossy as syrup, as smooth as silk, so beautiful you want to die the moment you see it.

He must have been stunning. He's stunning now, and that's without the other thing my heated imagination has latched onto: how dazed he must have looked, under the pressure of all that lust. I think of those blue eyes of his, near-blank and foggy with a thousand thoughts of her, and I can't imagine how she didn't jump on him immediately.

Though I'm guessing I'm going to find out.

'Back then, though,' he says. 'I honestly thought I was being real subtle. That she had no idea about the private sex sessions I was having with her, in my head, in her bathroom. I pictured myself suavely seducing her – giving her exactly what her puny husband never did. I'd seen him around, in his shitty suits, as skinny as a reed.

'Whereas I was ... well. I was six-two before I graduated junior high, and had already hit two hundred pounds of mostly muscle. I just knew I could give her what she wanted. I'd grab her and throw her onto the antique Italian silk couch, then pound her until she screamed for more. Then I'd bend her over the kitchen counter, the way I'd seen some guy do in the electric seven minutes of porn I'd dared to watch in my parents' basement – then shove myself inside her. She made me feel electric.'

I flick from this to that, in the maze of all the things he's saying – the idea of him swaggering around, contrasting with the expression he has on his face now, as he talks about it. He thinks he was ridiculous, I can tell – and I like him for that.

But I like him more for the last little bit. The way he says the word *electric*, as though some probably pilfered dirty movie sent a charge direct through his body to his dick. I know how that feels, all right ... oh, I remember the delight of digging through all kinds of movies and books, searching for that one illicit scene.

We have something in common there, I think – though I suppose everybody does. I'm not about to get excited over it, or anything. I mean, his next words *are* these:

'I spent actual hours trying to imagine what she would feel like, around me, so I could emulate the sensation exactly. I'd slick my hand with every slippery product known to man, then fuck my fist into the mattress. It was a real time of sexual discovery, for me.

'Does that sound sort of foo-foo?'

He's laughing at himself, a little, but I hope it's clear that I'm not joining in. I can't even answer him. He just talked about fucking his fist into a mattress. I mean, the image of him standing naked in front of a mirror was bad enough.

This is turning my insides purple.

'Well, maybe it is. But that's how it was. I started understanding stuff I liked – slippery things, obviously. The amount of times I imagined oiling her all over with that suntan lotion of hers, then getting to ease myself between her soft thighs …

'Though that wasn't the only lesson I learnt. I realised pretty quick that holding off made it sweeter, when you finally let it happen. Sometimes I'd keep myself on the edge for hours, until my orgasm felt too intense to take. I felt feverish, too on edge. I felt like pheromones were leaking out of my pores. She *had* to notice me, eventually.'

I think he's right. I'm noticing him, and I wasn't even there. I'm fifteen years into the future and a million miles away from whatever American town he's talking about, but I'm sure I can smell that earthy, saltwater scent from here. And though it's never been something that particularly interested me, I find myself tingling at the idea.

What would it be like, to see him aroused and in this state? I don't know, but I'm no longer content to wait and find out more.

'And did she?'

'It'd be a pretty weak story if she didn't, right?'

He pauses, and for that one second I think he really means it. This is just some tale of for ever wanting and not getting. He could call it *The Madcap Adventures of Kit Connor*.

But then he continues – like a warden, granting his sexual prisoner a reprieve.

'So, the longer this went on for, the worse things got. And the bolder I became. I stopped being satisfied with the bathroom, and makeshift masturbatory aids. I started wanting the smell of her perfume, the feel of her silk underwear against my skin. I turned into her stalker, slipping into her bedroom when I knew no one was around. Running my hands over the clothes in her wardrobe – the works. It got so bad I could get hard by stuffing my face into one of her couch cushions.

'I was pathetic – but when I finally got caught, I tried

to bluster it. I turned on the ridiculous swagger I thought I had. Think I even told her, "You want it, baby?" God, I was such a punk.'

'You still *are* a punk,' I say, but I don't know if I really mean it. I don't think punks talk so openly about their sexual habits, before admitting that they are one. And I definitely don't think they look hurt, when some chick hurls the word at them.

Because that's what it feels like I've done. His eyebrows draw together briefly, like a flicker of an expression he'd like to have, if it didn't make him seem so vulnerable. And then it's gone as quickly as it came, leaving me to wonder if it was ever really there at all. I mean, guys like him ... they don't care if girls like me think they're a little ... douche-y. Right?

And if they do, oh, God, if they do, please let him just say. I'll apologise if he just says. I can't do so without it, because then I'll just look like an idiot who's imagining feelings that aren't really there. It's the first step towards lovesickness – wanting to be sorry for hurt you might have caused.

And he'll know it, and laugh.

He's laughing now, as he plunges on into the story.

'Yeah, I thought I was hot stuff. So when she said, "Oh, I want it all right," I preened like nothing else. I didn't think a single thing to her telling me to strip. I thought my body was hot and she just wanted to see it, so I took off my T-shirt, I took off my shorts. By the time I was down to nothing, I was practically mute with excitement. My cock was almost touching my belly, and everything felt real swollen down there, you know?'

I do know. I'm so swollen in that same place I can hardly keep my legs closed. It's like trying to fit myself around a burning coal – though I think I keep the signs to a minimum. I'm so hot I'd love to fan myself with my notepad, but I resist. I don't even run a finger around my clammy collar, and I definitely don't remove my jacket.

My nipples are too stiff for something like that. They're showing through my shirt, and I know it – though I've got less idea about the *why*. The story isn't even that exciting, really. I've heard lots like it a dozen times before. He's going to nail her, now, then write. 'Dear *Penthouse*' on the top and mail that sucker in. He's going to show me what an incredible stud he was, because he could fuck her like her husband never could.

Or at least that's what I'm sure of, before he tells me the rest.

'But she didn't touch me. She didn't sink to her knees the way I'd always imagined she would. She said: "Do you know how to make a woman come, Dillon?"

'And now, every time I'm flicking through the catalogue of every sexy thing that's ever happened to me … every time I'm on the brink and I need to pull out something intense to really get there … that's what I think about. I think about that one sentence, like a siren's song. "Do you know how to make a woman come, Dillon?"

'I couldn't even tell her yes. I knew it was a lie. In every fantasy I'd ever had about her, she'd screamed like a porn star and lapsed into unconsciousness the second my cock touched her, but I never stopped to think how or why. I assumed my dick was the magical key to a winter wonderland, but when I tried to show her I could do it, when I tried to climb on top of her like some fumbling fucking idiot, she stopped me in my tracks.

'She waved her red-tipped finger in my face – and I always

remember that, too. I remember her pressing me to my knees with just that one talon on my big shoulder.

'Then she said more words that still send a burst of arousal through me, now: "Lick your fingers. Lick your fingers, baby." Like she was the one with swagger, and I was just her little cutie-pie, ready to be serviced. And I can remember feeling like I didn't want to – I was sulking, then, I guess. I was thinking she was messing around with me.

'But the weird thing was – that didn't make it any less hot. In fact, it made it hotter. My cock actually jerked when she said those barely-anything words. I was kind of bothered by the mess I was making all over her carpet – I was absolutely dripping by this point.

'And I was shaking. I was really shaking. Putting my fingers in my mouth felt like the most erotic thing I'd ever done. Like I was sucking myself. Like I had nerve-endings there that I didn't know about. I actually got lost in the feel of them, sliding in and out of my mouth.

'Until she lay back on the bed, and spread her legs.

'Of course, I'd seen pussy before – in magazines. In pornos. But it's kinda not the same, don't you think? Have you ever looked at yourself, when you're aroused? It's not the bleached, waxed, perfectly positioned and pert thing from porn, as dry as the Sahara and hardly a notch above pastel pink. It's flushed, and slippery, and so swollen, like a beating heart between your legs – or at least, that's how it was with her.

'All of her folds were coated in her clearly visible wetness, and her clit … oh, Jeeze, her clit. I'd always thought it was something kind of mythical, you know? You couldn't really make anything out in dirty movies, and no one ever talked about doing anything to it. There's no locker-room talk about banging some chick's clit last night.

'But seeing that stiff little thing up close ...

'I actually leant forward, thinking she'd want me to lick it. Hell, that's what I would have wanted, in her place – and that's the first time I understood that particular concept, too.

'Women want the same thing men do. They want to get off. They want what feels good, not necessarily what feels good for *you* – though I think some girls like that idea, too. I think you do, if that squirming you started doing when I told you about stroking my own dick is anything to go by.'

And I thought I was being *so* subtle. I thought I looked composed, but I can see now that I didn't. And I certainly don't, now. I feel like there's a wrestling match going on inside my body. My eyeballs are boiling alive inside my head. I try to sit still – but it's almost impossible with this constant pulse thrumming between my legs.

I have to move around just to keep it from beating me right off the chair.

'You like hearing what turns me on, right? Don't be embarrassed. There's nothing quite like a selfless lover – someone more interested in your pleasure, than their own. But somehow, I think you've had a lifetime of that, and not very much of the other way around, am I right?'

I've *never* had it the other way around. *Never*.

'Yeah, I'm right. I bet you've laid beneath a dozen guys called James or Jake or Jack, counting ceiling tiles over their shoulders as they fuck you like they're doing their tax return. And then when they're done dealing you out your two-minute portion of passionless sex, you wonder why people go crazy for something that feels like getting a shot at the doctor's, for some disease you don't actually have.'

I'd laugh here, if it wasn't so awful. And so dead on, oh, God, he's so impossibly dead on I could cry.

Instead I briefly close my eyes, and tell him:
'Just tell me the rest of the story.'
In a voice like dried leaves.
Only that just means that he does.

'She didn't want me to lick her there, however. She didn't
want me to touch her there, either. I felt almost swamped
by the scent of her body – like coconut oil and something
furtive, something secretive – and it made the urge to stroke
her so strong ... so incredibly strong. It was like a compul-
sion – but she stopped me there, too. She said to me: "Not
like that, not like that," while I wondered what else there
could possibly be.

'And then she took hold of my hand, and forced it down,
down ... until those two fingers I'd sucked on simply slid
into her warm, wet hole. So easy ... man, it was so fucking
easy. I didn't even know what was happening until I was
already halfway inside her, and after that I didn't think about
anything at all.

'Finally, finally I was getting to feel what that slick heat
was like – and, oh, it was better than I'd imagined. What my
own hand always missed was that sense of being pulled in,
of being sort of ... sucked on, almost. I thought of my own
mouth as I slowly eased into her – the tingling feeling I'd
gotten when I'd licked between the webbing of my fingers,
the slippery sense of my own tongue ...

'That was what it was like.

'And it blew my fucking mind. I got pretty close to passing
out with pleasure before I'd even done a thing – though I
figured she'd have slapped me awake, if I had. She was all
commands, by that point, real bossy about things – but I'd
stopped caring about three decades prior.

'"Fuck me with them, then," she said, and I did. I did

what I thought fucking was, back and forth, like a piston. I had no more sense than a dog – but that turned out OK, too. Because I think, more than anything, she liked the idea of teaching me. See what I mean? She'd cluck her tongue and tell me, "No, like this." Or she'd nudge me with one of those incredible thighs, until I went where she wanted me to go. And all the while I'm getting hotter and hotter and more frustrated, the frustration like some other layer of arousal I've never encountered before.

'Which was when I *really* started to appreciate patience. Not some five-second hold-off in my own bed, thinking I'm hot stuff 'cause I don't come right away. Not fantasising at three o'clock then waiting 'til seven to fucking do it, everything all tight down there and just ready to fucking come. No, no, no. *Real* patience. Really holding it off. Just … revelling in that feeling you get, when everything's too much and there isn't a thought in your goddamn head. Getting a sense of your own body, and every tiny little sensation it goes through.

'Yeah, that's what I learnt from her.

'But I got something even better than that, too.'

I can't imagine what's better than seeing him in this theoretical state of sexual euphoria, but I'll hold off on my verdict, for now. He's deep into his story, by this point – eyes all far away, body practically sprawling back against the boxes – and I'm just as far into it with him.

No sense in distracting him now.

'After a while, she started sighing and tossing her head, as though I was the most useless person in the world. And then she said something else I've never forgotten. She said: "You don't get anywhere by banging on the door. You want a girl to come outside? Beckon her over."

'Of course I didn't have a fucking clue what she was talking about. I started wondering if this was some hint to go down and answer the doorbell that wasn't ringing. Maybe she didn't want a sex slave, after all – maybe she wanted some guy to run her errands and do her chores for her.

'And I fucking hate admitting this – but I would have done it too.

'Lucky for me that she didn't mean that at all. She gave me a demonstration, when it became pretty clear that I was lacking most of my higher brain functions. She crooked her fingers, like this –'

He makes that exact gesture – of the kind I've seen a thousand times before in everyday life. Teachers used to do it to me in staid classrooms; my elderly Nan was a fan, for those times when she wanted to give me a boiled sweet.

But it's different, when he does it. For a start, I don't think he's got a sack of pear drops waiting for me in his pocket. And then there's the way he goes about it, all seemingly innocent, with a layer of lewd on top. It's kind of like ... he's stroking the air with the tips of those two crooked fingers.

And the air really, really likes it.

'– and told me to do it that way. "Do it hard," she said. But when I did she only wanted it harder. I couldn't get the pace right, the rhythm right ... nothing I did was what she wanted. I fucked her in a way I was sure should hurt, and held myself back a dozen times.

'Until I realised that it didn't matter what I thought. It mattered what *she* thought. It mattered how she responded when I did something. Yeah – that was the thing. That was what I started to pick up on. I didn't have to tiptoe around, waiting for her to say or me to guess. I could see it in her, if I only took the time to look for the clues. Her face gave away almost nothing – but her body did.

'When I pressed upwards, just a little, her back would arch. And if I just kind of ... drummed my fingers against that soft, sweet spot inside her, I'd get a sound. A faint one, but a sound all the same.

'I tell you, I could have lived for a month on that barely-there sigh. I'd have worked on her pussy until my arm dropped off – which it wasn't far off doing, anyway. I was drenched in sweat, exhausted, aroused to the point of hallucination, but I didn't want anything else, right at that moment.

'I wanted to hear her sing for me – though I wasn't really prepared for it, when she did. You know what a woman looks like, when she comes because you've done her like that? She's not polite about it. She doesn't blow you a kiss and gasp a yes in your ear.

'She loses every bit of control of her body. She loses it so badly you can hardly believe it's the same person – the one who wore gold-rimmed sunglasses and gave you thousand-yard stares through their blank, black lenses. The one who could have graced the cover of an eighties fashion magazine: all power and money and long, blonde beauty.

'She went to pieces when I made her come. Every muscle in her body turned tight, in a way I can't forget. I can't forget the way she made a stiff little ball out of her perfect body, and begged me to stop where once she'd only known how to command. She nearly crushed my fingers, and ohhhhh the slipperiness of her. How *wet* she got. She practically came all over my hand, like a teenage boy, unable to help herself.

'Man, I was proud. I was so full of pride that I might have gone away from that encounter even worse than I was before – that stupid fucking swagger bolstered by my badge of honour, courtesy of her. I even stood up, cock sticking out like I'm flipping her the bird with it, most of me ready to get my reward, now.

'But she saved me from that fate. She waited, until she was calm and I was not. She took her time composing herself. And then she said the worst possible thing she could – the thing I'd based my whole idea of seducing her on, the thing that made me grin whenever I glanced across at the picture of her skinny little nerd of her husband, on her bedside table. She said:

'"I guess no one's as good as he is."

'And some part of me is still trying to be whatever it was that he gave her. To reduce a woman to a mess so helpless that it compares to the great and incomparable Mr Edwin G. Goldman – accountant, owner of some bitching hair plugs, sweats when he's nervous, Edwin G. Goldman, who had the hottest wife in my neighbourhood, simply because he knew what to do with his hands.'

There are many things I feel, once I realise he's finished with his story. Which I don't, at first. In fact, my faintly stupefied lack of realisation is so bad that he claps his hands together, and does a kind of semi-wince. He sucks air over his teeth, the way people do when they're bracing themselves for a horrible verdict.

However, I don't know how to give him one – horrible or otherwise. I'm still shell-shocked. And once I'm done being shell-shocked, I'm trapped between a whole bunch of conflicting emotions – and all of them are the most intense versions of those feelings I've ever experienced. My arousal is stalking around inside me like a rabid dog. No matter what move he makes – from innocuous chin-scratching all the way down the pervert scale to fairly obvious rubbing through the pocket of his shorts – the thing has to be yanked back on its choke chain.

And this giddiness I'm going through … it's of the hysterical kind. I feel like I might get up at any moment and start frantically shaking his hand, before offering him the grand prize for Being a Man.

Because he deserves it. Even I know that, and I kind of hate him. I hate him for making me feel this way – so inexplicably grateful to another human being, for doing things that probably aren't even real. I mean, they've got to be made up, right? Everyone's heard the 'Dear *Penthouse*' story of the pool boy and some hot older woman who looks like Chrissie Brinkley. And even if Chrissie was real, what's the likelihood that she'd do these things? That she'd instruct him in the ways of womanhood – ways that are even more ridiculous than the idea that bored housewives really do fuck the help?

It never happened, I think. It's all just another fucking fairy tale.

'I should probably go,' I say – though, in my defence, I'm an idiot. I know I am. I don't even know why I care that he might have made it up. At least he *told* it.

Telling something like that is more than I've ever gotten before. And yet somehow I'm still trying to pull my bag over my shoulder – wrapping the strap around myself several times in the process. I think I actually send it into orbit, briefly, and I know how stumbly and fumbly I must look.

I go over on one shoe – these stupid fucking heels I shouldn't have worn – and everything in his apartment is in the way. I almost trip over an old ski boot, just to make it absolutely easy for him to laugh. He's got to be laughing.

That's why he did it, didn't he? That's what he likes, isn't it? To reduce women to helpless messes? Well, he's certainly succeeded with me. My shoe has actually kind of come all the way off, and I can't seem to get it back on.

'Kit,' he says, but I'm not listening. I'm too engrossed in this shoe debacle. It's like *The Krypton Factor*, only with a leather-heeled Mary-Jane instead of an intense logic puzzle. My shoe *is* the intense logic puzzle.

'Kit.'

I think I shout, 'You stupid fucking shoe' in response.

'Kit,' he says. He won't stop saying my name. And he's stood up now, I'm sure of it. I can see him out of the corner of my eye. He has his hands in his pockets, and he's kind of casually sauntering over – as though he suspects that sudden moves and the appearance of his hands might incite me to attack.

I'm like a bear. A bear who doesn't know how to deal with sexual feelings – which is weird, because I'm pretty sure bears are really good at that sort of thing. Don't they just lumber up to each other and mount?

I wonder if he knows that I want to mount him. I wonder if he's going to try to make me feel like a fool, now, to make sure I don't make a pass.

'Kit,' he says.

And then he touches my arm in this oh-so-soft way, and I go all still. Just like that.

Likely he has a lot of experience with wild animals. I can see an Ocean World T-shirt slung over the dresser by the door – he's probably a shark wrangler or maybe a killer whale wrestler. Are those actually things? I don't know. But I do know I should be focusing on the here and now, instead of imaginary careers he might have. He's still touching my arm, and I'm still watching him touch my arm, and after a while the tension is just too great.

I have to look up at him.

Hesitantly, though. Maybe I even briefly slip into slow

motion – it kind of feels like it. I'm afraid to see his face, in case it looks too good for me to stand.

And sure enough, it absolutely does. His expression is molten metal, from those heavy-lidded eyes of his to his parted lips. The intense heat from the ironworks he's operating inside himself has melted any higher considerations, and suddenly he's just *this*. This greedy, lustful thing. He looks at me from underneath those thick, black lashes, and I don't think he's doing it so he can assess my shoe problem.

He's doing it because he knows it makes me weak in the knees.

'Come on,' I say, doing my best to hit the same note of incredulity he does, when he utters those two words. But the problem is – he has whole sentences to go after them. I don't. I just go, 'Come on, come on, come on,' over and over again, until he's forced to ask for clarification.

'Come on what?'

'None of that really happened.'

Shame that such sure words have such a faint voice to support them. I feel like I barely have any breath to push out the things I want to say, and the cocky pose I'm trying to hold is coming apart at the seams. It doesn't help that my right side sinks much lower than I expect it to, every time I sag beneath the pressure.

If only I hadn't lost that one shoe!

'I mean, nobody really loses their virginity like that, to some hot older woman.'

'No? So how do they do it?'

He's not looking at my face any more. He's looking at the fingers he's busy trailing up my arm – the ones that somehow end up at the collar of my suit jacket.

And then he ... then he kind of ... opens the material a

little bit, in a way that should make me very, very nervous. He's almost peering around the corner of my clothes, to get a look at what lies beyond – which sounds terrible, I know.

Yet somehow it's not. There's such a gentleness to it, and that way he sneaks a peek is so overt it's nearly cute. I like the way his mouth skews right, like he knows he's being cheeky. I like how his eyebrows mysteriously make everything playful, even when they should be turning my insides upside down.

I like *him*, I realise. A lot.

'In the backseat of someone's car, in under twenty seconds.'

'Yeah?'

'And it feels kind of like being thrown into a cement mixer.'

'Sounds awesome.'

'It sounds *real*. More real than anything you just said.'

'You think? And where exactly did I fall down, on the reality front?'

I debate whether to say, specifically. There's a chance it will lead me down some very narrow paths, to some incredibly uncomfortable cul-de-sacs. Most of them are marked *you don't know what the fuck you're talking about, and he's going to tell you so in great and graphic detail*.

But the thing about a cul-de-sac is: once you're in it, you can't easily back out.

'Well, for a start you can't make a woman ... do that. Like that. And I know, because I am a ... I am one of those ... I am a woman.'

Unfortunate that I sound so unsure on that last part. Kind of undermines my point, a bit.

'I see. You sure do seem to have it all figured out.'

'I do.'

'Mmmhmm,' he says – probably because my collar is so fascinating he can't possibly tear himself away.

'So you admit it, then?'

'Admit what?'

'That you just ... made all that up.'

He takes what looks like a thoughtful breath. Clears his throat, in preparation to deliver the truth. I should be pleased, really, only once I know it's coming I kind of don't want it to. Just give me another thirty seconds with that thing that could never have possibly happened, I think at him.

And he does.

In fact, he gives me more than thirty seconds.

'You know, Kit ... I think the lecture portion of the afternoon is over.' I pretend not to notice that he's unbuttoning my jacket, as he says this. I pretend not to breathe, too. I'm very convincing – I almost pass out when, he next speaks. 'I think it's time for the practical demonstration.'

I believe I reply with this:

'Oh. That's OK.'

As though he just asked me if I wanted something for Christmas, and I was too polite to say yes. I'm always too polite to say yes. My worst enemy could ask me if I'd like this knife removing from my back, and I'd tell them, 'If it isn't too much trouble.'

All of which makes it even more startling, when he says:

'I'm going to kiss you now.'

I mean, what on earth did I do to deserve such an honour? I'm fairly certain that a snog from a gorgeous man is not the standard reward for extreme courtesy. But I keep up with it, just in case.

'No, really. You don't have to.'

'But I want to. It's honestly no trouble,' he says, in an absolutely ridiculous imitation of my British accent. His top notes hover somewhere around the Queen of England, while

Addicted

his bottom ones blunder around in Boston. He could attach a tally-ho to the end of that sentence and it wouldn't seem out of place.

But I can't laugh. He doesn't give me a chance to. Once he's done with the verbal teasing he dips his voice back down low, and heads straight for the other kind. The more ... physical kind, that sort of makes me want to throw up.

'I want to taste that sweet little mouth of yours,' he says, but he's not done. He's just using a dramatic pause to build the tension for the next bit. And it's good that he does, because the next part is this: 'Before I make you come so hard you forget who you are.'

I think I actually gasp.

'I'd like to kiss you while you're still Kit,' he adds, but he's out of luck on that. I'm not Kit when he leans down and touches his mouth to mine. I'm a shell of myself, ready to crumble into dust and blow away. His kiss is just too gentle for me to stay together. It's too tender to go with his bristly stubble and his big body and his many tattoos.

I expect rough, horny tongues and lots of pressure, but he just traces his lips over mine, barely touching – and I think I know why, too. Because when he pulls away, I'm so desperate for more I could claw him back. I even put out a hand, to grab his arm.

But he still has no mercy on me.

'Take your panties off,' he says, at the most perfect point he possibly could. I'm all primed and suddenly starving, and I've made a fist around the sleeve of his T-shirt. I'm never going to tell him no, now, and yet I'm still electrically shocked when he says it. I'm electrically shocked by the *way* he says it – so low and syrupy soft. It's hardly a command ... but it's hardly not, either. It exists in some perfect mid-space between what I'd like to do and what I can be talked into.

Though I still find myself floundering. What does he mean, exactly? Take them off after I've removed my skirt, so that I'm completely bare down there? I'm not sure I can manage that, but the other option seems childish.

I *feel* childish, doing it. I immediately want to stop before I've started, though of course I can't. Once you've committed to pulling your underwear down, hitting pause is no longer viable.

So I keep my skirt down and do it under cover of darkness, like I'm out somewhere in public and I really need the bathroom. I squirm out of them, hoping that the embarrassment will fade once I've slid them all the way down my legs.

But it doesn't. My face is on fire, and my brain simply won't stop screaming at me. 'Why are you doing this?' it hollers, right in my ear. And I have no answers for it.

Especially after I've looked up with that little slip of cotton still tangled around my ankles, and seen the expression on his face. He glances off at something else, briefly, then closes his eyes. And he makes a sound, too – a little puff of breath, with a few 'O's on the end. Like someone shaking their head over something that costs too much.

I cost too much. My rudeness costs too much. He didn't mean it about the underwear being off – it was just a test! And now I've failed, I've failed.

'Man, there's nothing sweeter than seeing a girl take her panties off like that. Those cotton? Oh yeah, that does it for me.'

He sounds like he really means it. He sounds *shaky*, in fact. But I have to be sure.

'Are you messing with me? Seriously. Is this just –'

74

He reaches out and takes my hand.

'Does it *feel* like I'm messing with you?' he asks, in such a sweet, light-hearted way. He could be talking about picnics in the park or long walks in the beach, if it were not for the thing he presses my fingers over.

God, he's *so* hard. He's really, impossibly hard. I'm surprised I didn't see the thick length of him, straining against the zipper on his jeans – though that's just testament to how much I'm trying not to look. I don't even look now, while he fondles himself with my hand.

I don't really have to, to be honest. I can see just fine with my fingers. I can see that he seems to go on for ever and ever – to the point where it starts to get scary – and that the head of his cock is fat and thick, and very solid.

He could beat someone to death with that thing, I think, feverishly.

The fever probably explains why I actually voice this opinion.

'It feels like you dropped your nightstick down your pants.'

'Oh, so *that's* where that went.'

'I'm not kidding. Is this all you? Because if so, I think I may need to rethink a few things. I may need to rethink the shape and depth of my vagina.'

He gives me a dazzling, lopsided grin. I think I'd do anything for that thing. At the very least, I let him tow me through the veil of plastic between us and his bedroom, which is just as higgledy-piggledy as his living space. The sheets on his bed look clean and crisp, but the bed itself is tilted at a weird angle. And the tangle of clothes on his floor is so intense, I find myself thinking of the movie *Labyrinth*.

David Bowie is going to spring out of his discarded shorts, and thrust his crotch in my already overwhelmed face.

'No, you don't. Lie down on the bed.'

He gestures to that slanted thing with a sideways nod of his head. Like it's a route out of here, instead of the place where I'm going to get my insides rearranged.

'Really, I –'

'I'm not gonna hurt you, Kit. It's like I said: just a demonstration. And I know you want to see that demonstration, because you slid those sexy little panties down your legs in the hottest, awkwardest, most eager way I've ever seen anyone do that.'

My body flushes so hot it leaps off of me, and gets all over him.

'You like eager, huh?'

'I like awkward, too.'

'So it *does* get you off to see me making a fool out of myself. I *knew* it.'

I roll my eyes, only I don't truly mean it. I don't mean it, because he's not what I thought at all. Instead, he's the kind of person who laughs, and says:

'No, baby. It gets me off to see you not knowing a single damned thing about yourself, and getting to be the guy who makes sure you learn. Because I *am* going to be that guy, I promise you that.' He pauses – probably to give me time to faint. 'And we're going to start with a much-needed lesson in orgasms.'

There's very little protest in me, after that. I think I manage a dry-mouthed and very up and down:

'You're not going to be able to do this, you know.'

But I'm fumbling my way onto the bed as I do. And I can't blame myself for that. I think I'd give almost anything in return for words like those. He could probably ask me to climb on a sweaty camel right now, and I'd try. I'd run a million miles over mounds of molten lead, just to hear him say, 'I'm going to be that guy.'

He's not even *lying*. He grabs a hold of my leg – probably because I'm still clambering thirty minutes later – and then he just hauls me down the bed. He *hauls* me, the way other men haul other girls, when they really don't want to be that far apart.

He even stresses this concept.

'Yeah, we're going to have to be closer than that,' he says, as I do my best to get myself back into some sort of dignified sitting position. I know I'm not doing very well, however. I'm still breathless from the things he said and shocked by the manhandling – not to mention what's happened to my skirt.

It ruffled up when he dragged me, which would probably bother me at the best of times. But right now I'm *naked* under here. My knickers are still in a puddle on the other side of the curtain, and all that leaves is my suddenly bare pussy, exposed to his greedy waiting gaze.

I notice his eyes flashing all big and excited, whenever he catches a glimpse.

I notice it.

'Annnnd I'm probably going to see a lot of what you're trying to hide, pretty soon.'

'Really? Because I was hoping we could do this through telepathy. Like – you just *think* at my vagina and it spontaneously combusts.'

We're not far from that, as it is. He's burning a hole through my skirt with his heavy gaze, to the point where it's actually making me want to flash at him a little. Just a hint of shadow, you know … just a suggestion of the inside seam of my thighs …

But enough to keep that heat on me.

'While that sounds like fun, I'd prefer if you just slid that little skirt up your legs.'

He pauses, like he's daydreaming about doing that very thing almost in the middle of doing that very thing. We're two seconds away from the reality, but he's so impatient he can't wait. His eyes follow the path his hands haven't taken, all around the outsides of my thighs, ruffling the material as he goes.

By the time he actually touches me, we've fondled, fucked and I'm smoking a cigarette – which should probably take the edge off things.

Only it doesn't. My teeth clack together when he suddenly snaps out of his reverie and climbs onto the bed. He captures me between his two immense legs, and I'm shaking, I'm shaking. I can feel the bed rattling underneath me, despite the innocuous places he puts his hands: on my knees, really, rather than my thighs.

Though the tickle of his fingers on their outer edges … that's something worth being this nervous over, I think. The fizz that's flowing through my body is justified, for things like that. And for things like this:

'I'm not all waxed down there,' I tell him, partly because the thought is bothering me, and partly for something to say. He's making these circles on the insides of my legs – just a little way beneath the material of my skirt – and I can feel it pulling me down into silence. Soon I won't be saying anything at all, and then what?

Then I'll be like him.

'Uh-huh,' he says, distractedly, like he's forgotten how to make whole words. All his focus has transferred from things like conversation and my fluttery panic, to the inside of my thigh. He's practically gripping it, now – groping it, I suppose – in this graphic, possessive sort of way.

As he inches my skirt ever closer to actually revealing something. I bet he can see the outline of my pussy now, plump and pursed and so, so ready for this. A little more and I'll be completely exposed, and, oh, that anticipation is agony. I've never been undressed like this before – in parts and pieces. He just lets the material sag and stutter down my angled thighs, then right when I'm on the verge of saying no, he makes an impatient sound.

And spreads my thighs.

He has to kind of slide back a bit to do it, then crook my legs a little more, to give them room. Which seems like a long-drawn-out operation – only it isn't, in his hands. He does it all in one fluid move, like ripping off a plaster. One second I'm a nervous wreck. The next it's all over.

I can feel the air on my spread pussy.

Though I can feel his eyes on it, more. His gaze seems to weigh a ton, and it goes on forever – most probably because he's counting all the flaws. In fact, he must be counting all the flaws, because after a while of wandering all over everything he says:

'You always get like this?'

In a weird tone of voice I haven't heard before. It's short on breath and long on roughness, and I feel almost yanked into answering.

'Well … uh …' I start, but after that I'm unsure how to proceed. If I say yes, then I'm locked into whatever awfulness he means. But if I say no, maybe I can go away and do something about it. I can spruce it up a bit, add some Christmas decorations.

Though that would mean leaving; which I definitely cannot do. I'm too paralysed by his tractor-beam eyes to move.

'Was it the story?' he asks, and I know it's on purpose, now. He definitely baits his questions to get me to give the final push – right over the edge and into graphic sex talk.

'Was *what* the story?' I say, and he socks it to me.

'That got you this wet. Oh, God, you're soooo wet.'

The urge to glance down is great, but I resist. I resist because I know he's right – I can feel my own slipperiness all over me, and know how it must look.

Though it's not the story that made me this way. And it's not the way I am, either, because I swear I've never been this excited in my life. No, no … it's just him. It's his face and his words and the way he says them.

'Wet,' he says, like that's the best possible thing a woman could be. 'Sooooo,' he says, in a low drawl that sets me off again.

I could come, I think, like this.

I could come just hearing him talk some more.

'You'd never know that you were this aroused, baby, I swear,' he says, while I shudder uncontrollably. It's like I really am inside that cement mixer – only it's awesome. 'I mean, you get pretty flustered, but then there's the suit, and the wisecracks, and way you hold yourself off … Even I had no idea. Thought I'd at least have to warm you up a bit.'

He's touching me, now. Just the tip of his finger, trailing over the swollen outer curve of my sex. Barely anything, really, but it's enough to illustrate what he's saying. I can feel the glide between his touch and my skin. I can feel how easily he works his way in, through all of my slick folds and down, down to the place I want him most.

'But I guess not, huh? Ohhhh, baby, you're so slick. That feel nice, me stroking you like that? Maybe it feels a little more like torture, the state you're in.'

Oh, Jesus – *the state I'm in*. Apparently I'm a bombsite; I'm a disaster area. I'm all over-excited and soaked through and swollen, and good *God* I do not care. For the first time in my life, I don't care. All I want is for him to keep running his fingers over me, while he looks like this and talks like this. Oh, man, I could listen to him talk like this until the end of time. I've never heard any guy be this uninhibited in his speech, and it's bliss. It's unbelievable.

I'm writing thank-you letters to him in my head, for every single word he's said.

'Are you actually moving your hips in an effort to get my fingers a little closer to your clit? You know, I think you are.'

I think I am, too, but can he really blame me? He keeps circling that one agonising spot, without ever really touching anything. And sometimes it's so close that I'm sure he's there, I'm sure he is ... but then he moves away, and I realise it was just my imagination.

I'm having pleasure hallucinations. I'm so turned on I can't tell a real touch from a sly, teasing, non-existent one.

And then he makes it *worse*.

'Come on baby, work for it,' he says, because he's really fucking teasing me. This isn't me, going insane with lust. This is him, tormenting my aching body until I'd be willing to do anything, just anything to have him stroke me there.

Though I know he's not going to do it. He's going to do the other thing, instead – the one that absolutely will not work. I'm broken, I think at him, but he's not listening.

He's sliding a finger inside me, instead. Slow and steady, like he's trying me out. He wants to know if I can take it, and despite the tension in me, I can. I take it better than I ever have before. My pussy just opens up to him, everything so smooth and slippery and good.

Then better still, once I've seen the expression on his face. His eyebrows dip in the middle and his mouth goes slack, just as I imagined it doing in his story. And he makes a sound, too, as he glides into me – so much hotter than the one before. This isn't a puff of breath and a faint 'oh'. It's guttural and half-grunted, drawn out to the same speed as that finger sinking into me.

'Yeah,' he says. 'Yeah, baby, oh, you're so hot and tight.'

As though it's his cock filling me, rather than that single digit. He sinks it in all the way to the hilt, with just a little twist at the end. Then back out again, with as much pleasure as he seemed to experience over the long, slow slide in. I can see it in his eyes – narrowed to slits – and in the way his chest heaves up and down, as he explores me. It's in the deliberate stroke of his fingers, more a fondle than anything else, and the flicker of his tongue over his soft, wet lips.

I swear to God, when he licks himself that way … my body goes nuts. Because he was right about that. He was absolutely right. There's nothing I like better than knowing a man is turned on – and over me, of all things. He's this excited because of the simple feel of my sex, to the point where he can hardly stand to be away from it. Those strokes grow shorter and shorter, until I'm not even sure if he's leaving me at all.

He's just letting my soft, wet heat enclose him completely, as he takes in the sight of it. And then when the sight isn't enough, he uses his free hand to do something even lewder.

He spreads me open. He parts my folds and leans in closer, in a way that should definitely make me uncomfortable. I rarely like someone scrutinising my face, so I don't know why this feels so different.

It just does. A hot flush of pleasure gushes through me,

the second he does it. And it's followed by another as I think of all the things he must be seeing: the way my pussy clings to his deliciously thick finger, when he does force himself to slide it slowly back out. My clit, which feels just as stiff and swollen as he described in his story, and just as ripe for that wicked little tongue of his.

God, I wish he'd give me his tongue. Because as good as this feels, I know he's never going to get me there like this. It feels amazing – there's none of the usual burn and all of the pleasure I never normally feel – but I'm not really that close to orgasm.

I'm sure I'm not. I'm *too* sure I'm not.

'I think I'm going to win this bet,' I say.

Which is kind of a mistake.

I know it as soon as he looks up at me with that spark in his eyes. I know it before he slides a second finger into me, in a way that still feels good. I like the new feeling of fullness, more than most actual cocks I've had inside me. And I like the urgency suddenly in him, as he sits up straighter over me, and sets that impossibly firm jaw of his. He's going to give it to me now, I think.

So it's almost a disappointment when he doesn't. I even go to tell him again: really, this isn't going to work.

And then he spreads those two fingers inside me, and turns his hand, and my body just jerks all on its own. Like when you go to the doctor and he hits your knee with a hammer. Suddenly, your leg is not your own. My body is not my own – and the loss of control is so startling I think I tell him off.

'Don't do that,' I say, as though he's some naughty schoolboy.

But of course he isn't. He's not been caught with his hand in the cookie jar, and now has to be contrite. He's a sexual maniac, who doesn't have to do a thing I say. In fact, he goes one better than that: he ignores me. He spreads his fingers again, and gives them a little twist.

Such a simple move, really. I think of keys in locks and a dancer turning in her partner's arms, about a second before something grabs a hold of my body and wrings me out. I bite my tongue. I make this sound: 'Goh.'

And I have no more control over any of it than I do over him.

'Yeah, there, huh?' he says, from somewhere seven hundred million miles from me. 'Fuck, you're primed. You wanna come, honey? Tell me you wanna come.'

I writhe against his tormenting hand, helplessly, soundlessly. There's nothing else I can do. I'm so turned on I've turned mute – but he's not satisfied with that. He curls his fingers inside me and strokes hard, hard. Harder than I should like, and rougher too.

But, oh, the bloom of sensation that follows that vicious stroke … the way it makes me want to curl my body up and never straighten myself back out again … I can hardly stand it. Something's definitely going to happen *really* soon, if he keeps this up.

So naturally he doesn't.

He stops, right when I'm about to get my hands on the Holy Grail.

He *stops*, and says this:

'Oh, that's good, huh?'

Probably because he's sure I'll agree. He's sure I am. Of course, I try to be calm and cool about things – but I know how I must look. Every time he strokes over that one non-existent place inside me, I ball the sheets up in my fists. I go all stiff, like I'm not used to processing this sensation and kind of have a system malfunction, every time it happens. That weird, lowdown bloom of pleasure just goes through me, and I shut down.

And then just as I'm recovering, he does it all over again. Harder and faster, until it really is like he's fucking me. He's *pounding* me, which is good on two fronts. The first being how much I *fucking love oh God I love it oh Jesus that feeling*, and the second comes with a sudden and startling realisation.

This is why girls like that.

There's no sense of being pummelled into oblivion, while most of me dies of boredom. When it's done right, when someone's actually hitting the target instead of veering off on some irrelevant tangent, there's nothing that's too much.

I want this. I want him to do it again.

Though I'll be damned if I'm going to say.

'You want some more? Tell me it's good,' he says, only now he's just as breathless and half-crazed as me. This ... this resisting ... it's the only chip I've got left. After he's made me say it, what else is there? I'll be in his thrall forever.

I'll be his slave, and I know it.

He probably knows it. Some lady in a hut on top of the Himalayas knows it. She can hear me sobbing with pleasure from all the way over there, every time he drums his fingers against that absolutely existent place inside me. She's laughing at me for trying to get away.

Because I do that too. I attempt to claw my way up the bed, but he's having none of it. 'Where are you going?' he says. 'No, no, get back here. You said it wouldn't work, right? So come on, tell me if it's working. Oh, yeah, you like that, huh?'

I do, I do. I even like the slight sense of being brutalised, now. Of being forced to come against my will. He just grinds the heel of his free palm down over my swollen mound – moulding my pussy around those working fingers, forcing everything right down onto him – and I almost start crying. That lowdown feeling intensifies tenfold, and I know then. I'm definitely doing it.

Though that's not why words finally spill out of me. No, no. They burst out because of the way he looks, which really isn't all that smug at all. He doesn't look victorious. He looks fucked out and flushed with this monumental effort. He looks like he'd do this to me forever, until he died, until he lost his mind.

And I can't be bitter about that.

So I just let it out.

'Oh, God, yeah, I'm coming,' I gasp.

It's the first time I've ever done so and had it not be a lie. In fact, none of this is a lie. I twist on his bed as the sensation thuds through my lower belly – one pulse at a time, so slow and heavy. And each one pushes outwards, once it's done with me between my legs. It grabs a hold of all of me, and just when I think I can't take it, it releases.

Before starting back up again, at the beginning.

I've no idea how long it goes on for. Feels like days. He *makes* it like days. I try to get away again and he pins me in place. He gets his body over mine and drills me harder, until I'm gritting my teeth and trying desperately to grind sound through them.

I don't even know what that is. Is that a thing – grinding sound through your teeth? I don't know, but I have to do it. If I don't, I might die of this orgasm.

Though I suspect I'm going to anyway, whether I do or not. It's probably why I'm really crying, when he finally lets me go. Yeah, that's definitely why my eyes are wet, and my body is shaking uncontrollably. It's because I'm sure I'm going to be dead, soon. Here lies Kit Connor, I think. Died of sex at age twenty-eight.

Only it's not funny really.

I've lived my entire life without anything like this. All those years I've wasted on wan feelings and half-pleasures, satisfied with so little and thinking it was so much …

Lord, I didn't even believe him.

But I believe him now.

* * *

The first thing I do once I've composed myself is try to leave, but that doesn't work out so well for me. I wriggle my skirt down and plant my feet on the floor, but when I go to stand my legs have apparently forgotten what that is.

I actually drop to one knee – and even that doesn't know how to behave. I've just had an orgasm, leave me alone, it says, before sort of skidding across the floor. I have to grab onto the bed sheets – which are actually quite nice, for someone like him. I didn't notice them before because I was too busy being desperate for sex … though in truth I don't know how I'm noticing them now.

Maybe I just need something to focus on. White, and yet still crisp and clean, I think, frantically. And, oh, he has a real duvet and one of those memory foam mattresses!

I recognise the latter because the thing tries to suck my will to live, during my attempts to get back up again. Somehow I'm bum-skiing down the side of his bed – which basically means that I get all turned around and, in an effort to keep my feet, I brace my backside against the mattress.

Before sliding sideways along it.

'Have you possibly forgotten how to move like a human being?' he asks, after a while. I can't be mad, however. That's *exactly* what it looks like. 'I don't think you're going to make it back to your apartment by suction-cupping surfaces with your butt.'

I mean, he's got a point.

Shame he uses that point for evil.

'I'm doing fine, OK,' I say, which sounds ridiculous, even to me. I'm not suddenly trying to manage after a hideous car accident that robbed me of my inner ear. Nobody needs to be told that I'm fine.

So why do I say it?

'Maybe you should just come back to bed?'

Damn him. I'm still stunned from my orgasm, and that – combined with his lovely light-heartedness, his incredible state of happy-go-lucky – is really, really making me want to do what he's suggesting. He doesn't even make the suggestion sound smug.

Nothing he says sounds smug.

He's some sort of smugness-avoiding champion. Behold:

'It won't be a big deal if you come back to bed. I was thinking it could be a very small deal – a hardly noticeable deal – of possible light cuddling and a casual plate of home-made waffles.'

Lord, please let me survive Dillon Holt. He's not *natural*. He keeps saying stuff and saying stuff, and it's even more baffling than his ability to press a button inside me that apparently makes me come.

'I mean, the *amount* of waffles on the plate would be enormous,' he's saying. 'But the plate itself is very laid-back. It won't even make a comment on why you're here, or when

88

we might engage in more sex acts. Very easy-going things plates.'

Is it weird if I want to hug his face? At the very least, his sideways slanting commentary on the state of things makes me stop floundering. I parlay my butt-skiing into a mild sitting on the end of the bed.

Where things calm down considerably.

Most of my body's still going haywire – probably because it barely recognised any of the things he did to me – but the sex haze is clearing from my brain. I'm starting to stumble out into the ruins of myself, with the words *what the fuck just happened* on my lips.

I'm a war-torn survivor of Dillon Holt.

'I have to ... uh ... go to a meeting,' I try, but I've misjudged. It was way too early to attempt speech – my voice comes out all up and down and obviously stuffed full of lies, lies, lies. Though it's not my fault entirely that he guesses.

'At seven-thirty on a Wednesday evening?'

I jerk around, searching blindly for a clock or a watch or some other indicator that this cannot be true. The cat with the second-counting tail – the one on his wall, just above his head – won't tell me so, however.

Seven-twenty-seven, that fucker claims.

Probably because it's in collusion with him.

'It can't be that late. Wasn't it four o'clock when I got here?'

'Time has no meaning in my zone of sex.'

'Did you really just say that?'

'I'm hoping I didn't.'

I look at him, then – accidentally. I'm in the middle of a slightly shocked laugh, and then the urge to see his face just wrestles the rest of me into submission.

It's a mistake, however. Not only is his expression really

awesome – a self-deprecating eyebrow raise aimed entirely at himself – his fingers are just sort of ... trailing over his glossy bottom lip. And then as I'm watching, transfixed, he lets one slide a little way into his mouth.

He's tasting me. He's tasting me on his fingertips, as though I'm some exotic fruit he just finished pulling apart. I can even see the faint gleam I've left on him, honey soft in the dying light from his narrow window.

But there's nothing I can say. Telling him to stop will mean I'm acknowledging the lewd thing he's doing. Telling him to keep doing that – maybe harder, with more of a long slow suck so I can really see how he looks, when he uses that blow job mouth of his – will simply mean I've gone nuts.

Unfortunate, really, that the latter is what I most want to do.

'Sure you have to go?' he asks, after too long a time. He knows it's getting harder to say no by the second. All I'm thinking now is: what do I taste like on him? Can he make out the tang of his own skin underneath? Am I good?

He makes it look like I'm good. He strokes his tongue up and down the underside of his finger, then seems to sink – near helplessly – into something more. A long, slow slide into his mouth, just as I had imagined.

Only better. His eyes flutter closed as he does it, the way people usually do when they're biting into a gloriously rich cream cake. And he makes a sound, oh, God, he always makes a sound when he does these things ... does he know how that makes me feel? My mind empties of all other considerations the second he does it, before filling up with all the things he could possibly say and do.

I've only experienced a quarter of what he's capable of, it seems. Less – a fifth, an eighth, a piddling pathetic pinprick of an amount. And that's very bad for me, I know. It's a bad thought to have, when I'm trying so desperately to leave.

It makes my words come out like this:

'The ... place that I ... do workings ... at ... opens late. And my ... person in charge ... wants to ... to ...'

'Have this meeting?' he suggests, for me – because he's generous. He's very generous, and extraordinarily kind. I need an excuse to leave, and he's willing to let me have it.

Not to mention everything else that he's just done for me. I should really return the favour in some way and I know it, I do, but the trouble is ... I'm not like him. I've no idea how to start things up, just like he said. I think about maybe leaning forward to take that finger in my own mouth, but so many thoughts stop me.

The main one being: what if I do it wrong? Always, always: what if I do it wrong? It's embarrassing when other people do ordinary things – like making everyday chit-chat about the weather – and I don't know how to do the same. Failing horribly at something so filthy would be mortifying. Failing in front of *him* would be even worse.

Though I realise I already have. I made a bet, and I lost it. I bet I couldn't feel anything, and I did. I felt more than was strictly advisable, for a first date that wasn't even really a first date. And now, I'm making a second blunder. I'm trying to leave, when I know I should stay. I should stay and do all the things that other people do so easily, so easily.

But I don't.

I walk all the way home with the thought of every single thing I couldn't give him, in my head. Just because I'm so afraid, all the time! Just because I'm so very afraid of myself, and all the hopes and dreams I've never dared have.

But they don't matter, now. Soon, I'll be safe again. I'll be beyond the deep-red door that guards my apartment, and maybe I'll think of him from time to time, with fondness. But I know I'll never see him again. He won't call, and I definitely never will, and everything will be as it should, once more.

And then I realise, just as I step inside:

My manuscript isn't in my bag.

He *took* it.

Chapter Six

Of course I know why he did it. He's holding my book to ransom, like a master criminal who has designs on a wealthy widow's fortune.

Only I'm *not* a widow, and I don't have any money. I don't have a single thing that he should want – or at least, nothing I can think of. I spend the entirety of the next day trying to imagine, but the only thing I can come up with is my cat, Harold.

Harold is seventeen, blind in one eye and often farts in his sleep.

But Harold seems like a safer bet than *he wants me*.

He wants me so much that he kept the one thing that would make me return. He *knew* that I'd never come back. Apparently I'm so obvious that he can read me months in advance, and now he has something that's going to make that psychic effect worse.

He has my book. My book that's utterly filled with my every thought and feeling. Each chapter of it is filthier than the one before it; each word tells a tale about all the things I've ever wanted. And now he's got it.

He can't be reading it, can he?

He wouldn't.

He wouldn't.

And yet I know he has, the moment he opens his door to me. I might not be as good at this as he is – maybe I can't pick up on every little nuance and gesture that someone else makes – but I'm not an idiot.

I know a gleeful grin, when I see it.

'Kit, what a surprise!' he says.

It is not a surprise. Surprises have stunned expressions to go with them, and his is just bursting with unchecked delight and probable mocking laughter. Oh, God, even Lori laughed after she'd heard the first chapter. This guy is going to throw a party over my died-of-embarrassment grave.

'Yes. Isn't it?'

I try to keep my face nice and closed – but that just makes my mouth go tight. Now my words are coming out all funny. That 'Isn't it?' sounds like it was ground out by an animatronic version of me, rather than the real deal.

'You know … I sensed that we might not see each other again. So it's funny that you're here. I am at a loss as to why this might be,' he says.

'Are you? *Are you*? Are you really?'

None of these sentences come out like questions. They come out like bullets, fired from a really angry gun.

'But if you want to come in, I'm sure we can talk about it.'

'We cannot talk about it. I'm going to open my bag, and you're going to put my book in it. And then I'm going to go home and lie down in a darkened room where I can pretend that you did not read the equivalent of my diary.'

He does something then that I am not prepared for. I think I expect protests, but instead he makes the kind of expression I associate with some glorious victory. He even brings his fists up to his face, and half-bites on one of them.

Before saying this:

'Oh, honey, if that's your diary let me dive right into you. Let me drown in you, oh, praise be for your heavenly body of unbelievable sin!' Those fists unfurl and reach for my face – though to my eternal gratitude they don't quite make it. They're too excited to make it. He's like a kid who can't believe he got a trike for Christmas, and is so giddy about it he just makes grabby hands around its general area. 'God bless you, Kit Connor. You're the reason I almost masturbated myself to death last night.'

'You did not do that.'

He nods his head to one side, telling me what he means before he says it. He's made the switch to rueful in under ten seconds. He could compete in the Face Olympics.

'You're right, I didn't.' He pauses. 'But only because I'm saving myself for you.'

Oh, Dillon Holt. I'm swooning and you don't even mean it.

'I think you're about thirty years too late for that.'

'Hey – ouch. That's the exact age I am.'

'I *know*.'

'Oh, uh-huh, I see what you're doing there. You're saying you think I've been a slut since birth. Which is true. But I swear, I never knew how it could be before you.' He clicks his fingers, and I know what's coming. I pray that it isn't, but my praying does no good. God obviously wants me to fall under this guy's spell. 'I made it through the wilderness. You know I made it through …'

'Please don't start singing.'

'Didn't know how lost I was until I found you.'

'I'm begging you. I have no defences against this.'

It's true. I don't. He hauls me into a rudimentary dance

position, and I barely try to stop him. I just let him spin me around, drunkenly, both our arms joined together and pointing at judges that aren't there.

'All the better for me.'

'You want my defences to be down?'

He looks down at me from his very great height, face suddenly serious. There's still a hint of amusement there, and he doesn't let me out of this armlock, but his gaze is warmer. Softer. And I can feel him making those insanely good circles on my back.

'Well, it would make it easier to kiss you. Very hard when I have to barrel my way across a barbed-wire-riddled no-man's-land just to put my mouth on yours.'

'I don't mean to be like that.'

'I know.'

'I want to be more ... more ...'

'Open?'

'Or maybe just less ...'

'Angry? Because you know, I *did* steal your book. You should probably be furious at me forever for that gross invasion of your privacy.'

Funny thing is: he sounds like he's being silly. But his expression kind of says he's not. I feel like those eyes of his are wrapping me in a big, warm embrace, of the sort that this dancing is maybe turning into.

'Angry wasn't what I was going to say.'

'No?'

His mouth is getting closer to mine now. And he's looking at my lips, as though contemplating that last bit of distance. Will I open fire on him, if he goes for it? He's already encountered the mines, and that barbed wire stole one of his boots a while back.

Maybe he wants to turn around now, before it's too late.

'No. I was going to say inhibited. I want to be less inhibited,' I say, and I confess: I don't really think much of it, when I do. It's just a word, the same as *angry*. Both kind of end up at the same place – him at arm's length.

Me with seventy-foot-long arms.

But he goes kind of still, after I've said it. He holds his breath. This weird tension suddenly grows and spreads between us, until I'm sure I can see it there, crackling in the air. It looks sort of like a thunderous raincloud, only really, really awesome.

And then the lightning breaks, and so does he.

He goes for me, the way drowning men go for the life-jackets. I think his arm actually hugs my head, because I can feel his elbow close to my ear and his hand has kind of come up from behind to spread through my hair. I'm trapped in the cage of his body.

But I can't complain.

I'm trapping him right back. I'm doing some of the things I desperately wanted to do the day before yesterday, but didn't dare – like getting my hands on those fantastic fucking arms of his. I actually squeeze one of his biceps, just to see what it's like.

And it's everything that I could have hoped for. So thick and solid, barely giving under the pressure of my hand. Then his shoulders, his smooth, round shoulders ... Why didn't anyone ever tell me that shoulders could feel so good?

I'm rubbing them – round and round in circles – before I manage to get a hold of myself. I think he's even laughing about it, into my mouth ... though I don't particularly care. I've got his kisses to distract me, from petty things like embarrassment.

And they do the job sooo well. His mouth is just as soft as I'd imagined, from the look of it and that little hint he gave me. Though that's not the best part. The best part is how he moves those lips, insinuating them against my own in this rolling, insistent way. I knew he had rhythm, of course, but this just takes it to another level.

He presses against me when I'm ready for more, and pulls away when I'm not – leaving me just long enough to catch my breath, before coming back for more. And just as I'm lost in the sweet pull of his lips – just when I'm ripe for it – he parts them, and lets me feel the slick suggestion of his tongue.

He doesn't even have to persuade me to open for him – like before, with my warm and ready sex. I let him in without a second thought, thrilling at the sensation of his tongue darting over mine. It makes all these little tingles spark through my mouth, but there's something beyond the physical about it.

Some sensuous suggestion of other things he could do, if I let him.

And I want to. I'm trembling with excitement before we've done a single thing, and I tremble harder when he pushes me up against the wall. We just kind of stumble around until I'm somehow there; giddiness bursting through me at the thought.

I've never been handled like this, before. Hell, I've never done the handling. I've only seen it in movies, when the hero and heroine are so desperate for each other they don't know where they're going or what they're doing – they just end up somewhere, in the middle of blindly clawing at each other.

And then I realise something even sweeter, a second later.

My feet aren't even touching the floor. He's not just pinning me to the wall. He's holding me up – or maybe, oh, God, maybe *I'm* the one doing the holding. I've climbed him like a monkey and now I'm clinging to him, desperately, as he kisses me into oblivion.

He's at my throat now. Then back to my face, my lips. I can hardly keep up with him, only somehow that feels OK. I want to be swept away. I want him to leave these hot, wet marks all over me, right on down to the V of my shirt – and lower, if he wants to go.

Which he apparently does. He mouths at my breasts through the material, turning it wet and heavy. But that just makes the sensation more intense. The cotton clings to my skin, rubbing at me as his lips do, as his tongue does.

And then he catches one stiff nipple, and I cry out without meaning to.

'Sensitive there, huh? And by there, I mean all over. *God*, you're easy to get going.'

'I am?'

'Oh, yeah. You got going the moment I kissed you, right?'

He trails his mouth up over the curve of my throat – probably to illustrate this point. I squirm the second he does it, and end with another faint sigh, to feel him licking just below my right ear.

Who knew that could be an erogenous zone?

'Maybe.'

'Maybe? Maybe is all you're going to give me?'

'Yes.'

'Even though I could just slide my hand up your skirt and see.'

'See what?'

Lord, I do ask some stupid questions. But in my own defence, he *is* sucking on my earlobe in-between sentences. I don't think anyone could put two and two together under that kind of pressure.

'See how wet you are, baby. Did you get wet just walking over here?'

'No.'

'Did you think about all those things I must have read, and feel that heat starting up between your legs? In your pussy?'

In truth, I can't remember – not that it matters.

I can certainly feel it *now*. It started as a small flame, when he first put his mouth on mine. And it ends as a raging inferno, the moment he says that one wicked word. I actually jolt to hear it, said in so exciting a way. He strips it of every negative connotation, and leaves me without the ability to speak.

'Because I read all of it, every word, every dark little fantasy, and I swear to God I'm going to do every single one to you.'

'You *are*?'

I sound so helplessly incredulous. It's almost humiliating.

'Oh, yeah. And I'm going to start with chapter twenty-four.'

My brain immediately flicks to the offending section, and that incredulity increases tenfold. I'm trying to kiss him back, but it's really hard to when your eyebrows have disappeared into the stratosphere. And my eyes … I know my eyes are comically wide.

I just can't make them any smaller, in the face of chapter twenty-four.

I wasn't even sure people really did that. I just put it in because it sounded so outrageous, but he doesn't seem to think it is at all. He thinks it's a trip to the post office to get some stamps. For him, chapter twenty-four is a daily event – and now he wants to do it all over me. And even more terrifying:

I think I might let him.

Oh, God, I can't possibly let him.

'Not chapter twenty-four,' I moan, as though he just threatened me with a pair of pliers and a dentist's chair. But my hands are sort of in his hair, as I say it, and I'm making these little daring, darting forays into various bits of his body. I jerk forward and give his earlobe a little lick – maybe to see if he likes that as much as I do – and when he goes all shivery I get a little bolder.

I lick his throat, too – his delicious throat, that kind of tastes like Juicy Fruit. And he's so warm there, too, so warm and just a little bit bristly. The whole thing leads me on like a teasing little trollop, until I'm kissing him there all hot and wet. I leave a mark where that curve meets his jawline, and another once I'm sure he doesn't mind.

But then, isn't that what's so cool about Dillon?

He doesn't mind anything. I could probably get away with grabbing him between his legs, if I had the balls to go for it. As it is I've managed to get his T-shirt halfway up his back, and that's in the middle of the most terrifying conversation of all time.

Imagine if I was calmer, I think.

Imagine how I'd be if I didn't care at all.

'How about chapter twelve, then?' he asks, as he rubs my achingly stiff nipples through all that material and all that wetness. It's really hard to say no, with that sensation in the back of my mind. 'I feel like you really, really might want chapter twelve.'

'I don't think I ... I kind of ...'

'You kind of want to do chapter twelve.'

'Maybe we could start with ... something a little more like chapter – oh, God, don't do that. Don't do that. Why are you doing that?'

The 'that' in question is him rubbing the heel of his palm over my sex, through my skirt. And even though my skirt is made of tweed and has the density of a giant chunk of dark matter, the surge of sensation I get from the feel of him is just ... otherworldly. A heated pulse spreads outwards from the place he's touching, and I clutch at his body. I gasp for air.

'To get a better number.'

'You're not going to get a better number by playing dirty.'

'Are you sure? Because it kind of feels like I might.'

'You definitely won't, oh, God, you definitely won't.'

'Really? Not even if I keep rubbing you like this?'

'Mmmm yes ... I mean ... no. No. No.'

'Because that is your clit right there, isn't it? And when I just make these little circles ... that feels good, right? I bet that feels sooooo good. You came so easily when I fucked you like that, so I gotta guess that you can do it in seconds, when someone's rubbing you here. Even if it's through material like this. Even if I'm barely touching you at all.'

He's right. I've got my arm around his shoulders and I'm kind of squeezing him in these spasms, and I can hear the sounds I'm making. I'm moaning in these little fits and starts that get louder as I manage to get my feet on the ground and shift position a bit.

'Yeah, oh, yeah. Did you just spread your legs a little for me, baby? Huh? You like that, huh? Want me to pull your panties down and lift your skirt? Maybe stroke you skin to skin? When does that happen in your book? ... chapter three, I think. Yeah, chapter three is when he finds her in the copy room, and rubs her off while the whole office watches through the window.'

'Please don't let anyone watch,' I say, because that's all I can manage. I can't tell him I don't want him to take my underwear off, because I want it more than I've ever wanted anything in my life. And I can't suggest that he shouldn't stroke me with his bare fingers, as that is pretty much all I've dreamt about since he almost did it yesterday.

So this is the one bargaining chip I've got left: no insane voyeurism.

But apparently it's not really needed.

'Ohhhh, honey,' he says, as he takes my face in one hand, and kisses me long and slow on the mouth. 'You really think that's how it's going to work? That I'm the one who has to let things happen?'

I go blank, momentarily. Then think of all the guys in every story I've ever written. They're always giving permission and making things happen, and I guess I'd kind of thought the same of him. He certainly seems like a steam train, barrelling through all of my barriers.

But now I'm not so sure.

I'm not sure about anything.

'It's just you,' he says. 'And whether you'd be OK with chapter two.'

Chapter Seven

There's something worse about that one than all the others. Not because it's ruder, because it really isn't. Chapter two is just the introduction of my heroine to her Master – it goes back to when they first met, and she was too embarrassed to admit anything about herself. So he makes her lie on the bed, with most of her clothes still on, and then ...

And then she does the thing I'm suddenly petrified of.

I almost say to Dillon: *no, let's go back to the first thing you suggested.* If I'm really in charge and I'm truly the one with the power of permission, then maybe I can just say. I even form the words in my head: *I'd like you just to stroke me, if that's OK?*

So it's weird that I don't let them out.

Instead I unzip the side of my skirt, and let it fall. If I'm remembering correctly she does the whole thing in her underwear – but that's still so very bare to be. That's still much more naked than I've been in front of him before, and now there's an extra layer of exposure on top, too. There's his growing knowledge of me, so much more extensive than anything I've got on him. I don't even know if he likes seeing me this way.

105

Though I think I can guess.

He seems excited just watching me unlace my shoes – so excited that I'm surprised he can stay where he is. That heat is crackling out of him again, and he's breathing really hard, but he doesn't come any closer. He stays sitting in one of those little loveseats, as I strip off in front of his bed. He's swept the curtain aside and drawn the chair very near to me – just like in the story – but that's the limit.

That's all he does, as I start unbuttoning my shirt.

'You want me to talk?' he asks, after a second – probably because I'm shaking and fumbling with this last real barrier. He's not seen my love handles, yet, or my ridiculously big boobs, and the thought of him doing so is making me shake.

So I say yes, even though the hero of my book rarely said a word. He was all moody looks and angry sneers, steely in his silence like some Clint Eastwood character. But when I wrote that, I didn't fully realise what words could do. I'm used to quiet myself, during sex, and have never really had the benefit of anything else.

But now I'm starting to understand.

I'm starting to understand how it feels to have someone say words like this, when you're stumbling around in the dark, unsure.

'Ohhhh, man, those tits of yours. Oh, baby, it's a crime that you hide that body under so many clothes. Come on. Come on, take that shirt off.'

They'd probably sound crude, to most people. They're gruff and half-grunted, and he uses words like 'tits' and 'fuck'. But somehow they're a thousand times sweeter than the poetry Bobby Tate tried to write for me, or the halting 'I like you very much' I got from David Lerner. They make my heart thump in my chest, and a flush spread over my body.

And then he puts a hand between his own legs and squeezes the thick shape he finds there, and the effect is magnified. The effect thumps me in the face and knocks me unconsciousness. I barely even think about the shirt I'm sliding off my shoulders – because he gives me so many other things to consider.

By the time I'm standing there in my mismatched underwear, all of my focus is on his jeans-clad cock, and what he's doing with it as he watches me.

He's stroking himself, I think. He's stroking himself over the breasts that barely fit into this ridiculous bra, and my silly cotton knickers that could put anyone off. The fact that the top bit is black and the bottom bit is white is just the icing on the cake, really, but apparently he doesn't care.

'Ohhh, yeah,' he says, as though I'm some peephole stripper, lithe and lovely, ready to dance for his delectation. The idea doesn't even make me feel tawdry, though I know it should. Whenever I'm writing a scenario like this, those are always the words I want to put into it. They're the ones that Lori thought was missing – the real ones – that tend to hover on the periphery of my fantasies. *Cheap, silly, slutty, wrong* … they stand in a ring around my heroine.

Only they don't stand around me now. I'm fluttering with nerves and they're showing in my shaking body and my flushed face, but that's about it. The rest is excitement, real excitement, of the kind that gets stronger when he says, 'Get on the bed, then.'

By the time I've fumbled my way there I'm breathing jaggedly, and my pussy feels so hot, so swollen, I can hardly move around it. I can't put my legs together, because putting my legs together feels like it might send me over the edge. And I can't keep them really open, either, because once I'm lying down I'm very aware of the view.

He'll be able to make out the plump swell of my sex, straining against the material, and the curving shape of my bottom, below – all of which he's already seen, I know. He's seen it all bare, in fact, so I should be absolutely fine about this.

And yet somehow I'm not. I'm more nervous, in some strange way, with my underwear still on, and him over there, just watching me. He's not standing over my body, making everything happen with his hands. I have to do it myself, and doing it yourself is hard. It's ... more real. I reach down between my legs and find the material soaked through, and immediately want to hide the fact.

Even though he's seen that before, too. He knows how I get. *I* know how I get. I shouldn't be the least bit surprised to feel all that wetness, making my knickers thin and clingy and really, really rude.

But I am, all the same. I make a little startled sound and a thick surge of arousal goes through me, followed by that desire to close my legs. Thankfully, however, arousal wins, and I just manage to hold them open, as I force myself to keep stroking over that slippery shape beneath the material.

And then after a while I'm no longer forcing things at all. I'm fondling myself, I realise, just like he wanted. I'm doing what feels good – like a long slow rub over my plump outer lips; that soaked material making everything more sensitive and alive to sensation. Just like his mouth did on my nipples, I think, and then I touch myself there, too, without thinking. I slip a hand inside the cup of my bra, and run the tips of my fingers over that one stiff point.

While my other hand gets bolder.

My other hand isn't content with teasing any more. I don't think it was content five minutes ago, to be honest, but I held it back. I kept it captive with nerves, and now they're falling away – along with my awareness of the story that sits behind all of this. The heroine had to be made to, if I remember correctly. He had to force her to touch herself, when she simply wouldn't go the whole way.

But I guess I'm not really like that. I'm more the sort of person who gets so turned on that they can no longer think straight – who gets over-excited, just like he said, and can't be shy about things any more. I want to come, I think, I really want to come, so I just slide my hand inside the material and ease my fingers through my own sex.

Much to his amusement.

'Couldn't wait, huh?' he asks, and I wonder what he's thinking of. Is he picturing that shy girl in the story, so much sweeter than me? I'm doing the exact same thing she did: masturbating under the cover of her pretty cotton underwear. But it's different, and I know it. It's different because he tells me so, a second later: 'Oh, you love it,' he says.

And I do. I love those first teasing strokes over my little bud, and the feel of my own wetness in-between. I love how hot I feel, how hard I clench around my finger when I briefly sink inside … But most of all, I love knowing that he's watching.

I never thought I would. I've never so much as stroked my own inner thigh in front of someone else without feeling self-conscious … but, God, I do. I do.

And I love hearing him, too.

'Are you rubbing your clit?' he asks, and I nod. I can't answer him. The sensation is so intense that I'm pinching my lips together, in case some of it leaks out and takes down a small city. I can't even touch myself directly, there, because it's far, far too much. I just have to circle around and around that one place, until I can feel it starting up inside me. I can feel that long, low stutter, that little hook that gets a hold of me and draws my orgasm out.

But I don't want it to happen just yet, because he's still talking.

'Tell me what it feels like,' he says, then hardly waits for the answer. 'Does it feel good, baby, huh? It looks like it feels good. It looks like you're gonna come all over your hand – oh, yeah, that's fucking sexy when you arch your back like that. That's it, that's it, rock your hips ...'

He's still talking, and I'm still going crazy over it.

'Moan for me, baby,' he says. And you know what? I do. I make this frantic, desperate, ridiculous sort of sound, all drawn out and far too loud. Then once I'm done with it, I do it again. I moan again – this time higher and more protracted – because, by God, it's a great thing to do. It's so freeing, in a way I'd never really considered before, and when I hear my own voice I don't want to curl away from it.

It spurs me on instead. It makes me stroke myself harder, faster, and after a while I actually prop myself up so I can watch whatever he's watching. I want to see what's making him gasp and say such filthy things, and when I do I kind of understand. The material has slid to one side and you can see little glimpses of me. And the way I'm working myself is just so ... out of control. It's like I can't get enough, like I'm completely lost to this pleasuring of myself.

And I can't deny how good that looks.

Or how good he looks, standing over me.

I don't know when he got up, but he's there when I open my eyes. And he's watching me with such intensity that it's hard to bear at first. I almost squirm away, before a million things drag me back: the sight of his erection, straining so

And then I realise I'm invoking the defence of sex pests everywhere, and have to pull myself up short before I get eight to ten in the sex-pestery wing of the nearest prison.

Good God, he makes me nuts. He makes me so nuts that I seem to have lost the brain power necessary for figuring all of this out – though, in fairness to me, he doesn't exactly make it easy. After I've laid there for a while in my underwear, absolutely mystified and unsure how to proceed, he calls to me from the kitchen:

'Hey, what do you want on your pizza?'

And I just don't know how to answer that at all. I'm too unaware of the rules and parameters. Is getting a pizza proper post-orgasm etiquette, in the world of normal sexual behaviour? I just don't know, because last time I did this with him I skied down his bed and then fled. And all the sex I had beforehand occurred when I was already living with the person, so once sexual contact had taken place we usually just went to sleep.

But I can't go to sleep now, because he randomly wants to eat a pizza.

Unless he wants the pizza for reasons other than eating, in which case I really am in trouble. I've never had to use a stuffed crust to get a guy off before, and am pretty sure I'd be really bad at it. I'm not even good at the ordinary stuff, like persuading a guy to let me take his pants off. I'm sort of secretly hoping he'll have already done it when he finally emerges from the kitchen – but he hasn't.

He's still completely covered in clothes.

Which only makes me feel more naked. It's like I turned up for a date in just my underwear, even though that seems really unfair. He didn't tell me that we were going to suddenly switch from sex to whatever this is, and now I'm totally

unprepared. I'm caught midway between a million things –
standing and sitting, pulling my shirt on and leaving it off
– while he continues being all casual and blasé.

He even hands me a Coke, while I'm still standing there
with my hand in one sleeve. And then he takes a seat, and
puts his feet up on the coffee table that wasn't there the day
before. He's had a hard evening's work, I guess, and now
it's time to ... relax?

I don't know, I don't know.

But, dear God, I wish he'd say.

'You gonna sit down? Pizza won't be long.'

That probably counts as saying, right? At the very least,
he doesn't want me to leave immediately. It's not as if he's
done his business with me and now it's time for me to go.
I'm supposed to sit – maybe in the chair opposite in him –
and that's a good foundation for me to work with.

But it still lacks one crucial point.

Am I supposed to be dressed or not? It feels kind of weird
for me to not be, at this point, but at the same time I can't
shake the sense that it would send a signal. Putting my clothes
back on means that I'm all set, and couldn't care less what
happens with him. I'm ready to walk right out of the door,
and he *still* hasn't had a single thing from me.

And that just seems crazy. It's completely backwards. Right
now, I should be the one unsatisfied, and yet somehow I'm
not. Or maybe I am, but it's really different from the usual
sort of vague disappointment.

I'm not sad for myself.

I'm enraged for him. I'm full of five thousand things I
could do to him, right now – all of them tumbling through
my mind one after the other in a great orgiastic burst of
tangled limbs and wet mouths and, ohhhh, God, I bet he'd

like that. Would he like that? I bet he'd *love* it. I bet he'd like it so much that he'd –

'So, Kit. You work in a library, right?'

What is *happening*? I can't even answer without putting an ellipsis in the middle, because I'm so unsure. Is he really wanting me to talk, or is this some kind of test? It feels like a test, but if it is I've no clue about the answers. This is what I go with:

'I ... guess.'

Like some timid pupil, who wishes they hadn't raised their hand.

'That's pretty cool.'

'... thanks?'

I don't know how a question mark gets on the end of that word. It just creeps in, without my permission – and of course it says so much, once it's there. It's says that I find my job so dull I can't even accept a compliment about it without asking someone if they're sure. *Are you certain you meant cool?*

I think you should have gone with utterly mundane, completely mediocre ... the job of a person who's afraid to forge a path through life, and instead settles for cardigans and catalogues and unsatisfying relationships with a man.

Like this one, only the *other way around*, it's the *other way around*.

Why can't he see that it should be the other way around?

'Do you wear little glasses?'

'Um ... sometimes.'

'And your hair pinned up.'

'Well, it's best for work, so ...'

'With strands falling out all over the place.'

'I guess, but, you know, it's just because my hair is so

unmanageable and there's this one kind of piece that never wants to ... wants to ... Wait. How do you know all of this?'

I have a sudden flash of him staring in through the tiny murky ankle-level windows that look down into my little basement lair – my section of encyclopaedic tomes and books of historical importance that no one bothers to come and see.

Except for him, with his imaginary peeping.

It has to be imaginary, right?

'I don't, really.'

Oh, thank God, it's imaginary.

'I was just listing all the attributes of some sexy librarian cliché I have in my head.'

I think I was a little hasty with the 'thank God'. Peeping I could have probably dealt with, but some ghost of me who might actually be sexy ... that's a tougher call. Especially when I'm still standing here with half a shirt on, unsure whether I should sit down or not.

And when I finally do, it's certainly not a sexy thing to see. My legs are still quite rubbery, and they fumble around on the way there. Then once they're seated, they're not sure how to place themselves. I've always been really bad at crossing one over the other – my legs are so short and chubby that they never seem able to do it right. But of course I can't sit with them gaping open, because my shirt barely grazes my underwear.

So in the end I settle for knees primly together.

Like a librarian.

A sexy librarian.

A sexy librarian who's just realised she's buttoned her shirt up wrong.

'Oh ... uh ...' I say, and go to sort them out. Somehow I've put the top one in the third hole, which is bad even for me. I tend to go to work with the two sides just a fraction out of alignment, but this isn't a fraction at all. I'm practically showing boob on one side and stomach on the other.

Not that he cares.

He stops me before I can fix it.

'No, no,' he says with a laugh. 'Leave it like that.'

'Why?'

'Because it's cute. You're cute.'

'I don't think cute is the technical term for what I am.'

'No? Then enlighten me.'

'I think it's called *being a disaster*.'

'And you don't think your disastrousness is the least bit adorable?'

I've no idea what to say to that. Mainly because I've never considered the concept he's talking about in any way whatsoever, but also because he seems so certain. He's a very certain person, Dillon. He kind of bulldozes you with his total conviction, until you find yourself somehow sitting on a chair of his in a badly buttoned shirt, unable to think of anything but sucking him.

Just ask, my brain whispers. But my brain can't be trusted. It's turned into a total idiot, and besides … there's something else I'm starting to wonder. Because he did say that thing about loving patience and holding off. So it could well be that this is all just part of his master plan, to possibly have an orgasm so intense it collapses the fabric of space-time and turns the Earth into a giant black hole.

In which case I'm all for it – despite the bit where my body gets spaghettified due to the intense pressures of his insane gravity. I mean, that's kind of happening to me anyway. So, really, where's the issue?

'You know what else is adorable? When I can clearly see you having a furious discussion in your own head.'

'That's *visible*?'

Oh, God, how mortifying.

'Kit, you practically mouth the words.'

'I do *not*,' I protest, but now I'm not so sure. No one's ever said this to me before. I was always certain that my silence was taken for a lack of things to say, instead of the opposite: sometimes, there are so many things I want to say that they overwhelm me. I've got years of unsaid conversations in my head. Decades of sentences that never slipped out; centuries of words I couldn't quite form.

That's got to put some pressure on your pressed-together lips.

'No, you don't. But it's a close thing.'

Or maybe he's just fucking with me.

'Stop fucking with me.'

'I'm not, I swear!'

'Then what *are* you doing?'

'Trying to have a ... a talk with you.'

The weirdest thing happens, in the middle of his words. They seem to sort of fail him briefly, and so does the smile on his face. In fact, the smile on his face falls all the way off, for a second, in a way that actually worries me. I think I get a little pang, seeing it happen.

Though I've no idea why. I don't even know why he might be sad, because he's absolutely fantastic at having a chat. He's so good at it that I'm saying all sorts of things without really meaning to, and am now somehow at a point where I'm *wanting* to tell him more. His bizarrely disheartened face just makes me blurt stuff out, apparently.

'I do have conversations in my head,' I say, and the sun comes out all over him. That grin comes back as though it never went away – and for what? A confession that means so little? I'm so little, I think, but he makes me feel like I'm so much.

118

'Yeah, I know it.'

'Sometimes they go on for a really long time.'

'I guessed.'

'They're usually about how rubbish I am at pretty much everything.'

'Guessed that, too.'

'You did?'

'Uh-huh. You're not as hard to understand as you think, you know.'

'Really? Then why has no one else ever figured me out?'

He grins even more broadly at that.

'Because they weren't as dedicated as I am. I'm the Professor of Kit Connor Studies, at Some Insane University. I did my doctorate in you, and possibly published a paper.'

'That's … the stupidest thing I've ever heard,' I say, but I'm smiling all goofily as I do so. I think I have hearts in my eyes, but here's the best part: I don't even want to get rid of them. I'm perfectly content to stare at him like a lovesick idiot, because he doesn't mind in the slightest. In fact, I think he's going after that very effect.

'Yeah, but you kind of like it, right?' he asks, and then he *bites his lip*. He bites his lip, as though he's a little unsure but oh so hopeful that this is the case.

I can't let him down.

'Of course I like it. Anyone would like it. That's the goal in life: to have someone else actually understand you. Though I suspect you know me less than you think you do.'

'Try me.'

'OK: how many brothers and sisters do I have?'

'That's not a fair question! We're talking about … existential stuff.'

'We are?'

119

'Absolutely.'

'Are you completely sure you know what existential means?'

'*No*, but that's not the *point*,' he says, and, oh, I love love love the way he does it. He puts this half-amused-at-himself emphasis on two of the words, so full of self-deprecation and ruefulness that I could just devour him whole.

I'm not the adorable one.

He is.

'The point is that I know a lot about your secret feelings.'

'You do, huh?'

I make my voice all big and blustery and sure of itself – but only to hide what I'm really thinking. Which is mainly: Oh, God, I hope he doesn't know that time I accidentally slipped a finger into my butt in the shower, and kind of liked it.

'I do. For example: I already know half of the things you think you're rubbish at.' He laughs, but not about anything I'm afraid of. Instead he just says this, as he shakes his head. '*Rubbish*. What a great British word.'

'I don't think garbage would have had quite the same effect.'

'Yeah, it sounds a little harsh. And you're harsh enough on yourself as it is.'

'I'm really not.'

'You sure? Because you seemed mortified about the wrongly buttoned shirt.'

'Well … that's a big deal. To no one else.'

'And you definitely don't know how hot you are.'

'That's … a very subjective … thing …'

'Oh, and there's your book, that you seem to think is so terrible –'

'I won't deny that I suspect it has probl–'

'– even though it's amazing.'

I swallow instead of speaking, then. You know, one of those really hard swallows that kind of feels like there's something in your throat? Only there isn't anything there at all. It's just me, being kind of shocked by something someone else has said.

Usually it happens because I've just been backhandedly insulted.

But I'm happy to experience this version, too.

'I bet you've written others, too, right? That's not the only one. You've got, like, ten of the same, somewhere under your bed.'

He's completely wrong.

They're in the bottom drawer of my wardrobe.

'And they've all never so much as seen the light of day, because you're so sure that they're not worth anything. You were so sure that you came to a meeting of sexual misfits at the word of one other person, and continue to see someone as ridiculous as me in the vain hope that I can make you better.' He puts the rim of the bottle to his lips and takes a sip while all of that sinks into me. 'Which is a pretty terrible plan, when you think about it. I can't even make myself better. No idea what help I'd ever be to you.'

I've had some time, now, and it still hasn't sunk through me. There are just so many crazy things he's packed into one paragraph that I don't know where to start. I feel like I've just been on a rollercoaster of words, from the elation of *being worth it* all the way down to the depths of *no idea*.

He has *no idea*?

I can't let that stand.

'Dillon … I'm not really sure you *need* to make yourself better.'

'Oh, Kit – you have no idea, seriously.'

'Well, I'll admit I'm not as good at this as you are. Most of the time I can't read you at all, and I've no clue what you've got under your bed. But you've ... you know ... you've ...' Oh, God, I can't say it. I can't say that he's been cooler to me than anyone I've ever known. That's just the saddest thing of all time, after three damned days. 'And even if you are ... not that great ... you should probably give me a chance to know that. I'd like to know that. I'd like to know more about you. We keep talking about me, but what about you?'

The moment I say it something happens to his face. Something much more noticeable than the loss of a smile, because even when that happened there was still stuff going on there. He always has stuff going on there. His features rarely stay still for more than a second, so when they *do* go still ... when there's a sudden lack of emotion on his face ...

It's unsettling.

It's so unsettling that I want to put a hand over his, and ask him ... really ask him if he's OK – even though he'll definitely think I'm silly when I do. He's the kind of guy who probably is OK, all the time. It's just a momentary lapse in his laddish armour, and in a second he'll snap right out of it. Any second now. Any second ...

Oh, Lord, he still isn't coming around, and now it's been forever. It's been an eternity of that blank look and those dead eyes, and I just can't let them go any longer. He said all that stuff about me, and seemed so concerned. I have to show him that I'm concerned about him, too.

Only just as I do ... just as I work up the courage to maybe ... pat his leg a little bit and say something soothing, like 'Dillon, you know you can tell me anything' –

The doorbell rings, right in the middle of it. All I get out is this:

'Dillon, you know you can.'

Which means absolutely nothing at all. It has zero comforting value, and probably very little worth as a set of words too. It's not even a complete sentence, and I can't make it one now. He's just yelled, 'Pizza' and dashed to the door, and when he comes back he's so excited about the food that the blank-faced thing is forgotten.

But I at least get to file that one away:

Dillon Holt *loves* to eat. Ohhhh, man, does he ever love to eat. He practically inhales half the thing before I've finished a slice, and he makes such a meal of it as he does. He licks his fingers and runs that wicked tongue into the corner of his mouth. He makes noises ... the kinds of noises I've previously heard him reserve for sex stuff.

And while he's doing all of that, I take in some other things, too. I learn about him in bits and bolts and fits and starts, from the pair of roller skates he's got in one corner to the life-sized figure of Captain Picard in another. There's a picture of Boston on one wall that makes me think he comes from there, but of course I can't be sure.

I can't be sure because of something I realise, a whole hour too late:

He didn't jump up like that because he's so in love with pizza.

He jumped up because I started to ask.

And he didn't want to say.

Chapter Eight

I realise what's happening about three hours into the next day, when I accidentally file an F in the N section because I'm thinking too hard about him. In fact, I'm thinking about him so hard that I forgot to eat lunch. I'm just sitting at my little desk, daydreaming about him, and suddenly it's half-past one. I've lost the whole morning to thoughts of what I could do, if only he'd let me, and guesses about what he didn't want to say.

I bet he's a drug dealer, my mind says, but that's not any more helpful than my other imaginings. It doesn't separate my thoughts from him for ever. I just start picturing myself on the back of his badass drug dealer's motorbike, on the run from the law. A whole elaborate scenario plays out in my head, with him as the star. I tearfully accept his life of crime, and move with him from motel to motel in some random American landscape that doesn't exist outside terrible movies.

And that's when I know I'm in trouble. Around that sort of fantasy – which isn't actually a fantasy, in truth. It's more like a nightmare, and yet somehow I'm still living it out, in my head. I'm living out a lot of things to do with him in my head, because apparently I'm obsessed. He's snared me with mysteries and things he didn't want to do, so neatly that I suspect he's done it on purpose.

Like with the book, I think. He's guaranteed I'll go back. I can no longer stay away under my own willpower, and instead have to return just to see. Just to know what might happen next. He's a book I haven't quite finished, yet, and I'm compelled to get to the end.

Though, I swear, I resist for a while. Once I've realised the problem, I do my best to minimise it. I force myself not to think of him for long stretches of time, which sometimes works and sometimes doesn't. Occasionally I can almost feel him, breathing on the back of my neck – to the point where I actually turn, to see if he's there. It's dark down here and the rows of shelving stretch on for ever, so it's entirely possible for someone to sneak up on you.

It's just that it's crazy to imagine he would. He's probably not thinking of me half as much as I'm thinking of him, and every time I consider this idea it strengthens my resolve to be saner. I'm just not used to someone talking to me so avidly, that's the thing. I'm not used to his questions and his intensity and his passion, or any of those things, full stop, if I'm being honest. I'm starved of attention, and it's showing in my embarrassing desperation.

So I decide: I'm not going to see him tonight. I'm going to show him that I'm cool, so completely cool and collected. He doesn't have to worry about me going all Glenn Close on his ass. I'm reasonable and rational – so much so that I make it into day two.

I get all the way into day three, before I turn into a junkie.

My hands actually shake whenever I try to make them do anything normal. They resist my cups of orange squash and go nuts over the keys on my computer. I attempt to type the words 'it's better when you don't' and end up with this, instead:

Ziiiiiizzzzzzz emmma nenuuuuuooonnnnt.

And I put symbols on the end that completely don't belong, too. Before today, I didn't even know some of these symbols existed. One of them looks like a really stiff fishing rod, with a fish on the end. Another has a hat on it, even though none of my keyboard keys were big on headgear, before today.

They've just turned against me now, in my hour of need.

And, apparently, so has my sense of sight. There I am, getting angry at my computer for inventing symbols that don't exist – even though the problem all along was my eyeballs. They're so intent on the screen that they barely notice when someone walks up to the counter, and by the time I glance up it's so much more of a shock than it should be. I jolt so violently I knock over my cup of orange juice, and of course he laughs when I do.

Of course he does.

'I didn't mean to scare you, Kitty-cat,' he says, but really he doesn't have to apologise. It's all my fault for being so certain that he'd never turn up here. I spent too long focusing on other things and dismissing every shadow and daydream, and now I'm sure he's the same way. He's just a hallucination, brought on by extreme Dillon Holt withdrawal.

God knows, he looks like it.

He's wearing … things. And the things are very … tight. I can make out the exact shape and weight of his pectoral muscles, underneath material so obscenely thin it should be outlawed. I've seen strippers in more than he's got on, even though he has actually covered most of his body.

It just doesn't *seem* like he's covered most of his body.

It seems like he's come to torment me.

127

'You OK? Kind of seems like you're drooling a little, there.'

'I'm not drooling.'

I *am* drooling. His eyes are a deeper blue in the dim, secretive light down here, and those black lashes surrounding them look nearly sinful. And, as I'm watching, he licks his lips a little. He licks them so that the lower one goes all fat and glossy looking, and I lose most of the saliva in my mouth down the sides of my chin.

'Hoooo, baby, you're gone. You been missing me, huh? I kind of wondered, to be honest, seeing as how you haven't been around. But now that I'm here and can see that look in your eyes ... that look is *hot*.'

'This is just ... my normal gaze.'

'Really? Then how come it's giving me wood?'

'It's not giving you wood.'

'You want me to stand away from your desk and prove it?'

I eye the edge of the desk – the one that's hiding most of him from view. And I swear, I've never been so thankful for its size. Usually I curse the fact that it could stand in for the Ark if Noah got into a spot of bother, but right now my desk is all that stands between me and certain destruction.

'Absolutely not.' I pause, as other words try to wrestle their way out. Sadly, it's a fight my rational side loses. 'Not at my place of work, anyway.'

Really, really shouldn't have said that. I know I shouldn't have said that. It's like a clause on the end of the Contract of Me. *Kit Connor does not want to look at Dillon Holt's penis, unless both parties fulfil the addendum in section B subheading seven. 'Not while she's in the presence of people who could possibly fire her.'*

'Ah, so you'd like to see my enormous erection at other times.'

128

'Well …'

There's something about the way he's just said it that makes me think I should say no here. Just something – devilish, maybe – about his voice and his face, and his everything. I feel like I'm about to make a bargain with Satan himself, but the problem is … I can't really think of a compelling reason why I shouldn't.

Which is probably why my next word comes out sort of like a question.

'… *yeah?*'

And of course he finds that utterly hilarious. His mouth skews sideways and he looks to his left, briefly, like he's trying to hold it in. But I can see it bursting out around the corners of the fist he brings to his lips.

'Is that so weird?'

'No, no, God – no.' He waves his hands and does his best to straighten his face, but I can still see how amused he is. 'It was just the way you said it.'

'And how did I say it?'

'Like you were asking me if it's OK that you want to see some cock.'

'Can you blame me? You keep it hidden like it's the Ark of the Covenant. I feel as though I should hire Indiana Jones to drop down into the snake pit in your pants, to get it back out again.'

This time, he doesn't even try to keep his laugh in. It just bursts right out of him, louder than any sound I've ever heard in here before – so loud, in fact, that I almost run to the stone steps that lead up to the main library, to see if anyone has heard.

Not that they would have, of course, because the main desk lies approximately three miles from here. In fact, it lies so far away that sometimes I wonder what would happen if I died. Would I be found five hundred years later, as perfectly preserved as some of the dusty old tomes I look after?

I suspect so.

But that's never seemed like a positive thing before. It mostly just scares the life out of me, instead of what it's doing right now. It's giving me permission, currently, to actually keep talking about this – though I still keep my voice to a tentative whisper. I have to, and not just out of deference to the silence down here.

There's also the personal library environment that's constantly in my head. It tells me not to say what I then do, but I manage even so. I get out what I've been wanting to for days and days and years and, oh, God, I'm sure it's been centuries.

'Seriously, Dillon, I was starting to wonder if you were deformed down there,' I finally squeeze out, and only realise that it's kind of a funny thing to say when he laughs again. I'm being a hilarious idiot without really meaning to, apparently.

So, you know: in for a penny, in for a pound.

'Or maybe you have, like, only one ball. Or balls that look like three balls. Or ... or ... it could be that you have one of those really big thingies that kind of droops down instead of pointing up ... I just don't know. I don't know.'

'But you've apparently thought about it a lot.'

He crouches down a little and leans over the desk. Puts his chin in one hand, in this adorable sort of way. Like he's my friendly therapist, or teacher, or some other fatherly figure. Only really, really bad.

So bad I can't say yes to something like that.

'Not really.'

'You just suggested re-enacting *Raiders of the Lost Ark* to get at my penis.'

'I was just … joking.'

'So you haven't been obsessing over what I've got in my pants.'

'Not at all.'

'You don't think about my hot, hard cock day and night, sliding through your slippery fingers, filling your hot little mouth, fucking your sweet, tight pussy … ohhhh, that pussy of yours. Don't think I haven't imagined that last one myself.'

I dart a look at the doorway, again, though this time it's not because of the noise. It can't be because of the noise. His voice is barely above a whisper – my *breathing* sounds louder than him. But, oh, the *words* he's saying. Those filthy, forbidden words, in a fusty old place like this …

I'm surprised the books don't leap off the shelves in protest. Upstairs, Eileen Dorridge is probably fainting, due to the psychic sexual energy he's throwing out all over the place. Hell, *I'm* close to fainting, and I've had all the time in the world to get used to it. I'm practically an expert by now in the lascivious ways of Dillon Holt, and yet I still can't manage more than this, in response:

'I might have … considered those things.'

'Come on, baby. Be a little more specific,' he says, and I shake my head.

'I *knew* you were just doing it to torture me.'

'Doing what to torture you?'

'Keeping your pants on.'

'Actually, I just enjoy patience – as I've told you in some detail. Now you tell me in detail: what have you been thinking about, huh?'

I can't believe he actually assumes I'm going to say, amongst all of this oppressive quiet. In my workplace, with my happy little mug not a foot from me and that sign on the wall above my head. *Silence Please*, it says, and I've always obeyed it before.

How on earth am I supposed to change now?

'I can't really tell you *here*.'

'I see. And there's nothing I can do to persuade you?'

He has this look on his face that makes me want to tread carefully. This heavy-eyed, predatory sort of look that reminds me of crouching animals getting ready to pounce – though I'm prepared for it if he does. I've braced myself against my desk, and folded my legs one over the other.

He couldn't get in if he tried.

I'm impenetrable. I'm a fortress.

'Absolutely nothing.'

'So if I stand up and come around there, it won't loosen your tongue,' he says, and suddenly my battlements are looking a little shaky. One of my hands drops off the desk and my body turns halfway towards him, like a flower seeking the sun. Instead of Fort Knox, firing at him with machine guns.

'Don't come around here, Dillon. Don't come around – no. Stay there.'

I point to the spot I'd like him to remain on – around seventeen miles from my current position. But of course he doesn't pay the slightest bit of attention. He just keeps coming until he's all the way around my desk, and once he's there he doesn't leave a comfortable distance between us. He leans right over my chair, and puts his hands in places that hem me in. I'm trapped between my seat back and his body.

'What's wrong with me being round here? I mean, if you're so certain about your ability to stay silent.'

'I am certain. I just ... I just ... uh ...'

132

'You're really not finishing that sentence, Kitty-cat.'

'How am I supposed to finish it when your crotch is in my face?'

'Oh, come on. It's hardly in your face. No, no. *This* –' he yanks the back of the chair and I know what's going to happen. I know, but I can't stop it. I just have to let the wheels on the bottom do their work, skidding me right up against him before I've had chance to get a hold of myself '– is in your face.'

He isn't wrong. My cheek actually smushes against the shape of him, briefly, and oh, Jesus, it's just as hard as he claimed it was. The sensation is sort of like running into someone's forearm, only much, much sexier than that. It's someone's really rude and arousing forearm, thick and stiff enough to nearly knock me unconscious.

And that idea leaves me far less calm than I'd like. I actually rub my cheek against him, without really meaning to, and it's only when he moans that I realise what I've done. It's only when he puts his hand in my hair that I realise I'd love to do more. Another thirty seconds and I would have probably pulled down his zipper, so it's good that I get a grip right then. I sit back in my chair and put a firm discouraging hand on his belly.

But that's a mistake.

As is thinking I can maintain control under pressure like this.

'You like the feel of my body, huh?' he asks, but only because he knows I do. The muscles in his stomach are gloriously firm and, even better, they've gone all jumpy and tense. Like he can't stand to hold himself back like this.

So it's really no surprise that I'm stroking all over them, when I fully intended to stay completely still. I thought I was fending him off, but apparently I was just fooling myself. I wanted to touch him, and any old excuse did the trick.

'Tell me what you want to do to it.'

I think it's fairly obvious what I want to do it. I'm almost under his T-shirt, by this point, and thirty seconds ago I rubbed my face all over his erection. The message couldn't be clearer, though I don't know how it's leaking out. I cut off all access to my vocal cords, and still I'm sending him signals, loud and clear.

I should have chopped off my hands. And maybe my legs, too, because they've somehow uncrossed themselves, and now there's all this open space between my thighs. He could just dive right in, if he wanted to, but I think I know why he doesn't.

Because it can't be him, I think.

Because it has to be me.

'I can't,' I say, even though that's half a lie already. I've pushed his T-shirt up and am quite blatantly snogging his stomach, and my right hand is definitely somewhere it shouldn't be. I'd like to call that place the top of his thigh, but several anatomy books would beg to differ. It's quite clearly his backside that I'm squeezing – much to his delight.

'Even though you're doing most of it already?'

'This isn't anything.'

'Groping my ass isn't anything?'

'You can hardly fault me for that.'

'Oh, really? And why not?'

'Because your ass is really amazing.'

'It is?'

Of course, I realise what he's doing here. He's trying to get me to talk by stealth. He's creeping in some unguarded

134

back door, to take me unawares – but I'm on to his game.
I'm not going to talk dirty to him in a library, no matter
what tricks he tries.

'Maybe.'

'Ah. So it more than likely isn't. You were just trying to
make me feel better, then, about my completely unspectacular
backside.'

'No – I really wasn't. I –'

'Actually you think it's kind of ordinary. Dull, even. Flat
and featureless.'

'Oh, God, no – are you kidding? Your ass is amazing,
honestly. It's so firm and round ... I swear, I can hardly get
enough of it. When you bend over or ... or when you were
just wearing that towel ... it's all I can do to stop myself
crawling over to you to bite it, you know, to just bite it all
hard and –'

Goddamn him.

I glance up – mid-poetry recital to his ass – and of course
he's laughing at me again. And he deserves a triumphant
giggle, too, because he got me without even trying. I was
busy watching the South entrance, and he snuck in the one
marked *make Dillon feel better about his flat ass*.

'You're a fucker.'

'You just said fucker in a library!'

'I'll say more than fucker, in a second.'

'Ohhh, I'm hoping so, baby. I am really hoping so. Think
I can get you to babble breathlessly about my cock by going
all emo about it, too? *I'm so small and flaccid, Kit, I don't
know what I'm going to do,*' he says, in such a ridiculously
false way that no one could possibly be fooled. And I'm not,
I'm really not in the slightest.

So why do I get the urge to tell him otherwise, anyway?

What is *wrong* with me? I'm so polite I want to respond seriously to a joke.

'I'm hardly likely to fall for that a second time,' I say, but I just sound so unsure. He has to know he's got me on the ropes now – and a second later he confirms this.

'No? Then I guess I'll have to try something different to get you to talk.'

'Like what?'

I shouldn't have asked. I should have gone with my first instinct: *since when did this become an interrogation in Communist Russia?* Then maybe he'd have thought of pulling my teeth out or breaking my kneecaps, and totally killed the mood.

But I didn't, and now the mood is sky-high. The mood is so thick and intense; it's become a supernatural fog bank, rolling in from a James Herbert story. I can't even see the door any more, and I'm definitely not paying any attention to what Eileen Dorridge might be doing. I'm only thinking of him, and the answer he then gives.

'Like lifting you onto the desk.'

I'm swooning before he's even done it. In fact, it's so swoon-worthy that I kind of suspect he won't. He's just having me on with words I last heard in some romance novel – words that never happen to the likes of me.

And then he gets his hands underneath my arms and just hauls me up. Right out of my chair and off my feet – as though I've turned into someone half my size. Tiny, sylph-like girls get thrown around like this. But girls with size seven feet never do. They're supposed to stay completely rooted to their seats at all times, composed and kind of like a block of concrete. They don't fly through the air with the greatest of ease.

Even though that's kind of what happens. I think I actually feel the breeze above his head, briefly. I'm reminded of *Dirty Dancing* and a dozen movies I've always wanted to re-enact, before he brings me back down to earth.

Only it's not earth he brings me back down to. It's another dimension in which I'm sort of sprawled across my desk, and he's planted himself firmly between my legs. And I can't right myself. I can't bring myself back to normality.

Because he won't stop asking.

'You want to talk now?' he says, and I do my best to seem unfazed.

'For a slab of wood beneath my ass? Come on,' I say, but then I feel that treacherous spark of anticipation in my chest. That little thing inside me that really wants to know what he's going to do next to persuade me. It wouldn't have to be very much, I don't think – and I'm right.

I sigh just to feel his big hands on my thighs, sliding underneath my skirt. He's done it before, of course, but I can't deny that it's different here. There's this extra knot of tension that turns to arousal as it unravels, though I try to deny it does.

'Any closer?' he asks.

'Not even slightly,' I say.

I swear you'd never know that I'm going out of my mind.

'And if I slide your panties off?'

'I'd probably slap you.'

I'd probably thank you, I think, and luckily it's my thoughts he hears. He always hears my thoughts. They must be written on my face in large print. I'm like *See Spot Run*, only with exhibitionism instead of happy dogs.

'You're never going to do that,' he says, and of course he's right. My hands stay bunched at my sides, slick with

137

perspiration and so tense. I don't think I could unfold them and crack across his face if he said disparaging things about my mother. I'm too wrapped in a dozen different sensations: the restriction of his body between my legs, forcing them to stay open ... the stroke of his fingers over my thighs ... his gaze bearing down on me like this ...

How does he do it?

It took so much more to get public indecency out of my heroine. My hero had to go through pages and pages of info-dumps, just to convince her it was a cool, safe thing to do. Dillon comes around my desk, lifts me up and plonks me down, and that gap between me and her is suddenly a chasm.

She would have chopped his body in two, to get her thighs together.

Whereas I ... well ...

I come pretty close to helping him, when he eases my panties down over my legs. And I can't even berate myself for it, either, because he's just moving far, far too slowly. He does it like we have all the time in the world, which we definitely don't. Someone's almost certainly going to come down here at any moment, and I'm not sure what's worse about such a possibility:

That I might be fired, or that I might not get an orgasm.

At which point, I realise why he's moving at a snail's pace.

'Just go on then,' I say, because I can't not. I have to, now. He's made orgasms more important to me than my job.

'Just go on with what?' he asks, all innocence. Though the innocence is somewhat sullied by the skirt he's pushed up around my hips. For the first time in history, the air in this fussy place has been exposed to a vagina.

And neither the air nor my sensible self is happy about it.

'You *know* what.'

'I do. But I think it's important for you to say.'

'I've said plenty to you.'

'In a public library?'

'Well ... no.'

'With your pussy all bare? Look at you, you filthy little thing. Exposing yourself like this, when anyone could walk in.'

'I didn't expose myself! You did it!'

He shrugs, as though it's nothing. This torment is *nothing*.

'Sure I did,' he says. 'But you *liked* it.'

And this time I'm so frantic I can't even find the will to deny it.

'I did like it,' I say, because it's true, oh, it's so true. I liked him sliding my panties off so much that I'm still reliving it in my head. The glide of the cotton on my thighs, the thrill of being revealed, of falling so far ...

And of other things, too.

'You *love* lying there with your legs all spread, don't you?'

Yes, I think, yes, oh, yes.

'I do.'

'And you want more, don't you.'

'Oh, yes, please, yes, please,' I say, those babbling thoughts I had a second earlier suddenly forcing their way out of my mouth. Apparently, the barrier between my desires and my vocal cords has almost completely broken down.

Though it takes a little more to destroy it completely.

Like maybe his tongue slowly sliding over my clit.

'What are you doing?' I think I say, but it's hard to tell for sure. I'm so stunned by the sensation and the daring of it and oh, God, his *expression*, once he's done it ... I can't possibly say more. 'What are you doing?' is all that will come out, over and over again until he's kind of laughing around my spread sex.

'You tell me,' he suggests, and then he licks again, just to make sure I know what I'm being tested on. Cunnilingus, I think. Going down, I think. The beautiful art of oral sex.

But unfortunately, I don't answer with any of those options. I answer with a rather unsteady and completely mindless:

'You're doing things to my clit with your tongue.'

It's quite possibly the most embarrassing sentence I've ever uttered.

And you know what? I *love* it for being so. I love how it sounds in my mouth – so filthy and fun. I love saying that word, like the lewdest thing this room has ever heard. And most of all, oh, most of all, I love love love my reward for speaking aloud:

A long, slow suck of that very thing, that ends with me moaning.

And him grinning.

'Like that?'

'Oh, yeah, like that,' I say, and then suddenly I'm spilling out more words, without any prompting at all. 'Do it like that. Suck me there.'

'Uh-huh. And then what?'

'Slide your fingers into my ... into my ...'

'Into your ... ?'

'My pussy. Fuck my pussy with your fingers.'

At this point, I've no idea what's more exciting. Him kneeling down between my thighs to do as I'm suggesting, or the words themselves. I mean, I just said 'pussy' in my library – a place that has never so much as seen me without my suit jacket on. I'm not even sure if I said 'shit' that one time I stapled my finger.

So this is ...

This is really, really ...

'Ohhhhh, yeah.'

'Yeah. You like that, huh?'

Is he seriously asking me if I like him licking me like that? Or maybe he's wondering if I'm enjoying the long, slow slide of his thick fingers into me? Either of these is an option.

But both of them are insane.

'Of course I do, oh, God, of course I do,' I babble, because really, isn't it obvious? He's started stroking the flat of his tongue over the tip of my clit now, and he's doing it in time to these unbearably steady strokes, in and out of my body.

I'm only surprised that I'm not humping his face. At the very least I'm rocking my hips. And as for my vocal cords ... They're completely out of control now. They've gone rogue, and started up their own splinter group.

Project Dillon's Cock, I'm going to call it.

And apparently my vocal cords agree.

'Oh, God, oh, God, I want you to fuck me,' I say, and I don't mean with his fingers. I mean with that big thick thing between his legs. I've lost all sense of space and time, it seems, and I couldn't care less if someone catches him doing me. Would that really be any worse than what he's doing now?

I don't think so.

So I just say:

'I want you inside me.'

Even though I kind of know that's not going to do the trick. If you want to get the best prize you've got to play a bigger game, and so far I've been playing so small. I need to take a leaf out of his book – a lewd, lovely leaf – and surprisingly, it's not as hard as it looks.

'I want you to fill me with that stiff, swollen thing … oh, God, I bet you're so hard right now. Are you? Are you hard for my little wet pussy?' I ask, which sounds so silly, on the surface. I'm sure it does. In fact, I almost get as far as an embarrassed blush.

Before I realise he's gone all still, between my thighs.

He's not really licking me any more. He's just sort of … resting his mouth there, while I do my best to twist him into as many knots as he's twisted me.

'I bet you just want to sink right in, don't you? And ohhhh, baby, I want that too. I can't wait for you to fill me with that thick cock of yours,' I say, and I can't believe the rush that goes through me when I do. It doesn't sound silly any more. It sounds like the most arousing thing I've ever heard – and I'm the one spelling it out. I'm the one speaking.

How can that be an exciting thing?

And yet it is. I'm making myself all wet, not just with the images I'm conjuring up and the rudeness of the words, but the sound of my voice wrapping around them. My timid, pathetic little voice, going on about cocks and fucking.

I'm not surprised that he glances up at me, incredulous.

I'm doing the same thing to myself. His expression probably mirrors my own, all giddy and shocked and, best of all, shuddery. Ohhh, man, he's shuddering. And *I* did that to him. I turned Dillon Holt into a shaking, disbelieving mess, unable to speak or move or function in the way he did before.

I've never been prouder of anything in my entire life.

Or loved a slow, knowing smile more than the one he then gives me.

'I see what you did there,' he says, and I practically burst.

I have an actual secret in-joke with someone! A little thing that we both share, ridiculous and rude and naughty, but still: *ours*. Just mine and his.

And, for one fatal second, it sort of feels better than all the sex.

It feels so good, in fact, that I have to manoeuvre him back on track, immediately – before I start composing sonnets to him in my head, and imagining things he's never said.

'Well, what are you waiting for?' I ask him, but that affection for him is still in the back of my mind. So much so, in fact, that when he says 'soon' I think he's referring to the feelings we're sort of falling into, and I almost make a fool of myself.

I almost say, 'Really?'

Before he saves me by burying his face between my legs. And this time ... this time he totally goes for it. He doesn't hold back in the hope that I'll say more. He isn't polite about it, in deference to my ladylike feelings. He licks around the fingers he's still got inside me, as he fucks and fucks and fucks me with them. And when I moan and squirm, he spreads me with his free hand.

He gets me all nice and open, before he works his tongue back up to my unbearably swollen clit – because he knows, I think. He knows how sensitive it makes that little bud to expose it like that. To make it stand proud of the slippery folds around it, as he laps at the tip of it, over and over.

And he knows, too, I think, that I'll forget about what I wanted. I'll forget about his cock, in that one sharp moment of bliss ... though that's not really what I want to focus on, as the pleasure builds. I'm focusing on my first instinct, instead – that one word he said – 'soon' – and how warm his expression had looked when he did.

He *did* mean something else, I think.

Not just fucking. Not just his cock sliding inside me.

He meant what I feel as I call out his name: that we're going to be more than this, whether I'm capable of it or not. It's like a promise, I'm sure – as crazy as that seems, from someone like him. But even crazier ... as I shiver and shake through this insurmountable pleasure ... as I go boneless for him, just in time for him to kiss me with his red, wet mouth ...

It doesn't seem crazy at all.

Chapter Nine

That word is in my head now, and it can't easily be removed. Soon, I think, soon, as I sip my hot chocolate before bed, or attempt to get on with my job in the place he once was. He pulled me to pieces at this desk yesterday, I think to myself, and then that word just slithers its way back in. It suggests all kinds of things, from fucking to feelings to all the stuff I want him to tell me ... and all the stuff he won't.

And worse:

I can't wait for any of it. Soon is not soon enough. I'm beyond that stage of trying to keep my sanity, and all the way into *I don't give a fuck* – which is probably how I find myself at his door, again, despite my lack of excuses. I'm not here for the book, or because he looped a noose around my neck with some mystery.

I'm here because I want to be.

I want to be.

I want to be so much that my heart actually soars in my chest when he opens the door. And, even more alarming, I think the same thing might be happening to him, too. He actually goes up on tiptoe and his face does this crazy thing – this beaming-like-a-ray-of-sunshine thing.

Then, just when I'm doubting my sanity for believing such a thing, he falls on me. He falls on me and kisses me like I'm the Second Coming, if the Second Coming was something you greeted with groping. His tongue is in my mouth before we've even said hello, but of course that thought just excites me.

I'm actually beyond words with another human being. We don't need to speak. We just need to kiss. We communicate through our tongues in each other's mouth, and our hands all over the other person's body. My fingers digging into his ass mean *I missed you*, his palms sliding underneath my shirt and over my back mean *I missed you more*.

And I'm so sure about this – absolutely, impossibly sure in a way I've never been before – that I'm quite startled when he pulls away. I thought we were on the same page, but apparently I was wrong.

Very wrong.

'Whoa, hey,' he says. 'Why don't we … uh … why don't we …'

I hope he means to end that sentence with 'have sex'. But to my horror he doesn't. He wants to do the thing I thought we didn't need to, for some inexplicable reason.

'Maybe we should just talk, for a second,' he says, in a way that should make me feel like a complete fool. He's turned me into the guy, in this scenario, so hungry for his body I'd climb on top of it without a word of negotiation – and I should be mortified.

But when I go to check the box marked embarrassment inside me, it's not there any more. I rifle through pages and pages of me, from falling flat on my face during P.E. to that time my boob popped out of the dress that Lori lent me, but there's no shame to be found. There's nothing.

And that realisation is just so overwhelming I don't know

how to bypass it. Part of me really does want to chat with him, if that's what he wants. There are things I want to know and so many little pieces of him that I want to unravel. I still remember the way he went blank, when I asked him to share something about himself, and I'd dearly love to know why.

But this new-found freedom simply overrides it all.

'I don't want to talk,' I say, like a completely different person from the one I was before. Then, even wilder: 'I want to suck you.'

And I know it's wild, too, because his answering expression is ... impressive. I'm impressed by it, and I'm the one who made it happen. I think his eyebrows reach mid-air, and his single-word response is rather faint.

'What?' he asks, like an old lady who maybe misheard.

I *love* that I made him an old lady who maybe misheard.

'I've waited long enough, and now it's my turn. So get those pants off.'

And OK, I don't sound quite as convincing as him. I'm missing some of his rough assurance, and I know my gaze isn't as sultry as his. My eyes feel quite wide and guileless, so I'm guessing this is a little like being ordered to strip by Milly-Molly-Mandy.

But he does it, just the same. His hand goes to his belt, and then I get the utterly arousing sight of him slowly easing it out of the buckle – because, oh, I've always enjoyed that. The clink-clink sound of metal against metal, the whisper of leather ... that sense of someone loosening a constraint ...

It's all very, very good.

As are the words he says to me, once he's almost there. He's got a hand on the top button of his jeans, and he's maybe a hair's breadth away from undoing them. And then he just tells me, in this husky tone of voice –

This *madly arousing* tone of voice –

'You know how big I am, right? 'Cause otherwise I'm gonna warn you now.'

I don't think he could have said anything better if I'd given him a script. My head spins at the sound of it, and that seed of an idea in the back of my mind takes root. Is this part of the reason why he kept putting this bit off? He said it was something else, but there's a quality to that one word 'warn' that makes me think it wasn't, not wholly.

And if so, I really have to put his mind at ease.

'I have a pretty good idea.'

'You sure? Other girls ran off screaming over a pretty good idea.'

I almost grin. *So I'm right, then.* I'm right! I'm actually starting to know him, just by watching his expression and taking educated guesses. I'm learning from the Master, and applying my lessons well.

I even get some of his confidence into my answer.

'Baby, I am *never* going to run away screaming,' I say, so suddenly sure of myself. So full of the kind of seduction I've always aimed for, but typically missed.

And then he worms his way out of his jeans and his underwear … and oh, God, I wish I'd been a bit more cautious. What was I thinking, taking on a persona I simply wasn't ready for? I should have known that something like that only fits massive, handsome people like him. Put it on me and the arms trail on the floor … the shoulders sag around my stomach …

I'm a mess in it. I'm like a melted waxwork.

A melted waxwork who's been really startled by someone's enormous penis.

'Oh. Well. That,' I think I say. Mainly because I've forgotten what sentences are. I can't even manage an ellipsis, or possibly an em-dash. I just stamp out those three words, complete with very final-sounding full stops on the end.

And of course he's disappointed when I do.

Amused, but disappointed.

'Knew you weren't ready for that,' he says, half-smiling, half-chagrined. And in a way he's absolutely right. I'm still trying to speak properly, and I'm having to force my hand to stay away from my mouth. Most of the muscles in my legs seem to have disappeared, and I can't stop staring.

But in another way ... oh, praise be for Dillon Holt. Oh, let me immortalise his name in song. Can I compare his penis to a summer day? Because I totally would, if doing so didn't sound insane. His cock is not only impossibly enormous – so enormous it's like an optical illusion – it's lovely to look at, too. There's no kink that makes it veer off in an unexpected direction, no odd shift in colour halfway down or weird flap of skin where it shouldn't be.

He's simply smooth there, perfectly smooth and gloriously shaped. The head flares in just the right sort of way – one that makes me think of him filling my mouth so completely, so thickly – and at the tip he's so deliciously slick. Oh, he's so glossy and slippery and swollen, like he's been hard for days and days.

Which I suppose he has.

I admit, I doubted it before. But now that I'm looking at his erection, pointing skywards despite the extra weight ... I can't really doubt any more. One stroke of someone's finger could probably get him off. I think I'm pushing him close to it just by staring at him this way – and his expression confirms it. The smile has dropped almost completely off his face, and it's been replaced by a sort of slack, flushed longing.

But in case I'm still not sure, he's got some things to say. 'Jesus, Kit, I feel like you're fucking me with your eyes. You want this, huh? Come on and get it, girl. Come on.'

Some really, really arousing things, with a few gestures just to finish me off. He puts a hand up to his mouth and actually licks his palm – the way he licked me, I'm sure – and then he strokes himself, just once.

But once is enough. It's enough to send a spike of sensation through me, and enough to make him push out this delicious sound. It's like an *oh* with the smooth bits sawn off, all rough and guttural and so good to hear. And after it's out he does something even better – something that turns the spike of sensation into a lance.

He takes his hand away, too quick.

Like he's on fire there, and can't stand to linger for long. Doing so would only lead to him making a mess, I think, though I'm not sure that's what he's concerned about, exactly. His own touch seems to make him all jumpy and jerky, and he spends a good few seconds gasping in this shocked sort of way.

And of course that's what gets me going:

The idea that the pleasure is so strong, and so intense … he can hardly take it. He can't stand it. He shakes that one hand as though he really did burn himself, before getting himself back together.

Though when I say *back together*, I really mean *falling apart*.

He looks the way I feel: like he wants to sprawl on the floor and never get up again. But he does better at resisting this than I do. He keeps on his feet, manfully, while I sink to my knees. And it's only when my motives become clear that he starts to lose it a little.

'Oh, so you're really gonna ...' he says, though he seems to struggle for the rest of the sentence. He ends up beginning a new one, without finishing the first. 'And on your hands and knees, too? Yeah, you're just crawling over to me on your hands and knees ... Jesus. Jesus, look, Kit ... you should probably know before you do this that usually I can go for hours and hours. Honestly, I swear to God I can. So you know, if I kind of do it all over your face before you've even ... licked anything ... it's really not indicative of my overall abilities.'

I wonder if this is why he wanted to talk first. But, if so, he should really know: the idea only excites me. I think of him doing what he's just suggested and I almost lose my balance. I sort of slide over to him at an angle, then find myself a little stuck.

I'm jammed up with excitement. I'm going all nuts inside, and can't really trust myself to touch him. Just the feel of his heat on the side of my face is enough to make me close my eyes and reach out a steadying hand, but unfortunately my steadying hand winds up on his thigh.

It's just like I'm groping him. And after I've thought of that word – *groping* – I'm even more excited than I was before. I'm getting great handfuls of him, squeezing and rubbing like I just ... really, really need to.

But not as much as he needs to put that hand in my hair. That shaking hand, so close to being something other than a caress. I think he's almost desperate to urge me on ... to maybe guide my mouth to him ... and yet he holds back. He keeps himself in check, as though I won't like it if he's forceful over something like this.

And unfortunately I don't know how to tell him he's wrong. I just have to kneel there, shivering with anticipation, as he *almost* touches the side of my head. As he *nearly* tilts his hips a little, so that this big thick thing strokes along the side of my face.

And then I turn just a touch, in order to make it happen.

I can't help it. I want to feel him sliding over my cheek, and the heat of him ... ohhhh, the heat of him. I suddenly understand why he ripped his hand away from himself, once he's there against my skin. It's like he's branding me with that heavy flesh; it's like he's searing himself into me. And he smells so sweet, too, so rich with sex ...

How can I resist? How can I resist the sounds he's making – these soft, breathless sounds? Or the feel of him shaking as I lean back a little and look up at his flushed face? He's completely lost now, completely gone in a way I never thought he could be, and I kiss his cock for that.

I kiss it, slow and soft and wet. And when he doesn't object – when he goes briefly weak in the knees and utters a curse word that I've never actually heard before – I do it again. Only deeper this time. I take more of him into my mouth, craving the sudden salt-sweet taste of him on my tongue ... or the heavy feel of him pushing in.

Because he does, a little. He can't seem to help it, any more than I could help my recklessness in the library. He just groans, and rocks his hips, and suddenly my mouth is full – though I'm not complaining. I like this role reversal. I like this loss of control.

And I like it even better when he puts it into words.

'I'm sorry,' he says, as he slowly pushes into my mouth. 'I'm sorry, I'm sorry, it's just, God, you have no idea what that looks like. Oh, you have no idea what it does to me to see you taking it like that. You've no idea how often I've thought about you doing this to me.'

152

I wonder if it's as often as I've thought about giving it to him? Probably not, if I'm honest. I've thought about it so many times I'm almost greedy for it, now that I've got it. My mouth is slowly getting sloppier and sloppier around that impossibly swollen head, and when I can't take as much as I'd like – when I try to deep-throat him and end up with him telling me, 'No, no, take it easy' – I use my hand to devour the rest.

And then I use both of them, once I realise that one won't do the job. I can't circle him with a single thumb and fore-finger. I have to clasp him like I'm in the middle of a prayer. I'm beseeching some deity, in a very pious way.

Aside from the giant penis, of course.

And all the slick sounds, and my frantic sucking, and the dirty words he chooses to say, about a second after I've taken him in my hands as well as in my mouth.

'Oh, yeah, that's it. Jerk me off, baby. Jerk me off just like that – ohhhh, right there.'

By 'right there' he means the sensitive spot on the under-side – the one I'm rubbing, with my thumb. The one I'm barely sure about until he tells me it's right. Other men I've been with? I could have stroked them there all night, and never known I was hitting any kind of jackpot.

But Dillon's just not that sort of guy.

No. He's the sort of guy who will say, if something feels good.

And he's also the sort of guy who will quite shockingly show you more, if there's something else that feels even better. If there's something else that makes him sort of crazy – because this undoubtedly does. He takes hold of one of my hands and groans, 'Like this, like this', and then suddenly I'm stroking him really, really far back between his legs.

Rudely far back. Arousingly far back. So far back I think he's going to do something else, for one thrilling second, and then I get what he's aiming for. I've read about it in books, during my more desperate moments – though I've never quite dared to put any of my seduction schemes into effect. I've never quite known how to go all out.

But it's easy, when someone makes you.

He just presses my fingers into that soft strip of skin – hard, really hard, harder than I would ever have dared – and once I've done it, and got the hang of it, he's ever so grateful. And by ever so grateful, I mean he grunts like an animal in heat and fists his free hand in his hair, which kind of feels better than a thank-you card, if I'm honest.

As do the things he says, once he's regained his senses.

'I'm gonna come. Ohhhh, man, I'm gonna come so hard. Fuck. Fuck. Oh, it's gonna be way too much,' he tells me, though he really doesn't have to. I can tell it's going to be too much by the way he sort of tries to curl right over my body. His foundations are collapsing, and he's losing all coherence – not to mention control over his breathing. I think he might actually be hyperventilating, and then there are long stretches where he doesn't breathe at all.

He forgets to, in such an alarming way that I have to glance up. I have to see if he really is about to faint on top of me, which sounds stupid in my head, but less so once I see him. His face is as red as mine feels, and his mouth seems to be open around words he can no longer get out.

He's stuck, I think … until I stroke my tongue one final time, over and around the slippery head of his cock. And then he goes stiff all over, just like I did, for him. He goes rigid, about a second before his thick shaft jerks in my mouth.

This is it, I think, in a rush of pleasure and excitement, but I'm still not quite prepared for it when it happens. He doesn't make a sound, you see. He doesn't cry out, the way I expect him to, or maybe pepper me with filthy words. All of his words are still trapped in the back of his throat, as he spurts in thick, prolonged bursts over my tongue.

Then all over my lips, when I pull away – perhaps because I think he's done. I'm certain of it, in fact, so it's a shock to hear his sudden groan, and feel that hot liquid coating my face. He doesn't even let me move back to let me get away from it, which should probably offend me terribly.

And yet all I can think is: I'm glad. I'm glad that he's this way. I'm glad that he shows me and tells me and puts his hand in my hair. I'm glad that he moans when he sees what he's done – what a mess he's made of me!

Chapter Ten

He sleeps like the dead. Which I suppose is appropriate, after an orgasm like that. For a while I'm sort of concerned that it's actually killed him, and then I get close and can feel his breath ghosting against my face. I put my hand on his back, which is going up and down, the way some great heavy beast's would – slow, and ultimately reassuring.

Everything about this is reassuring, even though it probably shouldn't be. I'm used to being somewhat disappointed by the sudden unconsciousness of my sex partners, and can't quite pinpoint why I'm not disappointed here.

Because I've had around eight thousand orgasms to his one, perhaps? The scoreboard is looking pretty top-heavy in my favour. And besides ... it's sort of nice to just be here with him, in calmness and quiet. It's nice to look at his face without any self-consciousness – no thoughts about whether he's noticed me staring, or what he thinks of my probable adoration.

Because I do, of course. Adore him, I mean.

How could I not? Even in sleep, he's utterly lovely. Those eyelashes of his fan out across his cheeks, soot-black and so soft looking. His mouth has made an inadvertent pout, that

157

lower lip all plump and just ever so slightly glossy. I kind of want to run my finger over it, before other things catch my attention.

Silly things, like the T-shirt he's still got on. He didn't take it off during the whole of whatever that was, and it's the goofiest thing to see him half-dressed like this. His ass is completely bare down below, and the material is far too tight up above. Plus, it's sort of rucked up a bit – in a way that reminds me of little kids who've spent too long playing, and just collapsed without any attention to where they are.

Or what their clothes might reveal. Because that ruffled-up T-shirt – it's revealed something I've not really noticed before. Of course I've taken in his tattoos. I know they're there. Sometimes I know they're there so hard I have dreams about them peeling off his arms, to swell and settle all over my body. I occasionally imagine his tattoos having sex with me, so it's not that I haven't been observant, or appreciative. It's just that this one is so small, compared to the others. And it lines the base of his spine, so you could almost mistake it for something else – the shadow of his bones, maybe. His backbone has made a dark trail through his skin.

A dark trail of words. They're words, I think, and then I can't resist lifting his shirt a little more to see the rest. The only one visible is *OK*, which seems like a mysterious thing for a man to have written on him.

But the other words don't make it any clearer.

You will be OK, it says, without explanation or elaboration. There's no hint about *who* should be OK, or why they need to be. And as I'm in the middle of figuring it out he makes a sound – so I can hardly continue. Just the thought of him waking up and catching me doing this is enough to jolt me. As though I'm spying, instead of innocently looking.

I even brush his T-shirt back down in this hurried, guilty sort of way – but I've no real idea why. He doesn't have the combination to his security deposit box under there. It's just a tattoo, like all of the rest of the tattoos on his body. I didn't just steal his soul.

So why does he look kind of unsettled, when I glance up at him? He actually turns over, too, and straightens his T-shirt, in a manner that reminds me too much of myself. It's a furtive, uncertain sort of gesture, of the kind I would make if I wanted to hide a part of my body. And it's only after he's on his back and looking at me full in the face – so easily confident – that I start to doubt this impression.

Maybe he was just sleepy. He *looks* like he was just sleepy. He even yawns, lazily, and says a bunch of stuff that confirms it.

'Oh, Jeeze. Did I pass out? I committed the ultimate cardinal sin of passing out after sex, didn't I?' He covers his face with his hands, and I swear it's so adorable I almost stick him in a gif and post him to Tumblr. At the very least, I forget my silly angsty feelings, in time for him to add: 'Did you even get a hug?'

The muffled voice only makes it funnier.

'I did not get a hug,' I say, in a mock-grave voice – one that he seems to find so amusing he almost cracks. His hands come down and that spark of laughter flashes across his deep-blue gaze, before he gets it back under control.

'Seriously, how can you ever forgive me? I should be punished. Deeply, deeply punished.' He pauses just long enough to catch something, as it flickers its way across my face. Though I'd perjure myself rather than admit what it was. No matter what he thinks, I won't admit what it was. 'You kind of like that idea, huh? What was that – chapter seventeen?'

'There's no chapter where she punishes him,' I say, laughing. Inside, however, I'm thinking of how electric it was, having him at my mercy. Seeing him lose it like that, seeing him give up control …

Yeah, I liked that.

It's almost disappointing, in fact, that he so abruptly changes the subject back to the thing we were talking about before. Disappointing, and a little … something else. A look drifts across his face that I can't read, but it's gone so quickly I could almost imagine it wasn't there at all.

He makes me *believe* it wasn't there at all.

'OK, so … hugging. How does that go? You sort of … stretch your arms out …' He does so too robotically, too broadly. It looks kind of like he's trying to find a boulder to slot into the space he's made between his chest and his hands. He looks like Donkey Kong, I think, and then I giggle. 'What? I'm getting this soooo right. I just have to clamp these things around you, now …'

He gets me in a headlock, one big bicep smothering my face, while his free arm flaps ineffectively somewhere around my stomach. Like he's searching for the correct hugging position, and completely failing to find it.

This time I squirm as I giggle – and not just because he's holding me weirdly. There are all of these odd feelings bubbling around inside me, and they turn me into this wriggling mess.

'Dillon, stop, stop – come on!'

'What? Am I doing it wrong?'

'I –'

'You need more bicep, right? More bicep smushed into your face. I knew it! I'm a hugging genius!'

He's a genius at making me wet myself – I'll give him that much.

'I can't breathe!'

'Isn't that supposed to happen when you hug?'

'Not unless you're into necrophilia. I'm turning blue, Dillon!'

'You are not. You looked beautiful, wedged against my armpit. Aside from the flailing. And the look of distress. And the amount of clothes you have on ... my *God*, woman, are you wearing your shoes while in bed with me? You do *not* have your shoes on.'

'I can't confirm that fact. I'm being smothered by muscles.'

It's true. I am. In order to talk, I have to nudge the heavy weight of his right bicep away with my nose, and do my best impression of a ventriloquist: mouth barely moving, sound hardly coming out of me. I'm surprised he hears me well enough to make the following offer:

'Here then. Here. Rest in this convenient nook I seem to have, right where my shoulder meets my chest.'

Which I accept with far too much gusto. Other people are probably really cool and nonchalant about it, drifting into his arms like a frost-covered flower. They don't scramble like a maniac for this tiny scrap of human contact.

But I don't care.

Because he doesn't, either. In fact, I'd venture to say that he seems quite pleased for a moment. A hint of a smile drifts across his face, before he's right back to the issue of the day.

'There. Now you can look down and observe that while I am completely naked from the waist down in a rather alarming fashion, you have on every item of clothing you possess.'

'I'm definitely not wearing seventeen pairs of shoes.'

'No, just these little cute ones. Lemme see those,' he says, all bluster and grabby hands. Funny, then, that he seems surprised when I actually do as he asked. I lift my legs and point my toes at the ceiling, in a way that shows my heeled Mary-Janes to their best advantage. They look almost cute, I think, with my smooth bare legs beneath.

And apparently he agrees.

'Oh, I like that,' he says, in a voice that shades just a touch too husky. It makes me glance down his body, checking for something I'm sort of sure won't be there, until my eyes reach their destination and it actually is.

'I can see that. Good God, man! Does it ever go down?'

'Not after head like that it doesn't. Not after waiting for it for that long. I mean, you understand that one orgasm was just, like, the appetiser.'

'I understand that you're crazy. Not yet, OK – we can't do sex things again yet,' I say, and I guess I expect him to argue here. So it's kind of weird that he doesn't.

'No,' he says. 'You're right. Post-coital holding, first. And talking! Let's do some talking.'

Which sounds a little like a joke, I think ... but a little like he's not joking at all, at the same time. I think of the pizza and the conversation he wanted to have, and how eager he'd seemed for both ... and then of course that just leads me to the one thing I've wanted to ask for a thousand years. Because if he wants to talk so badly, why did he suddenly stop?

I have to know. I have to.

'Are you sure?' I ask, in as light a voice as I can manage. 'You sort of seemed to lose your train of thought last time.'

'I did?' he asks, and I know he's being as falsely casual as I am. I suspect it may be catching – *get inoculated now against fake flippancy, before you too fall victim.*

'Yeah. I've been meaning to ask you about it, actually.' Boy, have I ever. 'You just seemed to go a little blank when

I asked you about yourself, and I wondered if –'

'Oh. Oh! You mean when the pizza came? Yeah, food can distract me from anything,' he says, laughing – but there's an obvious problem with that. He did the blank thing *before* the pizza came. It was way before, and I think he's aware of it. He's so aware of it that I can feel his body tensing just a little, and I'm afraid to look at his face – but about a second later he smoothes it over. 'I was thinking about it five minutes before the guy got to the door. Just zoned out, I guess – kind of like you do.'

It's a good patch job. I can almost overlook the cracks.

'I don't do it as badly as you did!'

'Kit. You're like JD from *Scrubs*.'

I give him a facepalm for that. He's earned it. He's working so hard to make what he's saying the truth that I want to give him something – something that says I believe, even if I don't exactly. I think there was a problem when he considered sharing. He ran into an issue of some kind, a memory maybe, and just wanted to leap right over it.

And that's OK.

We've only known each other for a week or so, after all. I can wait, I think. I can wait, as long as it's not *possibly murdered somebody*. Which I don't think it is, if the rest of him is anything to go by.

'But I like that about you,' he says, because apparently he's so awesome he can overlook my slight resemblance to Zach Braff.

I mean, come on. That's pretty amazing of him.

'You're so sweet,' I say, and then I give it one last go. You know, just to be sure he understands where we're at. 'But if there was something ... if there was ever something you wanted to tell me ... you could. Even if you don't think we're in that place, you could tell me.'

I can feel him looking at me, and it's making my face go all hot. But I won't take it back. Not even if he laughs, I won't take it back.

'You think we're in that place?'

'Maybe.'

'Awesome. I'll take maybe.'

Now I have to look at him. I want to see what level of joking he's at, and am shocked to find it's a minus seventeen. His expression is all sort of ... warm and fuzzy around the edges, with just a hint of surprise.

Whereas my surprise is a dump truck's worth, all over my face.

'You will?'

'Hell, yeah.'

'And you'd tell me, if there was something.'

'Kit ... I hate to break this to you but ...'

I hold my breath. I'm holding my breath so much, in fact, that when I exhale I practically punch him in the face. He finishes with this:

'... I'm just not that deep.'

Goddamn him and his face and his eyes and his everything. I give him a whack, when breathing out doesn't finish him off – but that just leads to him moaning and complaining in a way that doesn't sound like moaning and complaining at all. It sounds more like he's really enjoying me cracking my hand against his massive bicep.

'I'm as shallow as a puddle,' he insists, as I move down to other bits of him. I really want to see what happens when you slap your palm against one of his big, broad, sort of ... cushiony pectoral muscles, and it doesn't disappoint. The flesh is so firm and taut, and he looks so shocked once I've done it.

Shocked and kind of ... something else.

'Did you just smack my tit?'

Did he just say *tit*? And if he did, why is it making me cry with laughter? Honestly, tears are streaming down my face before he's even made his next move, which is not the one I expect. I fully anticipate a spanking of some type – it is, after all, a big part of my novel.

In fact ... I'm kind of bristling all over, just waiting for it ... that big, hard hand on my backside or my thighs or ohhhh, yeah, maybe the side of my hips as he takes me from behind ... oh, *God*. Oh, God, why did I say that thing about not having sex yet? I must have gone temporarily insane. I want sex so badly that I'm apparently prepared to butt my body up against his – because that's what I'm doing now.

I'm butting up against him, like some bull in heat. And what does he do?

He *tickles* me.

'You're gonna get it now,' he says, and he's right. He's not content with a dig in the ribs or a finger in my armpit. It's an all-out assault on my poor body, from the bits behind my knees to that awful, awful place between my thigh and my groin. I didn't even know anyone was aware of the ticklish qualities of this forbidden spot, but of course *he* is.

He's read the book of me. He can tell I'm going to squirm before I do.

Though I have to wonder if he knows I'm going to wee before I do.

'You have to stop,' I tell him, between breaths. It takes an effort to get words out, but he has to be told. Otherwise, we're going way into golden-shower territory before we've got to our personal chapter thirty-nine. 'Please, please.'

'Oh-ho, was that begging? I think that was begging!'

'That's not begging. That's not begging. I don't know what it is, but it's not begging.'

'Lost the ability to think of words, huh?'

'Can you blame me – oh, my God, not there. No no no don't tickle me there, seriously, I am going to wet the bed.'

'And it's not even chapter thirty-nine yet – Kit, you filthy little thing.'

How on earth does he know what I was thinking? I think our brains might be converging. And I definitely know that our brains are converging when he says:

'Come on, baby, beg me.'

He doesn't even put the words 'to stop' on the end. The sentence no longer needs it. He progressed from tickling to fondling about thirty seconds ago, and I've just realised that my butt is pressed right up against something very appealing. Something that's pressing right back at me as he continues this playful charade.

Though it's less playful, by this point, and more like we're sort of … *wrestling*. He pushes his hand up my shirt and I think he's going for my ribs, so I push it down. But then it sort of slides sideways and aims for something that can't be a tickle-spot, and slowly the picture becomes a little clearer.

Slowly, slowly, like I'm crawling my way up a big hill to the sex that's definitely at the top. We're going to have sex, I think, with such a burst of excitement it's ridiculous – especially in light of the struggling I'm keeping up. And the refusals I keep giving out.

'Stop,' I tell him. 'Don't.'

Which should probably put the kibosh on things. It's not the kind of begging he's after now, and I know it. So how come it's suddenly so hot in here? How come his cock feels like an iron bar against the curve of my ass?

'Don't do what, huh?' he asks. 'Don't take your panties down?'

'Yeah, don't do that,' I answer, but we both know what I really mean. I really mean that scene where they play a little game … one where he's very forceful, and she's full of protests. And the only difference is that he's a hundred times better than any hero I've ever thought of. He's a hundred times clearer on how these things should go.

Because whereas the Master made no provisions, no get-out clauses, no safety nets … *Dillon* does. 'Say "fire", if you really don't want to,' he tells me, 'you understand?'

It's the only time I nod during the whole thing.

The rest of the time I'm just a mindless mess. I lie there shaking as he yanks my panties down, and shoves my skirt up. And then I shake harder, to feel him pawing my thighs apart. He's like some other Dillon doing it – some rougher, more desperate man than the one I'm used to – but man, is it ever a turn-on. I can feel his rough breath against the back of my neck and his thick fingers, opening me up.

Nothing prepares me for how they feel sliding in, however. He rubs once over my slick entrance, moaning and muttering when he realises how wet I am, and then he just fills me with two fingers, as easy as anything. All the way to the webbing, so thick and intrusive that I clench, hard, around him.

But of course that just makes it feel even better. A big glut of sensation radiates from that one place, overwhelming me before we've even got to the next bit. Which is a shame, because I really need all of my faculties for this particular pop quiz.

'You always so ready for me, huh? Or did sucking my cock get you all excited?'

Oh, God, I don't know, I don't know. On the one hand, yes – sucking him got me really excited. I practically came just feeling him do it in my mouth and all over my face. I'll definitely be coming over it tomorrow, when I masturbate while thinking of him.

But on the other hand ... I'm always ready for him. He doesn't have to put his hand in my hair or rock his hips or moan, as I give him head. I get wet just looking at his face. I got wet watching him eat pizza. I'm wet all the time now, and that's the truth – but I don't say it.

Because the connection between my brain and my mouth has been disengaged. And it's just lucky, really, that he doesn't need that connection to be there. It's lucky that he's so instinctive. That he's read all of the things he's read and knows all of the things he knows. I'm not sure what would happen if he didn't – probably the same thing that always happens, when I try to enjoy myself and do fun sex things.

Something bad, I think.

Just as he murmurs in my ear:

'I'm going to make you come on that cock.'

And then I think it's fair to say that I have a minor orgasm. Not a big one, mind. Just a tiny hint of one – the kind that happens sometimes when you're asleep, and you're dreaming about three guys going down on you and everything's awesome and suddenly you half-wake up as pleasure jolts through your body.

It's *that* kind of fuzzy, nearly-not-there climax.

Only it's still somehow better than most of the actual climaxes I've ever had. Better because it feels good, and better because he goes a little still after it's happened, before breaking out of this mean-guy persona, briefly, to ask an incredulous question.

'Did you just have an orgasm, after hearing me talk about giving you an orgasm?'

All I can do is sob helplessly in answer.

'I think you did. I think you just came 'cause I'm fingering your sweet pussy and talking dirty to you – you know why?'

I don't, I don't.

'Because you're so nuts for this. Aren't you, huh? You're so primed. I can feel that hot little pussy clenching around me every time I move a muscle or say a word – ohhhh, yeah. Yeah, arch your back so I can look at you going nice and tight around my fingers. Yeah. Yeah. You gonna do that around my cock?'

I think there's a definite danger that I may cut his cock in two, when it finally happens. Though naturally I don't say that. I'm still incapable of speech. It's all I can do to keep breathing and being relatively still. My body totally wants me to buck against his teasing fingers, and he does nothing to dissuade this sort of behaviour. He actually puts a hand on my hip to help haul me into the position he wants – and that position is *lewd*. My ass kind of juts towards him like a piece of shelving, and now my face is half in the pillow.

Plus, I know what he can see. I know without even thinking about it, because I can hear it in his voice. I can feel it in his shaky actions.

'Oh, man,' he says, so hot and breathless. 'Oh, man, I can't wait to get in that pussy. Spread yourself open for me, OK? Here, here, like this.'

He gets hold of my hand and forces it over the left cheek of my bottom – roughly, too roughly. And then he just pushes against my wrist until I'm doing what he asked: spreading everything open for his viewing pleasure.

It's easy to, when he makes me. Everything is easy when he makes me. It has a kind of freedom to it, just as I thought it would. I don't have to think about how I look, or whether

I'm reacting right, or where my hands should go. He simply manoeuvres me into position, just as the Master did for my heroine, and, after a moment of watching myself be this open and vulnerable for him, I hear the rip of foil and the snap of rubber.

He's going to fuck me, now, I think, and even though I knew everything was leading to this, it still feels so fresh and sharp and vaguely frightening. The manhandling and my silence just make it that way – they strip the experience right down to its rawest components. No sweetness, no niceties …

I feel the blunt, thick head of his cock against my entrance, and then he's angling my hips and working his way in. Slowly, at first, easing back and forth until I give … but by the time I do he's impatient. 'Come on, come on,' he says, but I can't blame him. I can't think badly of him. Personally, I just want him to shove right in. I want him to go further into that persona and simply have me, take me, whether it hurts or not.

And when he gets close to that – when he finds the right angle, suddenly, and slips right into me in a shockingly thick rush – I know I was right to feel that way. The sensation is incredible – like I'm being parted, slowly. Like I'm enclosing him too, tightly. I try to clench around him, but there's nowhere to go. There's no room to test him out, and apparently he agrees.

'Oh, man,' he says. 'Oh, man, oh, man, oh, man.'

As though he's forgotten that other words exist. I wish he'd remember, however, because I know he's looking down between my legs. I know he can see his erection spreading me like this, and I've only got my own idea of how it must look.

So slippery, I think. So rude – and even more so when he slowly eases back out again. I bet I seem speared by him. I bet I seem forced to take that big, thick shaft, which is an exciting enough idea on its own. He doesn't have to figure out English again and explain it to me.

Though I'm glad he does.

'Yeah,' he says. 'Yeah, baby – you take that soooo good. That nice, huh? You like getting fucked by this big cock?'

I can't even fault him for his arrogance. He *does* have a big one. It's so big you could persuade druids to worship it on the solstice, so there's really no getting around it. In truth, I don't want him to get around it, because when he says 'fucked' and 'big' and 'cock', I moan into the pillow. I try to tell him, 'Yes, yes, I love it,' but it just comes out as muffled sound.

Which he appreciates.

'Oh, yeah, you like it. That's it, baby. Work yourself on it,' he says, but my attempts are pathetic at best. I jerk my hips and that's way too much – pleasure actually jabs me, right in the gut. And when I try to do it slow and easy, just sliding myself back and forth over that stiff, unyielding thing, it's not quite enough.

I bunch the sheets in frustration, and make helpless noises.

Which he appreciates even more.

'Not sure how to go about it, huh?' he says, and then he just presses me down into the bed. He presses me right down on to my belly and lifts himself up over me, hands on my ass. And I think it's going to hurt, I guess. I brace myself for the pressure of him, for the force of that too long and too thick and too brutal feel of his erection. I don't believe it when he says 'like this', until he actually shows me what 'like this' means.

It means that he angles his hips down and just sort of rubs into me – barely leaving that tight, slick space with each thrust, but making sure that every single one is insistent. Really, really insistent, like the way he tickled me. Like two knuckles digging into my ribs, which I know sounds absolutely awful.

So it's a shock that this is somehow the opposite. There's nothing awful about it at all. It's not even uncomfortable, the way I kind of expect it to be. He just strokes the thick head of his erection over that place he found so unerringly with his fingers, and I make a sound like a moose dying.

Not that he's complaining. He's not alarmed to find himself in bed with a large, hirsute four-legged animal. Far from it, in fact.

'Right there, huh?' he says, because he's a smug fucker. But hey – he has every right to be. I'm a boneless, whimpering mess. Every time he hits that spot, pleasure pushes through me in a thick, almost oppressive bloom, rendering me essentially speechless.

But that's OK – because he's got plenty of talking to do now. He tells me how wet I look, how tight, how hot. He tells me how tempting my ass looks, and asks me if I've ever had anyone there – then strokes over that secretive place with two terrifying, slippery fingers, before I've had a chance to answer. Hell, he knows that I won't answer. He knows that I can't, and after a while I think that gives him a kind of carte blanche.

He could finger me there, if he wanted. He could slide out of me and push it into that virgin place, and I wouldn't say a word. In fact, I kind of want him to just do it. I want him to go as bad as he can, without questions or prompts.

Because I can never give them. I understand that now. I can only get them like this, with someone who knows so perfectly how to do things and say things. He grabs hold of my hips before I've urged him, and speeds up his thrusts at just the right point. Then, just as I'm settling into the safety of it, the rhythm of it, he grunts:

'Yeah, you like being taken, huh? You like being used like this, to get me off. Fuck, I'm gonna come so hard in that tight little pussy.'

And I lose my footing all over again. That one word 'used' just sends me to some place I barely want to go, head flooding with a thousand images of him working me over his cock, as his control dissolves. I can feel him shaking with it, and I know he's excited. I know he must be close, because I can almost make it out in the swell of his erection and the sudden urgency of his thrusts.

But still ... it's something else to hear it put like that. To think of myself as a something he can take his pleasure from, like that – without any real input from me. I don't have to make any choices, bad or otherwise. I can just let him drill me into the bed. I can just squirm and clench around him, moaning almost constantly now.

And I'm not just doing it insensibly, too. I'm saying his name. 'Dillon,' I gasp, 'Dillon,' and oh, he likes that. His grip tightens on my hips and his own words lose their shape – just as mine start to brim over. I actually manage an 'ohhhh that feels good that feels good oh it's gonna make me do it,' and in response he grunts, gutturally.

And that's enough to push me over the edge.

My body practically jackknifes, curling in on itself so fast and jerkily he almost loses his rhythm. His hips kind of stutter to a stop and one of his hands slides up my side, before he regains his balance – though I kind of wish he'd lost it for good. I wish he didn't have the wherewithal to keep fucking into me, because I can barely take the first burst of sensation, never mind the next seventeen of them.

I think I pass out about halfway through. I know I tell him to stop, at the very least – though I've no idea why I have to. I've gone so tight around him I'm sort of afraid I'm cutting off the blood supply, and he should definitely be keen on reeling things back a bit.

But of course he isn't. He's more frantic than ever. He jerks into me, over and over, until I'm almost beside myself. Until I'm squeezing my eyes tight shut around actual tears, too far gone to repeat the one word I need to.

Stop, I think, stop, and then just as it's unbearable … just as I'm sobbing with it, and broken with it, he lets me have this long, rough 'ohhhhhhh'. He tells me he's coming, that I'm making him come, and I don't know what's better.

The feel of him doing it inside me, or that singular concept: *Making him.*

I'm making him do it. I'm forcing him into an orgasm so intense that soon he can't even issue a sound. He goes all tense and wordless, the way I did thirty seconds ago – and when I turn I'm just in time to see it all over his face. His mouth is a big, silent O, and there's a gloriously deep line between his brows … as though his orgasm is causing him actual distress. He can't quite take it, but that's fine, it's fine.

I can't take it either. I can't take it; I can't take him. I can't take the aftermath of my orgasm, so intense it's almost like it's happening all over again. But most of all … most of all I can't take what happens to me afterwards, as I'm lying there in his arms. He doesn't make jokes about being unsure about hugging, again. He just hugs me. And he says things, too, like 'you sure that was OK?' and 'now's the time to tell me if I was too rough. I know you kind of want that, but I need to know how much you want that, you know?'

And they're all such cool things to tell me that I simply think it, unbidden.

I love you, I think, like a total idiot. I absolutely love you.

Chapter Eleven

It must be just a fluke, I think. A knee-jerk reaction to all the affection and the mind-blowing sex. He's hit the emotional equivalent of my central nervous system, and now my feelings are spasming out of control. I have to rein them back in before he notices, because Dillon ... well. Dillon is *definitely* not the kind of man who wants to randomly hear an 'I love you'.

No. Dillon is the kind of man who bursts out of his wardrobe while wearing my underwear, because I said he wouldn't dare. He even puts my bra on, and then in the middle of my stunned sexual confusion he persuades me to do things that would make a porn star blush. At the very least, they make me blush.

Which is practically his mission in life now. As I get hardier and more inured to sexual excess, he has to push harder to get me to go red. He has to go deeper into chapter nine hundred and twelve to get me to that point of 'please, no', and, by God, he's unafraid to. He's like an extreme spelunker in the cave of me. Just when I think he's reached an unchartable depth, he burrows his way further down.

And he's so sly about it, too. So crafty and ingenious. 'Let's go for a walk,' he says, which sounds so innocent I can't say no. I'm even looking forward to a variety of new and exciting things that he just seems to slip in there when I'm barely looking – like hand-holding and being together outdoors and spending a casual Saturday together.

It's not just my imagination, I think. We're sort of becoming a couple in some stealthy, sideways sort of way. I glance to the right, and when I glance back our fingers are laced together. We're taking in scenery. We seem just like everyone else who's made it outside on this lazy Saturday morning.

Apart from the bit where he jostles and cajoles me into going inside the Pennyside Lane church. He practically dares me to do it, as though I'm the Devil and might burst into flames the second I step over the threshold – though that's not why I'm concerned, of course. I'm concerned because he's giving me those narrowed eyes and that little half-grin, and he's doing all the things he usually does when he gets me to partake in something I never thought I could. He nudged and tickled me just like that last week, when he felt it was important for my wellbeing to do a 69 before I hit that actual age.

He'd had a point. I needed that push towards *being a normal person*. And the pushing is working, too. I no longer zone out and think about neurotic non-existent scenarios. I zone out and think of our bodies sandwiched together so tightly you couldn't have slipped a piece of cardboard between us; his cock in my mouth and my pussy in his. I think about how crazy it had made me … how utterly wild and uninhibited – and how he'd played on that for what had seemed like seventeen hours. All he had to do was work me up to the point of orgasm, and suddenly I was sucking and licking and running my hands over his body like a goddamn sex maniac.

I let him put a finger somewhere really rude. *I* put a finger somewhere really rude.

And I was so proud, too. I'm proud of the person I'm turning into – looser and more relaxed. Not so worried about a million things. Able to successfully take my clothes off during sex, and even occasionally suggest certain stuff without squirming.

Until he goes one step further. And then I'm not sure who I am or what's happening. 'No,' I say, 'don't, not in here,' but the trouble is … I'm starting to like that, too. I'm liking the edge that refusal provides; I'm liking the sting of saying no. It's ironic, really: the minute I discard some of my baggage, I want to set it back up again. I want to rebuild barriers – though I suppose the difference is that *I'm* the one in charge of them now.

I get to make them, just so I can knock them down.

And oh, I love knocking them down. I love him for helping me do it. He just hauls me over to the confessional, heady with the scent of furniture polish and forbidden things, and once we're sat on either side of the latticed partition he says something that makes me bristle all over. He builds barriers fifty feet high and thirty feet wide, and then he just waits. He waits, to see if *this* is the thing I'll really refuse to do.

It isn't.

'I don't know when my last confession was,' I tell him, because that's absolutely true. I don't. I've never confessed anything in a church.

Unlike my heroine. Oh, my heroine is pious and perfect; she wore knee-high socks and prayed every day in school.

But I didn't. In fact, I'm surprised this is such a thrill. I say the words and then I add one on the end – one that she said, one that she felt to the bottom of her soul – and an echo of the sentiment goes through me.

'Father,' I say, like *Master*, only more warped. All of this is warped, I think.

And he agrees.

'Well, that's pretty terrible of you,' he says. 'I guess you'd better tell me everything.'

Which is isn't very convincing as a priest. But it is very convincing as something that makes me go all hot and cold. I can just imagine the dusty conversations that have gone on in here before, and how this descent into dirty is about to compare. Please sir, I stole a penny sweet, I think.

And then I confess my own tale of torrid woe.

'Last night,' I tell him. 'I let a man take my virgin ass.'

There's a silence that I don't expect, once the words are out. As though I really did say them to a priest, and now he's wrestling with his shock. He can't quite believe I said such a wanton, wicked thing, and in that sudden quiet I can't quite believe it either. I get a little frisson of thrill and fear, so sure for a second that I've actually done the impossible:

I've stunned Dillon Holt.

Which has to be way worse than giving a priest the vapours. If you shock someone like Dillon, you have to be beyond the pale. You've got to be a lascivious lady of the night, or worse – and I really feel the impact of that, for a second. I feel all sorts of things, for a second. A flash of shame, so familiar to me and yet so far away from the person I've become. A bloom of heat between my legs, as I consider any number of unlikely things: his cheeks flushing, his mouth falling open, his erection stiffening against his will between his legs.

And the worst part about it is: I like it. I love it.

Go on, I think, pretend to be outraged.

Only he takes it one step further than that. He doesn't

pretend. He sounds genuinely faint and faraway, when he speaks again. I've really somehow done it, though I don't know how. Because he thought I couldn't confess, and now I can?

Because I give it away more freely than he does, now?

He rarely tells me a thing that he fantasises about, or wants, or feels. But I'm deep into enemy territory now. I'm talking for myself, without the help of words I wrote some time ago, or his knuckles digging into my ribs.

'That's really ...' he says. 'That's really wrong.'

And I just answer without even thinking about it.

'I know. But it felt soooo right, Father,' I say, half in someone else's character, half in my own. My voice sounds high and plaintive, but it's all me dragging that one word out. Because oh, it did feel *soooo*. It feels *soooo* now, just to recount every little detail of it.

From this:

'But he was so persuasive.'

To this:

'And once he'd made me all slippery, I couldn't really say no.'

'You couldn't?'

'I tried, honestly. I thought of pure things, and pleaded with him to have mercy on me. But when he made me lie like that, with my legs spread ... when he suggested I lick and suck my fingers and just stroke myself there ...'

'Yes?'

'I found that I ... that I ...'

'That you?'

'Oh, I liked it, Father. I liked the stroking.'

'I see. And why do you think that might be?'

I picture the scene from the night before – my face in the

181

pillow, again. My skirt up around my hips. He'd told me to leave it on, this time, even though he usually prefers me naked, and I absolutely know why. It just made it so much naughtier, to have my bare ass framed and exposed like that. The contrast of my restricted body and my naked bottom had driven me nearly wild, before he'd even told me what he wanted me to do.

And I know why, too.

'Because I love making myself lewd for him.'

'You do?'

It's unsettling how genuinely curious and surprised he sounds. Can he really possibly not know? Does he think I'm lying when I moan for him, when I gasp for him, when I squeeze the sheets into my fists just to feel him easing into my tight ass?

I guess he does, a little.

And that needs to be remedied immediately.

'Oh, God, yes, yes. I loved fingering myself for him.'

'Because of how it felt?'

'Because of how it must have looked. Oh, I bet it looked so bad.'

'I bet it did. Yeah. Yeah. I'm sure it did.'

'And then he trailed oil all over me, there, and I'm certain it looked worse.'

'Oh, man, it – it probably would have done, sure.'

I love how he corrects himself, there. He almost couldn't help himself, I think, but he pulls the façade back just a fraction of a second too late. Which makes me wonder: is this my fantasy ... is it mine, or could it actually be his? He sounds so breathless and so unlike himself, and when I come out of my reverie for a moment I see his hand gripping the lattice between us. He's hooked his fingers through, and the knuckles have gone all white.

And that idea is so exciting me ... it's so explosive that I'm briefly stunned by it. I'm fumbling all over myself, wanting to do more, to get more, to push him into something the way he pushes me ... even as the backseat of my mind worries and worries.

Why does he seem to find it so difficult, to play outside the parameters of me? Where's his book for me to read and follow? – because, oh, man, I want to. If he wants it, I want to give it. I'm ready to do and say anything, to give it.

'And it felt ... it felt ...'

'How did it feel?'

He asked me at the time. In fact, I sometimes think he likes hearing more than he likes doing. But if that's the case, I don't mind reiterating.

'So big. So thick. I thought I was going to split in two.'

'But you ... you didn't like it, then?'

His grasp on this priestly role is really starting to slip now. I know why he started that sentence with 'But you' – he wanted to finish it with 'liked it though,' only that wouldn't have worked. No man of the cloth needs to be sure that you secretly enjoyed yourself in the middle of anal sex.

But Dillon ... oh, my Dillon wants to be sure. He pretends to be confident at all times, I think – and he is. He's perfectly, hugely confident, right up until the point where I might just be faking it. Apparently, that idea lingers so much in his mind he's able to somehow forget me wriggling and moaning and sobbing into the sheets.

Then stand on tenterhooks, waiting for the verdict.

'I'm afraid I can't say that, Father. I'm sorry to say that I loved it. I loved every second of it. I loved having someone take me there.'

'I see.'

He sounds relieved, but not enough for my liking.

'I loved being filled like that.'

'Uh-huh.'

'And just when I thought I couldn't endure any more, he made me take two fingers in my pussy.'

'He made you?'

'Yeah. He always makes me. He gets me so wet I just can't say no. And even if I want to, even if I struggle, he forces me to enjoy it.'

'It sounds like you need to get away from this sinner immediately.'

'Are you sure, Father? Because I think you like hearing me talking about him. Do you want me to tell you what he did next?'

'No,' he says, but I know it's *no* meaning *yes*. We've changed places, somehow, and now I'm the one in charge. He's the one who has to sit there and listen – while stroking himself, I suspect. I can hear some deliciously slick sounds coming from the other side of the partition, as the fake him falls to half-mast.

All I have to do is turn it around a little more, and I'll get what I've been hankering after.

'He came inside me, until it ran down the insides of my thighs.'

I don't know what makes me say it. It isn't true. We've never done it without a condom, and even if everything was perfectly safe I've no special predilection for the idea. It's just something dirty to say, I guess.

So his reaction is ... his reaction is *delightful*.

'You'd do that?' he says, in a voice that sounds both high and tight. And that slick noise is now extremely pronounced.

In fact – I don't even have to rely on that alone to know what he's doing. Through the grate, I see him lick his palm before he returns it to his cock.

'I would.'

'You'd let me come in your ass?'

'I'd let you come anywhere you'd like. Is that what you want, baby?'

Suddenly I know why he uses that little term of endearment so often, during sex. It somehow makes the dirty talk so much easier ... so much sharper and clearer. I'm not afraid to do it, when I'm him and he's me. When he's my baby, my honey, my sweetheart ... so ready to do my every bidding.

I don't even balk at saying the rest.

'You want to fill me there?' I tell him, and I'm proud of myself for doing it. No prompting, no nudging – the words just fall right out of my mouth.

So it's a shame that he responds with this:

'Only if you want me to.'

God, I never thought I'd find selflessness so frustrating.

'No,' I say, sharper than I intend. 'No. Tell me that you want to. I know you want to – is that a fantasy of yours? To fuck a girl skin to skin and then cream inside her?'

'I don't know, oh, God, I don't know.'

I think that's a yes, but admittedly it's hard to be sure. Just the idea of the thing I'm suggesting is enough to make him moan inside a church confessional. I'm not even certain if he cares whether anyone hears him, because a second later he actually says my name.

'Kit,' he moans, like I'm everything he so desperately needs. And if that's true ... if I'm right ... then God knows I'm not going to leave him hanging on that score. I don't know why he finds it hard to share his fantasies, when he's so free about fulfilling mine. But I've got no problems trying to rectify that – even in a church.

In fact, I don't even think about being inside a church, as I slip out of the confessional. I barely notice whether there's anyone sitting in those dusty, sunlight-dappled pews. I just go to where he is. I have to go to where he is.

And oh, boy, I don't regret it once I have. There's something doubly salacious about seeing him like this, seated on that well-worn wooden bench with his hand inside his shorts. He hasn't even taken them down, or taken himself out. He's being so secretive about this, so furtive, that only his hand on himself under cover of clothes and darkness will do.

Which is enough on its own to turn me on. I don't need the other stuff – though I take it anyway. His brief look of panic. The way he closes his eyes when I step close. The harsh rattle of his breathing …

Yeah, seeing Dillon Holt this excited, and yet this inhibited at the same time …

It's very compelling. It makes me wonder if he's at all religious, underneath his brash exterior. Or did he have other reasons for appreciating the game we've just played? I rarely use dirty talk, but it seems he enjoys it – a fact that drives me on even harder than any of his other persuasions.

Lord, if only he'd known. He could have gotten me to bum sex way before last night. I'd have probably given up my ass three weeks before I met him, with just a bat of those pretty eyelashes and an uncomfortable clearing of his throat.

'We can't do anything in here,' he says, but he's totally lying. He's *lying*. He's playing coy on purpose, because apparently that just excites him more. He practically arches up off his seat when I suddenly fall to my knees, and his 'no' is quite something to hear.

It has seventeen extra syllables. It's as elaborate as a game of Mousetrap, and it shows me clearly why *I* seem to like it so much. The word 'no' makes it forbidden, I think. 'No' makes it wrong, so wrong.

And it does it whether you're Kit Connor or Dillon Holt.

'Just say "fire", if you really want me to stop,' I tell him, with the wryest smile I've ever felt on my own face. Seriously, this is the most fun I've had in my life – and it's so easy, too. His eyes actually fly open at that sound of that one little word, and he remains speechless throughout the rest of my little explanation.

Then less speechless once I've done.

'I've created a monster,' he says, with just a flicker of amusement in his eyes. The rest is all red-faced flusteredness, to the point where I get that vertigo-inducing sense again. That sense that we've swapped places, just for a little while.

Just long enough for me to be even more daring than I was the day I told him what I was going to do to him, whether he wanted it or not. Maybe because now I don't care if it's *not*. I just slide his zipper down – so loud, in this closed little space – and then when he's at his most rigid, when his back's right up against the wooden wall and his Converse-covered feet are rubbing holes into the stone floor, I lick him in places he least expects.

Like over that strip of skin he loved me pressing my fingers into. Like the tops of his thighs, where he tickled me; like up and underneath his shirt to the sharp points of his nipples. I do all the things I've only guessed at or extrapolated from bits and pieces of information.

But apparently I'm getting good at doing so.

Because he definitely reacts, to almost everything. He moans at the flicker of my tongue in those secretive places, and rolls his hips to help me work his shorts down – even as he says no. He says no and no and no until I'm sure what each one really means.

It means the same as it does when I say it to him.

'You want me to suck this big thick cock?' I ask him, and when he shakes his head and peers through the little grating, I take the head in my mouth. I swirl my tongue around the tip, and then I say what I'm sure he wants to hear: 'I'm sorry, but I just can't help myself. You make me so horny, Father,' I say.

And he responds with:

'Oh my God oh my God oh my God we're going to burn in hell.'

'We are?'

'Definitely.'

'Well, I guess you'd better come in my mouth before that happens.'

'No.'

'Or maybe you'd like to do it all over my face.'

'Absolutely not.'

'Or between my tits.'

'There isn't enough "no" in the world for that – you'd better not take that shirt off. You'd better keep your clothes on. Do not take your clothes off in here.'

And I think we have a winner. He wants me to get half-naked in a confessional and rub my breasts all over him – something I would never have considered a month ago. But apparently I can be persuaded to do just about anything, with the help of two seemingly opposing techniques:

Either he makes me.

Or I make him.

Oh, God, I think I like making him. I think I like the way he looks at me as I undo the buttons, all wild-eyed and half-disbelieving. Suddenly I can see the appeal of myself, and how I've behaved for him – even though I rarely if ever understand why anyone might like me. I've spent my life feeling singularly unattractive and unspectacular, and it's there, on the stone floor of a church at 7 a.m. on a Saturday, that I finally and truly feel like something more than that. I feel voluptuous, and daring, and sexy.

He makes me feel all of those things, just by looking this shocked. By shaking, when I bring his hands to my bare breasts. By acting the part of an innocent so perfectly that I'm not even sure if he's acting right now. I think it really does stun him to be fondling someone's naked body in a church, despite his lurid past and his cocky swagger.

And that's so exciting that I'm pretty much shaking too, by the time I manage to get his mouth onto mine, and his slick cock between my breasts. 'Give me a pearl necklace,' I whisper in his ear – probably because it's the dirtiest thing I can think of to say.

Though I don't know how dirty it is until he presses me back onto the floor and rubs himself right there. He ruts, like he's suddenly out of control, hands squeezing and squeezing at my flesh. It's really the rudest, most ridiculous thing, when you think about it: his thighs straddling my body, one of them almost at my ear. Erection sliding and slipping between my breasts, mouth open, head back ... and me sprawled out like this with my head against the door.

So it's rather disturbing that those treacherous words enter my head at that exact moment. Just as he's about to give in and offer me that gift I've suggested, and then after it too. He lets out the most desperate groan of pleasure I've ever

heard him make, and I feel the hot spill of his come all over
my throat as I think it, stupidly, crazily, insanely:

I love you.

Chapter Twelve

There's not really any getting around it now. He came on me in a confessional, and I thought the words *I love you*. That's probably a marriage ceremony, in some cultures. We've done the sacred ritual – which means, at the very least, that we have to have some kind of chat about this. About him, and his weird communication issues.

And I suspect he knows this.

In fact, I'm absolutely certain that he knows this. Because when I turn up at his place with deep discussions about his innermost self on my mind, he heads me off at the pass. He performs a pre-emptive strike against my efforts. I'm about to burst in the door and just blurt out the first thing that comes to mind – something about religion, maybe, or his fantasies, or, hell … his job would do. I'm constantly wondering if he gets to manhandle the penguins or poke the seals, and by this point I really shouldn't have to. I shouldn't have to wonder. We're not just fucking any more, and people who aren't just fucking need to understand these kinds of things about each other.

Though I know as soon as I'm inside that he thinks otherwise. In fact, I think he might be actively avoiding divulging any information, in case me knowing him too well accidentally leads to a relationship. Somehow he's going to stumble into it, I think, unless he takes drastic measures.

And he has.

He's really taken some drastic measures.

He's laid out seven strips of red ribbon on the bed. Like the first chapter that's also the second-to-last chapter of my book. And because of that – because they're there at the beginning, but also at the end – they seem ominous. Exciting, true, and certainly as distracting as he's probably intended. But there's something else about them.

They're like a message. Keep going, and I'll completely shut down the way your hero does, I think; though the idea is more shocking than I expect. It's more blistering, like a wound I didn't anticipate, healing before I've got used to the pain. I thought he was fun, and silly, and full of light ... but when I think of it this way ...

He's not so different to the hero of my story. He's just as cold, in his own way. He's just as impervious. He doesn't say anything about his own wants and needs, exactly as the Master didn't. He won't share his life with me, and that's true of my cologne-soaked businessman too.

And yet somehow that's not half as sexy as it was in the story. It's not cool to be with someone so shut off. It's not full of thrills. I'm not going to ride off into the sunset with him, happy with a word or two about his feelings, for ever.

That's reality, I think.

That's what my story lacked: the sting of love. This sharp pain just under my ribcage, when he wraps the first ribbon around my eyes. Because it's blissful, of course it's blissful. It's almost unbearably arousing and so utterly lovely to have someone be this willing to make your fantasies come true.

It fills me with a shaking sort of gratitude, and persuades me to do as he's suggesting even as all my intentions turn to dust and blow away.

But it's not enough. It's not enough to live your life with a cipher. He said it to me the first day we met: 'I'm empty.' And that's what weighs heavy in my heart as he leads me to the bed. As he undresses me, piece by piece, until I'm just standing there, naked and sightless.

While he remains aloof and detached. He could be anyone, I think – and in truth he sort of feels like it, as he smoothes his palms over my breasts and my ass. I'm used to the slight roughness of his touch, and the startling sense of the size of his hands. But here and now his touch is almost elegant, as though he wasn't content with simply distracting me with the sharpest fantasy he could find in the book. He also has to be that man, utterly. He has to smell like something other than himself – not of fabric softener and sometimes of salt, but of thick, rich perfume.

And of course I can't tell him that I prefer the former.

Because I'm aroused, in spite of myself. I'm very aroused now. There's just something about a touch that's this imper-sonal ... like seven different men are doing the stroking. One of them dips his fingers into the V of my sex, testing my wetness. Another probes me, somewhere really rude. Something ghosts over my stiff nipples and I forget that I'm supposed to stand still.

And then I'm punished for it. A ribbon is wrapped around that place I've just quivered over – thick and silky and too tight around my breasts. So tight, in fact, that for a second I can't breathe ... though I'll admit it might be more to do with the situation than anything else. I'm all jumbled and conflicted, wanting more of this then needing to back down.

Just say, I think.

Dillon, we need to talk.

But it's easier thought than done. Of course it is. Everything is always easier in my head. In my head, my heroine didn't feel trapped by this act. She didn't want to say the safe word – she didn't even *have* a safe word. She just went along with everything like a good little lamb, and I confess: I kind of hate her for it now.

I hate her for being so selfish and so accepting at the same time. I hate her for moaning the moment he ties her hands behind her back – though I've no idea how I can be so unforgiving. Because I do the same thing when he does it to me. I moan his name when I feel him lacing that ribbon over and over around my wrists in an endless loop.

And when he leads me to the bed by the length of material he's left, I let him. I go willingly. I bare my throat for the ribbon there, too, though naturally I know what that means. I understand the connotations of a collar, even if I've no idea what I'm collaring myself to.

Mindless, mind-blowing sex, for ever? Awkward moments when he almost seems to know what a relationship should be?

Perhaps, perhaps. But in that moment I don't care as much as I should. I'm too busy enjoying the sensation of the silk sliding against my skin. In the story, it was more about the bite of those thick edges, the sense of being bound. But in reality it's so much sweeter than I would have thought. It's slippery and slick against my stiff nipples and the sensitive skin of my throat, and when he runs it between my legs, briefly …

Ohhh, my clit jerks at the feel of it. My back arches without having to be told to do it. He's got me on hands and knees on the bed, but it's me who puts myself into the right position. It's me who gasps and rocks back to feel the heavy press of him between my legs.

He's going to take me right away, I think – not like in the story. In the story the Master waited, because he could. But maybe ... maybe Dillon can't. Maybe he's so turned on he just has to have me, now, and the thought is desperately exciting.

Until I realise what it means.

I'm panting after his every tiny reaction, just as my heroine did. I'm sifting through him constantly, waiting for a sign of something. And though he gives me more than the Master ever gave her, though he shakes for me, and flushes for me, and tells me he can't wait, it's all just nothing, without the core of him.

It's nothing, I think, as he slides into me.

Even though my treacherous body believes otherwise. It always reacts the same way when he fills me with his thick cock – excitement slithers down and sensation slithers up, and both things meet in the middle in a big burst of pleasure. I gasp at feeling it, and immediately do what I hardly dared to before.

I fuck back against him, with all the desperation I'm currently feeling. I jerk and work and go for it, pushing him the way she pushed him, refusing to stay still. And when he gives me nothing but:

'Yeah, show me what you want. Tell me what you want.'

I think something cracks inside me.

And it definitely smashes into smithereens, once he's followed it with this:

'Why can't you tell me, huh?'

Why can't *I* tell *you*, my mind bellows, and then I do something my heroine never ever did: I rip the blindfold off. I turn without permission, and stare at him with all the incredulity I can muster. It's molten hot, this incredulity. It's burning inside me as hard as the edge of my orgasm is, and it doesn't take much to get it out of my mouth.

'I have. I did. I do, all the time,' I say, but that's not enough. I'm not satisfied with that. I have to move away from him and sit up, and maybe bunch his shirt into my fists, too. I have to wrench him down onto the bed, and once I have the rest comes out easier: 'But you don't.'

I think I intend it to come out quite accusatory, or at least to have a hint of detachment. But somehow I find myself kissing him in-between the words. And he kisses me back in return. He kisses me with the greed of someone who knows they're going to be starved soon, and I just can't help responding.

But I do my best to stay true to my course at the same time.

'You never say a thing,' I tell him, as he runs both hands down my body and gets a fistful of my ass. Before I know it I'm almost over him, his cock pushing against my belly, his mouth against mine.

And this sexual distraction isn't his only weapon, either.

He has other ways of making me not talk.

'I say plenty,' he tells me, and how can I say that's not true? He does say a lot – during sex and outside it. He's got the ultimate defence: 'I want to talk all the time.'

Though I'm starting to see that need to chat in a different light now. Maybe it's just what he thinks he should do, rather than what he can do. Maybe it's just more deflection from the real matter at hand.

'Yeah, but not about you. Not about things you want, and the things you fantasise about. Where's your book, huh? Where's your book for me to read?'

'I told you. I'm not that deep.'

'You're so shallow you can't tell me what you want?'

'I want you to fuck me.'

'You can't tell me what you need?'

'I need you to fuck me,' he says, and though I try I can't resist that. It's so close to what I'm asking for that I can't possibly deny him. In truth, it's so close to what *I* want that I can't possibly deny him. My body's still buzzing from the feel of him, and it buzzes harder the longer we kiss like this – so fierce and wet. And the longer we talk like this.

Like we're going to take each other apart with words.

'What else?' I demand, as I take him in my hand. He's still slippery with my slickness, and so hard it's impossible to resist. Only the struggle of straddling him – and the sudden sense of just how big he is, like this – stops me sliding right down on him immediately.

I have to work for it ... but that's fine.

Because working for it gives me a real chance to turn us both inside out. It makes it easy to keep this conversation going, with him all eager to feel me again and me all eager to feel him. All I have to do is keep doing this, I think. Keep teasing.

'Fuck me like you mean it,' he says, which isn't quite enough to warrant the long slow slide I'm dying for. It gets him a stroke through my slit, and nothing more.

Much to his consternation.

'Come on, Kit.'

'You want me to come on, you share.'

'And what if I don't have anything *to* share?'

'You did it well enough when we first met. You did it well enough in group.'

'That was different,' he says, and in a way I know he's right. Of course I know he's right. I even know why he's right, though I can't quite accept it until he spells it out, as clear as day and twice as large:

'It was just about meaningless sex,' he tells me, with the unspoken words left hanging in the air afterwards.

And this isn't any more.

This isn't some jokey anecdote that he can tell some stranger about one day. It's a river of murky water, full of sharp things and creatures with teeth. It's crazy and compulsive – to the point where I can't even stop him rolling me onto my back. I don't want to stop him rolling me onto my back.

I'm just as lost as he is, I think, feeling blindly through physical sensation, instead of dealing with anything deeper. I let him take me like that, roughly, passionately – until we're both drenched in sweat and criss-crossed by nail marks, and I don't say a single thing. I don't try to make it anything other than meaningless, even though I know it isn't, somewhere inside me. And I know we could see that, too, I know we could if we tried.

But I also know that we won't.

We can't.

We're too hopelessly addicted to everything else.

Chapter Thirteen

He says that he'll call me, afterwards. But it's the first time that I really suspect he won't. And I'm right, it seems.

He doesn't call, or come to my place of work, or stop by my apartment like I sometimes fantasise about him doing. Because we're not that sort of people really, and even if we were ... even if he was the kind of guy who *could* come to my apartment and have a movie night with me and eat dinner and take a bath and all of those normal things ... I've stripped him down to the bone now.

I've made him think about that word 'meaningless'. I've forced him to put it in front of 'sex'. He's probably at the sexual healing group right now, talking frantically about this chick he banged one time in a confessional, just to make absolutely sure that I'm not anything more.

And I'm right about that, too.

I wait outside the building and he comes out a little while later, like a sign I should have paid attention to all along. He's a sex addict. He's crazy for wild fucking, not fun-time sharing. I've probably been making him worse all this time – all of this lovely, lovely time of sexual exploration, and it's actually been a total nightmare of confusion for him. It's like I befriended an alcoholic by partying with him every weekend.

Which is probably what all the *trying to talk about ordinary things* was about. He can't go deeper, but he did try to go sideways. He tried to be ordinary, and I've just made him even weirder. I've fucked him up, I think.

And then I put my head on the car wheel, in utter despair.

Utter despair that comes with a side of car horn. A really, really loud and inappropriate car horn. I mean, let's be honest here. When people think of abject misery, they do not think of a big toot from a clown's nose, do they? No. They think of haunting cello music and maybe some sad ethereal girl moaning about the winds and the seas in Gaelic.

But of course, good old Kit Connor can't even get that right.

My life is a goddamn clown nose, I think – and naturally, just as I do so, it starts to get even worse. I glance to the right and there's Dillon Holt staring over at me. He even has a look on his face like I'm a slightly insane person, which, in all fairness to him, is probably true. After all, I did just follow him to a sexual healing group. And I am physically and mentally incapable of working any of this out, on any level whatsoever.

I can't understand my sexual responses. I don't get why I've done any of the things I've done. I don't know what my feelings are, or what his feelings are, or why it seems so desperately important to start the engine right now and drive away like I was never there.

There are several contenders, as an answer to the latter. But all of them just make me panic more. Behold:

You have to leave because now you look like a sad, pathetic loser who chases around a hunk when he doesn't call.

It might be best to leave, because he's clearly in pain and you put him there with your hunger for actual sex.

You just tooted a big clown nose. Well done.

See? All of them are awful, are they not? And they're making me sweat, and flood the engine when the car won't immediately start. They make me grind the gears like a maniac, and beg silently for someone to save me from what is undoubtedly going to be a horrible confrontation. *YOU MADE ME TRY TO SHARE!* he'll scream at me, while clawing at my window.

And then I'll have to kill myself, for crimes against humanity.

I'll have to kill myself, for crimes against Dillon Holt.

Or, at the very least, I'll have to kill myself for being this embarrassing. I think I'm crying a bit, and I don't even know why. It's not as though I expected myself to be successful at being with another human. I didn't really believe that we could work things out and talk things through.

I guess it's just ... it's just that I'd *hoped*.

I'd let myself hope, I think, for a little while – though I know that hope always ends the same way. It ends with books at the bottom of the drawer and friendships fucked beyond repair. It ends with: *You're useless and awful* and *I never want to see you again.*

I know it does.

So why am I getting out of the car?

'I'm so sorry!'

Probably because I want to do that. And then maybe cry a little, very manfully.

Or, if I'm really being honest: blubber a lot, absolutely ridiculously. In fact, it's so ridiculous that after a second he laughs – though I'm not going to put my name to that assumption just yet. I've covered my face with my hands, so it's entirely possible that what I'm hearing is his death rattle, as he dies of horror.

But then I dare to peek, and no, no.

He's actually laughing at me.

And that's not even the strangest part. No – *this* is the strangest part:

'What are you sorry for?' he says, and then quite suddenly grabs me by the back of my head, and yanks me into a bear hug. I get my face smushed against his left pec, which in general circumstances would probably be really uncomfortable.

But of course it's not, here. It's feels *wonderful*, here.

'Kit, you're such a goof,' he says, and that feels even better.

'I know I am.'

'Why are you so intent on thinking you've done terrible, wrong things when you haven't done anything at all? I'm the one who ... who ...'

I force myself away from him then. Because I'm strong, OK? I'm strong and good and I can do this. I can tell him that we can't party any more. Hell, maybe I need to not party any more. I've had more sex in the last two months than I've ever had in my entire life, so clearly something is going wrong.

He needs to know that I know that something is going wrong.

'Yeah, but I've pushed you there with all of my ... need for shenanigans.'

It sounded better in my head, I have to say. But even so – I don't expect the level of *what the fuck* on his face. It's sent his left eyebrow into the stratosphere. It actually makes him ugly, for a second – which is testament to how scrunched-up his expression is.

And then he laughs again, just to cap it off.

'Pushed me *where*? Into sexual ecstasy?'

'No! Into … being weird and addicted and probably unwell.'

I point in the general direction of the place he just came from, but that only makes him laugh harder. He's almost holding his belly by this point, and I swear he swipes away a tear.

'Oh, I see. So you think I've been secretly coming here all this time to work through the terrible pain of bonking you into oblivion.'

I'll admit, it sounds less logical when he puts it like that. Especially as he uses the word 'bonking', then chuckles after it and shakes his head over *mad British words*.

'Maybe not … exactly.'

'Kit, it's not an addicts' group. You went to it, right? You know it's all about healing your feelings and being positive and all of that shit. I'm just trying to get in touch with my … you know. Inner self.'

'Then how come you say "inner self" like it's a flying banana-coloured unicorn that farts rainbows and sings in stereo?'

'Maybe 'cause I'm not sure I have one.'

I can't help hearing the slight change in tone when he says that last bit. It's a little less *flying banana-coloured unicorns*, and a little more disturbing. So disturbing, in fact, that I feel I have to insist his inner self is present – despite barely knowing what it looks like. It could enjoy wearing striped pyjamas and dancing the fandango, for all I've been told.

But the thing is, I suppose … I know it's there. It's so big I couldn't possibly miss it. Whenever I'm near him, I can feel the hulking shape of it rubbing against my body, like an animal seeking warmth. I can make out its shadow at the centre of him, subtle and mysterious but still completely visible.

'You have one,' I tell him, because I can see it right now. It shifts restlessly beneath his skin, when I unwittingly poke it with my next words. 'Even if that one is a crazed sex addict.'

'Oh, Christ, Kit. I'm not a sex addict. Is that how I seem? Like a sex addict?'

'Well ... maybe. Sometimes.'

I'm thinking specifically of the times when he wakes me up in the middle of the night for the seventeenth time, with an erection like a constantly regenerating Duracell bunny. But of course I don't say that. I fear it would only muddy the waters, just as they're starting to clear. His expression is so open and honest, suddenly. I can actually see how that inner shadow matches up with his outer self, if I strain hard enough.

And to cap it off, one of the guys from the group gives him a sobbing hug, as he passes us on this little narrow and very wet street. 'Thank you for helping me actualise myself,' he says, which pretty much sums up what Dillon's saying. It backs up what I remember, too, about the crystals and the healing hugs and all the other hippy-dippy stuff.

But it still doesn't get to the heart of the matter. And I want the heart. I do. I don't care if it's black with despair and riddled with rot. I'd live inside the bits of him that are barely functioning, if I could. I'd spend the rest of my days trying to piece him back together, if he'd let me.

Which I suspect he won't.

'Honestly, Kit,' he says. 'I'm really not that fucked up.'

He even puts his hands in his pockets, and kind of shrugs – like *hey, I'm totally OK with the world and my place in it. I'm cool and laid-back, without a care in the world.* And it's convincing too. I could probably go on for ever with him like this, in a fantasy land of fucking and fun.

If it were not for the other him just waiting for me behind his eyes.

'Yeah? Then how come you can talk about meaningless sex with strangers but you can't talk to me about ... anything?'

There, I think. That's got you.

But of course it hasn't at all.

'Because I made that up.'

I'll admit, it's not the answer I was expecting. It's not even the answer that really goes with my main point, which is basically: *why do you avoid telling me anything real about yourself?* But it's there now, and it has to be addressed.

And I address it thusly:

'*What?*'

It's very articulate of me, if I do so say myself. My brain wanted me to go with *ffffffffffftttttt*, but I refused to let it get the upper hand. I stick to my guns, and only allow actual words to escape.

'I made that up. I don't find it easier to talk about it with strangers because I adore meaningless sex. I find it easier to talk about it with strangers because I totally made those stories up. They didn't mean anything.'

But I'm less successful after he's delivered that little doozy.

'Ffffffffffffffftttttttt,' I say. I think I'm attempting *fucking terrible*, though I could be wrong. There's nothing actually terrible or fucktastic about what he's just said, so who knows, really? I could just as easily be trying to tell him that he's the craziest, most spectacular person I've ever met, on so many, many levels.

Like this one:

'Yeah, I've never actually had a threesome.'

205

I'm so speechless that I sort of stand there with my mouth open, for a second. He made it up. One of the main instigators of this wild journey of sexual excess and he just pulled it out of his ass, for reasons that are not going to remain unexplained for much longer.

'Why would you say that, then?'

He shrugs again, but this one is even more magnificent than his last offering. It actually says whole sentences to me about his state of mind. It's full of that wryness he's always got all over him, that laughter he's always aiming in his own direction.

Only much more bittersweet now.

Oh, it's so bittersweet when he gives me his answer.

'Because you liked hearing it,' he says, as though it's the most obvious thing in the world. Of course he'd want to give me what he thinks I want, at the expense of himself. Of *course* he would. That makes perfect sense, in a universe where everything is completely different from this one in every way possible.

I almost want to glance around, in case the trees in the park beside us are suddenly reaching their roots towards the sky. Any second now the pavements are going to start losing their solidity, until we find ourselves sunk into them up to the knee.

Not that he'd notice if it did. He seems to have no clue that my idea of how life should be is slowing imploding, a piece at a time.

'You did like it, didn't you?' he asks, as though that's perfectly normal. It's absolutely reasonable for him to wonder and worry, even though no one else has ever bothered before. Mostly they just act as though I'm enjoying something even when I'm clearly not, and hope for the best.

So really I have to reassure him on that score. It takes me even further away from the point I was trying to make, but there's simply no avoiding it.

'Of course I did, but –'

'But what?'

'But now I feel like I know even less about you. Which was really not the aim of this.'

'You do know me, Kit.'

'Really? Because I think you just told me that you made up your entire sexual history because you thought I might like it. And although that's rather nice of you, it's not really what's missing from our time together.'

'And what *is* missing?' he asks, only he does it so desperately I don't know what to think for a second. He actually almost grabs me; the way the hero might grab the guy who knows how to defuse the bomb, at the end of a movie. Goddamn it, man, I think. You've got to tell me which wire to cut, before we're all blown to smithereens!

Even though the answer is obvious.

'*You*,' I say, without a single second to consider. '*You're* missing.'

He looks somewhat taken aback for a moment – as though he's really never considered that idea before.

And then he gets a grip.

'I'm not completely missing. I've told you things,' he says, which is perfectly true. He told me about his first time, for example, and he's occasionally nudged me down some dark alleyways that he obviously enjoyed.

Only those tiny moments of revelation are not really the problem any more.

This is.

'Yeah ... but none of them actually happened.'

He throws up his hands, then, but he's kind of laughing while he does it. And it makes me realise that I do know him in some respects. I know him in the here and now, in the little things he does and says. I know him as someone who so easily turns difficult things around and makes them easy.

I just don't understand why I didn't think of that, when I was so busy worrying about how to ask him this. I should have remembered his lopsided grin and his laid-back manner … his way of relaxing me even when I don't think it's possible.

'Some of the things happened,' he tells me. 'I *do* love pizza.'

And I love *him* for saying that. Some of the tension drains out of the conversation the second he does it. Now we're no longer facing a minor nuclear explosion because I don't know what wire to cut. We're just standing here, on this street, actually getting to know each other.

'And if I'm being honest … I *have* been with a lot of women,' he says, which should probably tense every muscle in my body. But of course it doesn't. It's something about him that I can hold onto – it's part of the foundation I've built him on.

And then he goes and detonates that foundation all over again.

'But the thing is … I guess … I don't *want* to be with a lot of women any more. I'm not some sex addict trying to sort myself out. I don't get a high from fucking everything that walks. I get a high from wanting someone as much as I want you. From actually thinking that for once … for once in my life someone actually cares enough to cry because they think they've messed me up.'

It's true. I did. But when he says all of that amazing stuff in a big fountain of incredible awesome-sauce, I don't immediately recognise it as me he's talking about. He says things like 'want' and 'you' and I imagine some other woman. Some other, Valkyrie-like goddess of unspeakable power and beauty. Seven feet tall with breasts akin to casaba melons, legs that could wrap once around the world ...

He can't mean me.

Only I think he kind of does.

'Do you have any idea how hard it's been for me to find anything even remotely like that? I'm quite aware of what I am, Kit. I know how people look at me. I'm the guy you see in some bar, being loud and obnoxious. I'm the jock at your college, throwing a basketball onto your desk as you're trying to study. I know I am. But I want more than that now. I'm too old to be playing games any more.'

His last sentence pulls me up short, but it's a good thing it does. For a while there I was in real danger of falling down a rabbit hole of his words. I've flushed from hot to cold about thirty times since he started saying all of this, and I only level out when I can focus on one thing. One small thing, that's not about me being fabulous.

'See, I don't even know that much. How old *are* you, exactly?' I ask, because quite frankly I'm now wondering if he's secretly one hundred and twelve. He's probably an android from the future, sent to destroy the sensible centres of my brain.

'I'm thirty-two,' he says, which is in the ballpark of my mental guessing. He looks thirty-two and mostly acts like he's thirty-two ... he just doesn't sound like he really believes he *is* thirty-two. He sounds like he believes he's five hundred and nine – and this weariness continues into his next words. 'I've had thirty-two years of feeling ... disposable. And I don't want to be disposable any more.'

Lord, what a thing to say. I think I actually clutch at myself, to hear it. I mean, even if I don't really know him

– even if I haven't gotten to some mystical core of him – he does realise how he comes across, right? So affable. So easy to share things with. I only realised he'd barely said a word about himself after he'd pried my every fantasy out of me.

And that's a good thing in one way. But such a sad thing in another.

Does he really think he means so little?

'God, honey, you're not disposable,' I tell him, because I'll be damned if I'm going to let him carry on believing something like that. I don't think my heart would allow it, even if the rest of me was totally cool with him feeling this way. My heart is trying to reach through my chest and hug him, and I am in full support of this initiative. 'You've got to know that you're not just some jock. Are you crazy? All the things you've done for me … all the things you've made me feel …'

I shake my head, boggled by the sheer volume of them. And by this sense I'm getting of why he might have been so keen on giving them to me. In fact, it's more than a sense at this point. It's a dawning horror.

'Is this why you've been so focused on me? Because you think I might *dispose* of you otherwise?'

It sounds absolutely crazy, once I've said it out loud – to the point where I almost take it back. No man is that weird and awesome and terrifying. He just has communication problems, that's all. He hasn't been trying to give me everything I want so that I'll stick around.

'Not exactly.'

See?

'But almost kind of.'

Oh, my God.

'You can't be serious.'

'I'm a little bit serious.'

I think he may be more than a little bit serious. He's smiling, but the smiling isn't exactly reaching his eyes – much to my alarm.

'But ... but *why*? Why? I mean ... have you *seen* me?'

'Of course I've seen you.'

'And you still think I'm worth this monumental effort? You must be mad. I'm genuinely afraid that you're completely insane.' I pause, considering. And I swear, it's only a *half-fake* reflection on the gravity of this situation. 'I should call an ambulance.'

'Kit –'

'You've constructed an elaborate fantasy world based around a person who regularly goes to work wearing odd shoes. Something has to be done.'

'Kit –'

'I'm not even sure what's real any more.'

He gets me by the shoulders for that. And then, once he's got me, he shakes me. He stamps his next words right into me, as though I really am the guy who doesn't understand that the bomb is about to go off. I'm too interested in my little petty concerns to see what's right in front of my face.

'Everything was real,' he says. '*Everything*.'

And my heart pounds, once he has. I don't even know why, really. It just gets all giddy at the thought of him being this sincere and this passionate. I have to rein it in a bit, before it gallops out of control.

'Are you sure?' I ask, even though I don't really want to. I don't really want to ask the next bit either – but I know it's a necessity. So I brace myself and let it out. 'Maybe you just wanted to play at relationships with the sad, safe librarian, to see how it fitted. To see if you could do it.'

Though, once I have, all I feel is this weird flash of guilt. It's giving him too little credit, and I know it. I know it before he explodes in a great cloud of outrage, and even try to apologise before he's done so.

But naturally I get absolutely nowhere. It's almost impossible to, when he's being this maze of wild gestures and wilder words. He actually pounds his fist on the roof of my car, briefly, and there's lots of pointing and squeezing of my head.

'*Kit*. Will you just fucking stop with this? *Come on*, man. Do you really think you're that uninteresting? That I just wanted anybody, so thought: Hey – she'll do? I didn't just want anybody, OK? I wanted someone who ... who ...'

'Who *what*?' I ask, but only because I'm so impatient for the answer. My mind is imagining a million things while he's stuck in this big, breathless feedback loop, and I want to stop it before it gets any further. I don't want it to fill in his answer before he delivers the real thing.

Because the real thing is, as I suspected, so very awesome. 'Who makes me feel the way you do!' he says, and I think my body actually jolts when he does so. 'Who makes me feel like I'd go fucking crazy if I lost you! So yeah. I did whatever I thought it would take. Whatever I thought you needed – because I swear to God the second I saw you ... I knew you needed something almost as badly as I do. I saw you that first night, with your shoulders all hunched and your eyes on the floor, and you know what? I wanted those shoulders to be back. To be straight. I wanted you to meet people's eyes and not be afraid ... I ...'

He can't seem to find his words between all the big, insane breaths – though I can understand, I really can. All the oxygen in the world has deserted me and made its way over to him. I feel like I'm going to pop or maybe implode, and my eyes are leaking again.

My whole body is leaking. I'm a shaking, perspiring, red-faced mess. If someone saw me, they'd probably think I was preparing to go in for the most life-changing exam of my life – which I suppose is true in one way.

I've got to work all of this emotional algebra out, and still emerge as someone sane on the other side. I've got to process what he's saying to me, even though I don't think I can. I think I'm going to fail, because, dear *God*, he's still talking. He's still saying this stuff.

'There are so many girls I've just let slip through my fingers,' he tells me, and I see them all in my head, leading back from him. Only they don't look like Valkyries any more. They're not seven feet tall with legs as long as the world. They've lost their substance, and faded down into nothing. 'Because I didn't care. But I cared with you. I cared so much that I would have done anything to keep you. Anything to make you think I'm a worthwhile guy.'

Suddenly I'm not just seeing the surface of this suggestion. I'm seeing everything he's done and everything he's said in a completely different light. And this light is *blinding*. It's dizzying. I don't even know how I manage to spell it all out for him, in brilliant, backwards clarity.

'Like the awkward attempts at segueing into conversation?'

'Oh, Jeeze. Were they really that awkward?'

'And the need to randomly have pizza.'

'I wanted to go for a four-course candlelit meal, but thought a Domino's might be more convincing as something I would do.'

'And the walks?'

'Well, you know I love walks. And the hand-holding! The hand-holding was awesome.'

213

'And the mind-blowing sex.'

'Yeah, that was a real hardship,' he says, and though he's trying to be kind of light about it, though it's kind of funny, really, when you think about it … I have to tell him now. I only half-thought it before, but it's been growing in my mind since the paradigm shift.

Until finally it's at this stage. This bursting, impossible, glorious stage.

'You're so stupid,' I tell him, because he is, he is. Didn't he realise? Didn't he get it? 'You should have known: it wouldn't have taken anything at all.'

He falls silent then. Spookily silent, if I'm being honest – though I guess that makes sense. He's just been stripped down to the bone – right down to the real and honest him – and then I just went and said something like that. I'd be shocked if he'd just said it to me. Or at the very least I'd be wondering why I made such an immense effort.

He's probably thinking, I could have clicked my fingers. He's probably seeing me in the light he should have done, right from the start: as someone who'd be happy with anything. God, why did he think I needed more than anything?

It's so ridiculous I almost ask.

Before he drops in a little clue.

'You say that but …' he says, and I get this funny, tingling feeling. This *nervous*, funny, tingling feeling. There's one thing he hasn't fully explained yet, and I think he's on the verge of maybe telling me all about it.

I just have to keep cool and convince him.

I just have to make sure he understands.

'But what?'

'But maybe you wouldn't feel the same way, if you knew everything about me.'

'Is *that* why you won't talk to me about you? About what you want? About what you feel?'

He shakes his head in an impatient sort of way.

'My whole life has been about me, OK? I just wanted it to be about *you*.'

'And how would I know that? You won't say,' I tell him, and then, oh, then, it really clicks. I actually pause mid-rant about his lack of sharing, and go over all the times he's changed the subject or started talking about something I've done or am doing or maybe might do sometime in the future.

'Oh, my God. You really *did* cut off before I could hear your terrible truth, right? You didn't zone out at all. You never zone out. You just avoid telling me some … big secret.'

He answers with silence again, but this one is worse. This one is really potent – full to bursting with all the things he could possibly have to conceal. He's secretly an alien, my mind whispers, which would in normal circumstances warrant a swift kick to the back of my mind's head.

But in these ones … in these ones, I have to wonder. I'm actually quite staggered to find that a man like him exists, so the extra-terrestrial thing hardly seems that farfetched. Maybe this is like *Starman*, and he's the dead husband that I've never actually had. He's my soulmate from outside the galaxy, here to teach me how to feel love and be wanted.

All of which he's succeeded at admirably.

Despite his obvious issues.

'Yeah, you know – I don't think this is just about giving me what you think I want. I think this is about hiding yourself away,' I say, and I know I'm right before he confirms.

'Can you blame me?' he asks, which is even stupider than all of the alien stuff I dreamt up. He hasn't even told me what it is yet, for fuck's sake.

'For being a fucking idiot. Sure I can.'

'It's not idiocy to worry what someone will think of you when you tell them something important about yourself. Something that worries you in the dead of fucking night,' he says, and I'm just about to kick his ass for really believing that, when he delivers the kicker: 'You do it all the time.'

Well. He's got me there. I worry about it so much, it's a wonder I manage to walk around and say words and function in any way at all. I can't even pretend I'm worthy of keeping the high ground here ... so I don't. I'd rather be on the same level as him anyway.

In fact, it's a step *up* for me to be on the same level as him. I feel as though he's held out his hand from the top of some high holy hill, and I can finally take it, and stand up there beside his exalted self.

'So I guess we're two halves of the same whole then,' I say, and only realise the full glory of that concept once the words are out. I've just somehow voiced an idea I joked about in my head five minutes previously – an idea that's just so crazy and improbable I had to attach an alien to it.

But it holds, once I've blurted it out. It shines like a beacon in the otherwise shambolic darkness of my life:

He really *is* my soulmate.

And my soulmate does not have to be quiet about a single thing. I don't care what it is. I don't care if he killed his own grandmother with a shovel. I'm not bothered if he's escaped from Broadmoor, and his real name is Reginald.

I have a *soulmate*.

'Only I've told you everything about me,' I say. 'So now ...'

'I can't do the same.'

'Why?'

'Because I'm scared, OK? I'm scared you'll run for the fucking hills.'

I can't even describe how painful it is to hear someone like him – someone so powerful and masculine and cool – say something like that. He sounds so raw about it, too. As though it really, really matters to him, and even worse ...

I think he truly believes it too.

'You really think I would?'

'I –'

'You think I'm so fickle?'

'Not fickle, Kit. Just ... worthy of more. More than my mess.'

Oh, he's making me angry now. He's making me a lot of other things too: swoony, totally in love with him, ready to lay down my life for him, etc. But chief among these things is anger, right at this moment in time.

'Wow. Do you have any idea what it would take to make me think you weren't worthy of me?'

'I can guess.'

I don't think he can. I don't think I can guess what I'm going to say before I say it. I thought I had all of this stuff locked down, but apparently not. It wants out, while we're in the middle of this conversation of unspeakable gooshiness.

'Nothing. There is nothing you could say to make me think that. Nothing you could say to make me walk away. I've wanted to ask you a thousand times why you stopped in the middle of the conversation that day, and held myself back a thousand times – but it's not because I was afraid to hear what you'd say. It's because I was afraid you wouldn't want to go to that relationship-y place with me. It's because I was afraid you'd think I wasn't important enough to tell.'

217

I feel as though I've run up a mountain, once I've gotten the words out. My heart is pounding right out of my body, and the rest of me is all up and down. None of me knows what's going on, but I can't really hold that against it. I'm simply not used to big gushy pronouncements like that.

And I'm certainly not used to ruefulness once I've done it. I can hardly bear to look at him but, when I do, that's what's on his face: rue. Which has the benefit of being a good deal better than all the things I was expecting: disgust, horror, a dust-shaped Dillon where he once was.

Though I guess I should know by now that none of that is going to happen. We're in this now, I think. We're really in it together.

'Oh, you've got me there, huh. See, how can I not tell you now? You've promised me relationship-y places and feeling like you're important ...'

'It wasn't meant as a trap.'

'I know.'

'I want you to trust me.'

'I do,' he says, but I can hear his voice wavering just a little. And he tries to change the subject a second later: 'Do *you* trust *me*? Do you trust that I want to be with you and do the relationship-y things and am not just a crazed sex maniac?'

I've got to admit, he's masterful at making people swerve left, when they want to go right. I almost fall for it, in fact. I nearly start talking about all the ways in which he fills me with joy and security, before I realise what he's doing.

'Yeah, I think so. But really, it doesn't matter if I do or not,' I say, then, before he can protest: 'Because now, everything's going to be all about *you*.'

Chapter Fourteen

We drive to his place in silence after that. Though of course it's obvious why. He's lost all of his armour and every one of his weapons of mass distraction. He can't ask me about my feelings or thoughts or what I did in school when I was twelve, because I'll know why he's doing it. And even if I didn't know why he was doing it, that time has passed. He's full to the brim with information on me.

It's his turn now.

It's his turn ... even if I still don't quite know how to make it his turn. Of course, I can ask him about obvious things – I find out that he does, in fact, hail from Boston. He has two brothers and a sister, he gets on well with his family, he misses them, etc. He likes dogs more than cats; comedies more than action movies.

But all of that stuff is easy.

It's far harder to say to someone: *so what's the horrible secret you're hiding?* Even if it now burns between us like a bonfire. It's there when he tries to laugh, and his laugh comes out all hollow and weird. It's there when I squeeze his hand, as we walk up the steps to his apartment, and behind every question I ask that isn't the right one. And, most of all, it's there when we wind up on his kitchen floor, tearing frantically at each other's clothes so that we won't have to go there just yet.

Though that's a little unfair of me to say, I think. Because I know that I desperately want to go there. And as for Dillon, well ... I'm pretty sure he does too. It's just that we've spent the last hour or so baring our souls in the middle of a street, and once we're finished with round one we're both a little ...

Greedy for each other.

More than greedy, in fact. My head is absolutely fit to bursting with him saying *I'd have done anything to keep you*, and his head is definitely full of me saying *nothing can keep me away*. And I know it is, because once he's between my legs, with his shirt half hanging off one arm and his jeans shoved to mid-thigh, he tells me so. 'Did you really mean it when you said ... ?' he asks, and when I tell him, 'Yes, yes, of course, yes' into his hot, wet mouth, he sinks all the way into me, too quick and too rough.

But too quick and too rough is bliss, quite frankly. One more bruise takes my mind off all of the others – and, unlike the others, the sting fades after hardly a second. By the time he's started fucking into me, I'm hanging onto the kitchen cabinets while gasping his name. I've forgotten most of what we've talked about and am intent on the feel of his erection, shoving nice and hard against that bundle of nerves inside me. And his mouth ... oh, God, his mouth on my breasts, on my throat, so hot and wet and then ...

And then he takes one of my tight nipples between his teeth, and I definitely make some undignified noises. I think I claw at his back too – though I only know for sure later on once we're sprawled against the kitchen cabinets, panting, and he tries to sit up a little straighter. He makes it about halfway to his destination, then winces and turns to show off the red lines I've drawn all over him.

It's like I'm a kid who went mad with a crimson crayon. I think, amidst the mess, I can see a house with a smiling sun above it.

He can hardly complain, however. I've got a similarly coloured bracelet around my right nipple, and another on my left shoulder. We've practically mauled each other in our mad dash towards orgasm, but somehow it still isn't enough. I can tell it's not enough just by glancing at his face. He's got that briefly-lost-his-mind look about him, right down to the foggy gaze and the parted lips. The lower looks kiss-bruised and still ever so slightly slick from all the licking I gave it, and it draws me in just as fast as I'm apparently drawing him in.

He gets a handful of my hair and a fistful of whatever clothes I'm still wearing, then suddenly I'm not wearing them any more. I'm completely naked on his kitchen floor, with hardly a care in the world – though naturally it's difficult to worry about anything when someone like Dillon Holt is forcing your mouth onto his. When he's laid-back, it's bad enough. When he's like this, it's impossible to step back and suggest we have some more chats about stuff.

I find myself completely lost in the smallest things: the curl of his tongue against the inside of my upper lip – just a little too tickly and yet still somehow exciting. Or how about the sound of him moaning into my mouth? It excited me before but now it's almost electrifying, when placed alongside all of the feelings he mentioned and the thoughts he expressed. It has an extra layer of longing that I can't really describe.

But I can at least understand the effect of *honesty*. This is his honest passion, I think. His true desire. I can't pretend it's some gimmick or gag. It's real and unfettered and so, so good … oh, it's so good I almost choke, in an effort to cram every feeling down into me all at once. I squeeze his hair into my fist the way he's done mine, and, when he attempts to manoeuvre us off the floor, I almost get in his way. I'm too busy trying to eat his face and his throat and his left earlobe to pay attention to things like lifting and pivoting, and it's really just a testament to his strength that we end up staggering towards the bed.

Or, more, *he* staggers. I just hang off his hip and his massive shoulders, like a misplaced Christmas ornament. And once he's in a position to put me down, he can't quite manage it. I won't let him manage it. I'm stuck on him now, and I can't quite detach.

Though he does an excellent job of working with what he's got. He somehow twists me around his body like a ballroom dancer, and it's only after I'm on my hands and knees with him inside me that I remember the promise I made, and the place we're now in. He doesn't get to hide from me any more. It's not going to be all about me – though, I confess, for a moment I'm almost seduced right into it, all over again.

He's fucking me just like he did in the kitchen; hard and fast and without room for interjections, those big hands tight on my hips, drawing me back and back and back onto his cock until I can hardly speak around the pleasure. It's difficult enough to think under circumstances like these, never mind question.

But I focus. I make fists in the bed sheets and brush off my building orgasm.

'Tell me what you want,' I try, though I know it's not quite good enough to get the desired result. He might have spilled the beans about this little poker game he's playing, but apparently it doesn't mean he won't attempt another hand.

He's still set in that groove, I think – the one that tells him I might run away or be less than impressed if he doesn't think of me first. And though I find that idea as wildly novel as I did when he first let me know about it; the urge is strong to be as selfless with him.

It's more than strong. It's overwhelming enough to make me take it further. I put a hand over his on my hip, in an effort to slow him. And when that's not enough I try to shift a little way up the bed – just to make it that bit harder for him to keep pinning my pleasure down like this.

Of course, I utterly fail. He's so strong and insistent ... not to mention persuasive. He even knows exactly what to say to keep me in place: 'just your tight pussy,' he tells me, followed by the kind of groan that would make a nun cream herself. He even adds a bunch of stuff a moment later, as though he's completely aware that one comment isn't enough. One groan isn't enough. One thrust of his thick cock isn't even enough.

But maybe this could be:

'All I need is what I'm looking at right now. You around me, making my cock so wet ... just taking me so easy. You like that, huh?'

Of course I like it. He's slowed the pace, and the sensation is a protracted, nerve-buzzing version of the thing he was putting me through a moment ago. He slides in and I flow forward as though I've turned to water, and then, even worse – I have to endure him pulling slowly back out again.

I think I actually judder at that. So I've honestly got no idea how I'm able to squirm away from him. It's a miracle that I manage to disentangle myself from his hands, never mind anything else – though my resolve is definitely strengthened by his expression, once I'm halfway up the bed. He looks like he did in the church: flummoxed and frustrated, ready to stop me or drag me back but unable to do either for a moment.

His hands are still holding the air where my hips once were. His cock is a rudder jutting out in front of him, seeking heat that isn't there any more. And though he clearly wants to say a word or three, I think he knows there isn't much he could go with. Something's shifted between us now. The dynamic is more level. He's not the cocksure Svengali, teaching me a thing or two about a thing or two.

And I'm not quite as shy as I would have been before.

The church got rid of most of that. And the conversation put paid to the rest.

'You can have it when you tell me what you want,' I say, and to my great delight, I even manage to point to the thing I'm talking about it as I do it. I flash that wet, flushed place between my legs at him, then watch his eyes go big at the sight.

I can make his eyes go big at the sight of my pussy, I think, which only spurs me on.

'I told you,' he says, but he doesn't sound convincing. For a start, he's kind of half-whining. And then there's the fact that he goes for one of my legs, when he thinks I'm satisfied by his rubbish get-out card.

I'm too quick for him, however. I'm fully prepared for any and all assaults on my senses at this point – whereas he's mostly stupefied and definitely on shaky ground.

'You didn't get anywhere close to telling me,' I say. 'But try a little harder and I might give you it.'

He comes close to putting his hands on his hips. At the very least, he rolls his eyes.

'What if what I want just happens to be what you want?'

224

'Then I'm probably going to doubt you.'

'You shouldn't, you know. I'm pretty sure I go nuts over some of the same stuff you do – like when I bury my face between your legs and you jump and jitter in my arms. Or how about all that storytelling I did ... yeah, you liked that. You think I didn't like it too, seeing you get so flushed and ready to fuck because of a few words?'

'Lying words. Was the tale you told me about your first time even true?'

I kind of don't want to ask it, for many reasons. If he says yes, I'm going to be too excited to keep this conversation going. But if he says no, I know I'll be disappointed. I can feel it spreading through me already – that little tale ... the one that gave me my only clues about him and his life and likes and dislikes ... all of it fake.

It can't be fake, can it? Oh, I'm hoping too much that it's not fake. And I know I am, because when he finally tells me I actually feel a kind of relief. I hadn't even realised that the lies were worrying me a little – as though everything we are has no foundation – until he answers, as calm as you please:

'Yes.'

'So you really did let her seduce you.'

'I did.'

'And you liked it when she teased you.'

'I loved it.'

'Like you might love it if I did it to you now.'

'It's a distinct possibility.'

'Then tell me. Tell me you want me to do something just for you. Be selfish with me.'

He shakes his head in this slow, deliberate sort of way that shouldn't give me the chill it does. But it happens, nonetheless. There's something dark about his expression, something deadly, and it sends a little frisson through my body.

'I don't think you really want me to be selfish,' he says, and I wonder for just the barest second – is that the secret? Is he into something nightmarish, sexually ... something so bad he can't stand to tell me? Maybe I'm right about all of his generosity.

Maybe it's just evasion in disguise.

'Why? Do you really think you're going to disturb me?'

'Maybe.'

'You didn't disturb me with any of your tales – true or otherwise. And the things you've persuaded me to do ... none of them have disturbed me.'

'Not even public sex?'

'Not even that.'

'And being your priest?'

'You could be the Pope ... I wouldn't mind.'

'I see,' he says, but he still sounds unsure. So unsure, in fact, that it's a little insulting. After all, this isn't just about fulfilling my fantasies and forgoing his own. It's not even just about evasion.

It's about him seeing me as too fragile to take whatever he can dish out. Apparently he's got a red room of pain that I'm too pathetic to see. He's into whips and chains, and I might run for the hills if only I knew.

And that makes my tone far angrier than I intend it to be when I finally ask.

'Don't you have faith in me? Do you really think I'm so weak – ?'

'It's not that I think you're weak, Kit,' he says, and then he sort of sighs. His tongue touches his upper teeth, as though he's searching for inspiration there. He's searching for inspiration anywhere except the place he's most likely to find it. And when he does finally wrestle with himself enough to get to the root of the matter, his words are just as daft as they were two minutes ago. 'I'm just a little worried that you'll think I am.'

'Are you serious?'

He can't be serious. He's six foot three. He told me earlier. And he didn't need to tell me about his enormous shoulders and his big-man hands and the thing between his legs that's still pointing right at me. No one could ever mistake him for weak. He's so strong he's managed to forge this insane path with me for months, without me having the ability to do anything about it at all. I couldn't even get him to share a fantasy.

He's like Fort Knox.

A crazy, ridiculous Fort Knox.

'You might not see me as the same person. Other people didn't when I told them about this,' he says, as though the person he is has such a faint, indistinguishable outline. Like he's not stamped on the insides of my eyes for ever.

'Honestly, Dillon, if your big secret is that you like to cross-dress, you really shouldn't have put on that show for me last Tuesday. I mean, wearing my bra and panties was a bit of a clue. But jumping out of a closet while dressed in them was a mammoth giveaway.'

He rolls his eyes at that one.

'I was just fucking around.'

'And you think that, if you weren't fucking around, I'm somehow going to be really upset here? Oh, no, my boyfriend likes to do something that may make other members of society question his complete and total burly masculinity! Whatever shall I do?' I say, expecting maybe a sarcastic answer in response. Or perhaps he'll be serious, and focus on the kink that he may or may not have … it's right there in the words I've just said, after all.

So really the last thing I'm anticipating is him lasering in on this:

'I'm your *boyfriend*?'

Yeah, that throws me all right. Here I am, blustering about his lack of faith and men wearing panties, so sure and certain of my own ability to cope with anything. And he lunges at the one thing that actually throws me for a second.

I don't think it could have been worse if he'd said *I like to bum goats while wearing a top hat.*

'Well … yeah.'

'Holy shit, I'm someone's boyfriend. Are you sure?'

'I'm sure.'

'And you're not just saying it because it pretty much means I have to tell you now?'

'To be honest, I'm kind of scared that the word slipped out.'

I love him for doing a little fist pump after I've said that. I love him for sounding so delighted about the whole idea. He keeps saying 'boyfriend' in this wondering, chuckling sort of manner, and then when he's done I love him even harder.

Because he tells me stuff.

'OK,' he says. 'OK.'

And then he winces, and I wince, and finally he explains in a great rush of unfettered shame and uncertainty and obviously mixed-up feelings:

'I kind of enjoy being … tormented.'

At which point, I'll admit: I'm a little disappointed. It's sort of an anticlimax. I'm really not sure what I was imagining, but I'm equally sure it wasn't nearly as untroublesome as that. I was thinking *illegal throughout most of Europe, banned in twenty countries as a war crime, so bad I can never look at his face again* levels of disturbing.

I was thinking I'd start spontaneously crying.

Instead I sort of deflate – which in hindsight is just as bad. They probably look like similar reactions: abject horror and mild disappointment. And of course the moment he sees it all over my face, he puts his hands in his hair.

'See, I knew you'd react like this.'

'No, Dillon –'

'You're appalled. You want a Master … a big, masculine, tough, bastard of a Master, and I've just confessed to you that I like to be slapped around.'

I can't help it then. It makes things worse, but I really can't help it. When he put it the other way, it was sort of like something I already knew. He'd confessed to liking certain aspects of torment, after all – the holding off, for example. But now that he's put it like this, it's all fresh and new and wild.

'You like to be slapped around?' I say, but I swear I only do it because of the great gust of God knows what that goes through me, once he's laid that idea out on the table. I've never experienced incredulity that feels arousing before, but, by Christ, does he ever achieve it. *He likes to be slapped around.* As in … maybe me smacking that gorgeous ass and those amazing biceps and oh … oh … what if he wanted me to crack a hand across his face?

Oh, my God. What would that be like?

I can't even think about it in a reasonable and rational manner. I'm too busy remembering how his flesh had felt under my hand when I gave him that playful slap. He reacted to that too – I can see it now. I can picture it in my head, suddenly clear and bright.

And then he goes and takes it away.

'Well, maybe not exactly that.'

'Dillon –'

'And even though I occasionally fantasise about stuff of that nature, I'm a fan of everything else too. In fact, I love everything else. I love being all masterful, and can totally be that way for you if –'

'Dillon!'

'Yeah?'

'I don't *care*. I wouldn't care if you were into bonking goats! I'm not the least bit bothered by your masterfulness, whether it's there or not. You know why I like you? Why you drive me crazy? Because of that word you just said: 'everything'. You're everything, all at once. You've shown me things that I would never have imagined, and been willing to go to places I was too afraid to venture. In fact, you've done more than that. You've removed that fear in me.' I take a moment to swallow my own heart, which is trying to make its way up my throat. It's always trying to make its way up my throat around him now. It almost succeeds, in fact, as I squeeze these words out: 'So I've got to ask: do you really think I'd back out now?'

'I –'

'Do you really think I'd *want* to back out? My book lacked something because *I* lacked something. I lacked the ability to see things differently, to be different; to enjoy the whole of life and not just the bits I felt safe in claiming. You really think I want to stay within the confines of something I wrote before I felt any of this?'

He's not quite ready to say no yet. But I can see him wavering on the brink of it. I can see it because it looks the same way I did, when I first started this crazy journey with him. It looks like acceptance, and giving in, and most of all …

Relief.

'It's OK to be you,' I say, and when I do I think of that tattoo on his back. The one that I still haven't asked him about, but which now seems much closer – was this what it was about? Did he wonder if he was OK, because of desires he couldn't reconcile with his outer self? I don't know, I don't know. But I'm not going to let him continue, if that's so. 'Because I like you. I more than like you,' I say.

And then the rest spills out, twice as brave as anything I've ever done, and so exhilarating for it.

'I love you.'

Chapter Fifteen

He's very quiet for a long time after that. But I'm used to this happening by now. We've pretty much lamped each other with the truth for the last five hours, so recognising shock when it happens is not exactly hard.

It's just that it's *worrying* here. It's very worrying. I didn't really mean to reveal that much, and yet somehow I've done it. I've given away more than he has, even though he looks like he's gradually handing out bits of his immortal soul. He's told me how unsure he is, underneath the bluster – unsure enough to believe that I'll only stay if he makes himself into someone he thinks I want.

And yet somehow I've just bested him.

'Well ... what I meant by that is –' I start, but he stops me.

'No, don't take it back,' he says. 'Don't ever take it back.'

'OK.'

'Do you want to take it back?'

'Not really.'

'And you feel it, even though I've just ... told you all of this weird stuff about me? About my need to please and my disposable feelings and the tormenting thing?'

233

'You'd already told me about the tormenting thing. I just didn't listen hard enough.'

'I didn't *want* you to listen hard enough. Especially after reading your book. I mean, I've had girlfriends who didn't write a book about wanting a Master who were kind of put off when I really started to share about myself.'

For the second time in my life, I'm sort of ashamed of what I wrote. Though at least it's for good, honourable reasons in this instance. And they're not feelings he's forcing me to have, either – they're just kind of there, admonishing me for not letting him know sooner that I don't care if he re-enacts page seventy-seven or not.

'So that's what all of this comes back to. Stuff that you think I want because it was there on the page? You don't think I can be anything else?'

'I didn't think you could say, "I love you."'

'And now that I have?'

'Now that you have, my heart is trying to escape out of my chest,' he says, while mine does that exact same thing. I think it actually makes it to Bristol, before it remembers that I'll die without it.

'Is that good or bad?' I ask, tentatively, and then watch as he rolls his eyes at himself. He slaps his own forehead, like he's a complete bonehead for not realising one rather important fact – though I'm imagining it's *I've left the gas on*, rather than what it actually turns out to be.

'Oh, fuck. I haven't said it back! Oh, man, I totally forgot to say it back. See what I mean? I'm such a moron when it comes to this stuff, seriously. And your book was absolutely no help on that score, I gotta tell you. All that emotionally stunted bullshit and *oh I can't possibly reveal my feelings because I'm so cool and manly* … gimme a break.'

I don't think I've ever been so happy to hear a bit of literary criticism in all my days. I actually giggle when he's done, despite the heart that's still in Bristol. He just makes this withering sort of expression, and amusement bursts out of me.

And then he straightens, and makes his face all serious, and something else bursts out of me. I think it's my soul, which sort of tries to hug him before he's even said the words.

'I love you,' he says, though once he's done it I can see he isn't happy with it. He shakes his head and clicks his fingers, then puts his hand on his chest as he makes the declaration. '*I love you.*'

'The second one,' I tell him, mainly because the second one gave me goose bumps. 'Definitely.'

'Or I could do it on one knee? Maybe add a bit of poetry? My love is a rare rose that blooms at the sight of you ...' he offers, but of course we're both trying not to laugh now. Something as terrifying as love, and somehow I'm relaxed enough to laugh. 'But that's not really me, right? If I was going to go with the honest version, it'd be more like this: my love is like a giant rampaging mutant from another dimension, intent on actually ingesting you in case you had any ideas about running away.'

'Bingo.'

'Yeah. You like that one, huh?' he asks, as he stalks towards me across the bed. This time, however, I don't mind him doing it. I don't even mind when he bites at my left thigh, because now it's tied to something so awesome I can hardly comprehend it.

He loves me. He loves me enough to turn himself into a monster who chases me across dimensions. What could possibly be more perfect?

'I'm more than happy to be ingested by you.'

'I thought you might be. You do seem to love being eaten.'

'It's true. I do,' I tell him, but I make sure I give his shoulder a nip, directly afterwards. Just to … you know. Keep things on track. 'But it's not about *me* any more, remember?'

I pinch him again – harder, this time. And lower down, too, in a way that feels a little like testing the waters. Is this the kind of tormenting he's kind of into? Or is it something a little more subtle and insidious, like his predilection for teasing? If his answering expression is anything to go by I'd say he's definitely not averse to the former, at the very least.

He actually bites his lip when I do it, and his hand jerks out as though he wants to restrain me. To stop me before I go too far and he gives away too much. But then he seems to realise that it's a little too late for denials – he's already told me everything there is to tell.

Or at least I *think* he's told me everything.

Until he tells me more.

'So you really want to go there, huh?' he asks, as though there's actually a chance that I might not. As though the mark I've already created just below his ribcage isn't making me flush all over, before that look on his face finishes the job.

The blue of his eyes has darkened almost to navy, made worse by those heavy lids. And as I drink every inch of him in, he just lets his tongue sort of … slide over his lower lip. Too quick to allow me to linger long, too slow to be anything but deliberate.

Then, to top it off, he takes hold of the hand he almost restrained.

And presses it to his throat.

'Because if you do, you're gonna have to be a lot meaner than that.'

236

'How mean?'

'So mean I barely know it's you.'

'I don't think I can choke you.'

'No? Then what can you do?' he asks, in this dreamy, creamy voice that almost makes me melt right off the bed. 'Show me. Show me what you can do.'

I confess: I was sort of hoping he'd carry on giving me hints. Little nudges in the right direction, just in case I'm wandering down the wrong path. Though the thing is ... once I've moved a little closer to him – once my mouth is almost on his mouth, and his breath is ghosting warm and rapid against my skin – it's actually much easier than I thought.

Or at least it's easier to go with my instincts. Because my instincts immediately tell me to move away, when he goes to close the kiss. And they also urge me to carry on, once he's made a slight sound of frustration. The slight sound of frustration is a good sign, I think. It's a sign that I'm getting this right.

And so is the move he makes, the moment I go lower.

He sort of sprawls onto his back in this excessive sort of manner, like he's luxuriating in whatever I'm doing. Even though I'm not really doing anything at all. I'm just nearly pressing kisses to various parts of his body, before dancing away at the last second. Occasionally, I'll let him feel the heat from between my lips, or maybe the slightest slick promise of something more.

And then I'll move on to another bit. The mark I made on his side, maybe, or the slant of muscle just above his groin. That last one in particular gets a good long groan out of him – though I think the noise has more to do with the obvious bypass I make around his rigid cock than with anything else. I don't even let him feel my breath in that particular place.

There's no hint of a kiss for that long, delicious curve.

Despite the overwhelming urge to do just that. Oh, God, the urge is so strong. I think my mouth actually starts watering the second I manoeuvre my way back up his body, but I resist. I keep true to my course, even though my course is sort of starting to make me tremble now. He just smells so good, and his body is so tempting … from the flat, many-muscled planes of his stomach, all the way up to that amazing chest of his.

I want to lick him there, I realise – but I'm not allowed to yet.

Because apparently I'm teasing myself as much as I'm teasing him. The air between us is like a living thing, and every time I move it brushes against my body. It makes promises I don't want to cash, such as *he'll feel so good when you slide down onto him. Just do it, right now. No one would blame you, if you did.*

And while that's true, it's still too early. It's too early for anything but these little tormenting nearly-kisses that are now making his body roll like the ocean. The movement starts at his feet and goes all the way up through his hips and thighs, until our bodies almost touch by accident.

Though I know it wouldn't really be an accident at all. He's progressed from muffled noises to outright grunts of indignation, and he's definitely trying to get me to do stuff by default now. He's trying, but the point is – he's not trying hard *enough*.

He's not doing the things he could do if he really wanted to. He could throw me over onto my back with a flick of his wrist. He'd hardly need to exert any strength to force our bodies together. So the fact that he doesn't …

It definitely suggests I'm on the right track. It's almost as though we're in opposite land, in fact. When he complains, it means I'm doing well. And if his hand comes up to grab me, but stops short by several inches ... well.

I should take it as a pat on the back.

And I do. Oh, I definitely do. I'm almost glowing by the time I get to anything substantial. I'm stuffed full of victory – of the sort I never thought I'd get to feel – and it only gets stronger, the longer I hold out. I honestly don't know what's more intoxicating: the sense of actually doing something sexual in a half-decent manner, or the waves of arousal that keep hitting me every time I ratchet this thing up a notch.

Though I suspect it's the latter. When I finally let him feel my mouth on his body – just around some place innocuous, like his right shoulder – it's akin to detonating a bomb between my legs. The taste of his skin is so much sharper after all that waiting. And oh, the *feel* of him. The give of his flesh, beneath the press of my lips ...

It's really no surprise that I do more than kiss. I think I've actually waited too long, and the thousand years of no touching have sent me somewhat doolally – because I swear, I only intend to leave a soft, wet trail over his skin. But once I'm there, I accidentally sink my teeth in.

I bite.

And even worse:

He *likes* it.

Though in all honesty the word 'like' is understating it somewhat. 'Like' implies something you mildly approve of, possibly. It could be applied to a can of mushy peas, or a Saturday-night light entertainment programme on BBC1. It cannot be applied to his reaction, which is roughly the same as mine on realising that I've done this to him.

I've turned him into a writhing, groaning mess. His back actually arches up off the bed, as though I'd licked the tip of his erection. And once he's done with the arching, he twists until he's almost completely turned away from me – until his face is buried in the pillow, and his body is this contorted sort of S-shape.

His upper half hides, while his lower half remains where it is. Though I suppose that makes some sort of sense. I don't think he could bury that cock of his in the mattress if we'd dug it a metre-deep hole, because, by *God*, he's so hard. He's so impossibly, improbably hard.

And that's pretty much the point where I go nuts too. I can feel my own wetness on the insides of my thighs. My clit is so swollen I'm sort of afraid to move, in case some random part of my body brushes against it and accidentally triggers my orgasm. Hell – I think my elbow could probably do the deed, with very little effort at all. It might be a good foot away from lady-parts and in a physically impossible position, but my clit's such a danger zone I'm fairly certain anything could do the job.

Including him, and his orgasm-inducing moans.

And even worse – he's actually using words now, too.

'Again,' he says, which is bad enough on its own. But then he seems to remember that talking really turns me on, and gives it to me both barrels. 'Do it again, just like that, yeah, just like that – make me come.'

I pause mid-kiss while that one sinks in. Though even after I've given it a good few minutes, it's still kind of lodged in the back of my mind. It keeps jabbing me between my legs with a red-hot poker, every time I ask myself the question: can he really come, just because I sink my teeth into him?

Until the question is three feet tall and surrounded by incredulous exclamation points. He can't, I think. No one can come because of a bit of biting.

But I can already tell I'm going to test that theory. The urge is in me, before my brain has even finished laughing about it. My brain's still busy being amused, while my entire body flushes hot, and then hotter, and then hotter again. If I get any more aroused I'm going to melt myself, and possibly the bed beneath us.

So I have to act fast. I can't go for half measures now. I need to feel him buck beneath my bite, and he does, oh, he does. I sink my teeth in just above his hip, right over that glorious dragon tattoo, and the moment I do he almost lifts himself clean off the bed. He pounds the mattress with his fist, and makes this almost giddy sound.

Then dissolves into actual elation when I bite a little harder than I'd intended.

I don't mean to, of course. I want to stop at just a hint of him … just the smallest sense of his flesh giving under the pressure. But his reactions are so beguiling it's hard to hold back, once I've seen them and heard them and felt them. He spurs me on with his squirming and his little half-laughs and his words, oh, his words: 'Go on, go on, make it hurt,' he tells me, which shouldn't sound sexy at all.

And neither should 'make me bleed', if we're really getting into it.

Yet both things make me shiver. They make me climb all over him, teeth bared, until he's a mess of raw red marks. Until he's shaking the way I'm shaking, and practically kissing the pillow in this desperate, lewd, open-mouthed sort of way, and then just as he's on some kind of impossible edge of control … just as he's begging me to be brutal …

I go in the opposite direction. I lick over some little dent I've made in his flesh, all soft and wet and soothing – then watch as he goes even crazier for that than he did for the biting. He actually goes all still for a second and snaps one hand to his cock.

But it's not to give himself the pleasure that I'm denying him. He doesn't stroke himself into a frenzy, without a bit of regard to all the careful effort I'm putting in. He squeezes himself tight around the base of his stiff shaft instead – so tight it kind of looks like it hurts – and once he's relaxed it, he lets out this series of panting, shuddering breaths.

And then I know exactly what's happening here. He's holding himself off. I licked him, and he almost went over.

So I lick him again. In fact, I take an even greater delight in doing it this time. This time it's almost like the first barrage in a battle, between his ability to keep himself in check and my greediness for his orgasm. I try more dangerous places, like the sensitive insides of his elbows and that place just under his ear, and when he complains, when he says, 'No, come on, come on, enough now,' I take that as my cue to make things worse.

I draw a slow, slippery circle around one of his nipples, until he actually gasps. He gasps for me, and those hips come again – only this time I'm right over his body when it happens. His cock slides over my belly, so hot and shocking that I do the same thing that he does when it happens.

I clench all over, and groan his name.

At which point he clearly believes he's winning that war. Or, at the very least, he's certain he's just triumphed in one of the lesser battles.

'Yeah, you want that, baby?' he says, and then he does it again, just for good measure. He bumps his hips up and that hot hard thing rubs right up against me – almost between my legs, in fact. 'You want that big cock inside you?'

I do, if I'm being honest. I really, really do. My pussy is

a perpetual ache, and it keeps clenching around everything that isn't actually filling it. And I'm now so wet I can hear it, every time I move. *He* can hear it, every time I move. His eyes keep drifting closed, and he makes this urgent, desperate sound at each little hint of it.

But whether he does or not, I don't care. I'm not ready to give in yet. I'm not ready to stop teasing. I haven't given him my grand finale, after all.

And my grand finale is *good*. I think he knows it is, too, before I even reveal it. He goes all tense again as I start sliding my way down his body, and I can't help noticing the hand he puts in his hair. It's a mean hand – a rough hand – and it only gets meaner as I carry on with whatever this is.

I outline the shape of his erection, as it rests there on his belly. First with my fingers, and then with my tongue – always promising that I'll go closer, but never quite delivering. And then just as he's bursting with it, just as he's actually saying no to anything more in case it proves too much, I let the very tip of my tongue flick over that glossy, swollen head.

Just the very tip of it. Nothing more.

But nothing more is enough.

It's enough to get him to fist his hand in my hair instead of his own. And once he's gone that far, he does something even more electric. Something that makes *me* buck this time. He pushes my face real close to his cock, and angles himself towards my mouth.

Then tells me, in no uncertain terms:

'Suck it.'

Of course, I think two things when he does. The first being: I guess he really does like things the other way around, too. And the second being: Oh, my God, I think I'm going to faint from arousal. I'm actually going to faint. It's not possible to be this aroused and maintain consciousness.

Though I'm proven wrong on that score. It *is* possible to carry on. It's just that all actions have to be done in a kind of mindless frenzy. He's barely finished ordering me to do it when I take him in my mouth. And my blow job technique could best be described as sloppy, with a side of enthusiastic.

I suck him as though I'm the one who's been teased for the last twenty minutes. I lick him like my life depends on it. And all the while he talks in a way that only spurs me on.

'Oh, yeah,' he tells me. 'Take that cock. You like that, huh? You like sucking me off?'

I do. But in all honesty I think I like it a little more when he turns my body so he can put a hand between my legs. Especially after he's parted my lips, and found that incredibly wet and wanting place.

'Jesus Christ, Kit,' he says, and I know why. He doesn't even have to work to slide three fingers inside me. He could probably get a fourth in there if he really tried. I'm just so slippery, and so flushed, and so ready to take anything ... it's easy. And clearly he likes easy. 'Guess you liked teasing me, too, huh? Did it make you all wet, seeing me suffer? God, baby, you've no idea what that does to me.'

I do have some idea of what that does to him. For a start, it makes his cock kick in my mouth, and his hand come down to grip the base of it again. And I guess it also gives him the green light, somehow ... as though maybe he'd started wondering if I'd had enough with the teasing. He didn't just lose control. He switched things back up – and, crazily, I let him.

I should have said no when he put his hand in my hair.

I should have gone as far as he goes with me.

Though at least I know that now. I know it enough to

stop sucking his cock, and I even manage to move away from his maddening, stroking fingers. I sit up straight and position myself a little further down the bed – almost out of his reach, but not quite.

Still, he doesn't reach for me. He makes a protesting sound, but he doesn't go for me in the way he could if he really wanted to. Instead he simply lies there, eyes gleaming with realisation, body as tense as it was a moment before.

'What?' he asks, but he knows what. And even if he doesn't, he gets the picture when I toss him a condom.

'Put it on,' I tell him, then, just in case it isn't absolutely clear: 'I'm going to have you now.'

Of course, I haven't the slightest clue where words like those come from. I only know that they really, really excite me, once they're out. There's just something so ... insistent about them. Something so rough and rude. And that's before I've even reached the idea that these are the words a man would more typically say, to a woman.

In fact, I think *he's* said that very thing to me before now. So I've no real clue what makes it this exciting to hear it the other way around. And I definitely don't know what makes it exciting to him.

I only know that it does. Oh, God, it really does. His head goes back against the pillow and his mouth falls open, as though he's coming just at the thought of it. He even makes an orgasmic sort of sound – all low and guttural.

But he doesn't neglect what I've asked him to do. He gets the condom on in a frantic, fumbly sort of rush, and then he just waits. He waits for me to fuck him.

And I think I like that part best of all.

I probably wouldn't have before. There's so much onus on me, you see. So much that I have to do on my own initiative

– without shame or uncertainty. I have to straddle him and hold his cock in my hand. I have to stroke him through my folds – until his face goes all taut and strained again, and his words turn into the ones I liked, from before. 'Stop, no, don't,' he says. Then finally: 'I'm gonna go over, if you keep teasing me like that.'

And of course, once he's said that, I have to do one more thing. One more thing that I would definitely never have dared to do, before the glorious and unending freedom of him.

'If you come before I do,' I say, 'I'll punish you.'

Then I simply sink down on him, as his expression shifts from dismay to delight and back again. For a good long while he can't seem to decide what to feel– but in the end he settles on a kind of heavy-lidded, lust-slackened awe, which I have to say I appreciate very much.

I appreciate it so much, in fact, that for a second it's sort of hard to do anything. I'm too turned on to trust myself with this task, even though it's supposed to be him holding off. He's meant to lie there and wrestle himself under control, while I take my time with my own orgasm.

But the thing is, I don't think it's going to work out that way. I'm close right now, before I've even begun. His erection is so hard, and thick, and swollen, I can feel it shoving against that sweet spot inside me, without even really trying. And when I try a graceful glide up and then down, all I can manage is a sort of clumsy jerk.

Followed by an almost-grunt of shocked pleasure.

Though all of these things do sort of work out better than they probably should. Because once I've revealed that I have even less control than he does, I get to carry on down that path of total abandonment. I get to be greedy and rude, and somehow all of it sort of matches up with that first idea.

The one about *having* him.

'Oh, God, yeah, your cock feels so good,' I find myself saying, and once I have it's really easy. In fact, the urge to debase him further just sort of ... takes over, until I'm telling him stuff like this: 'I'm gonna use it to make myself come. I'm gonna do it all over this big, thick thing. Mmmm, that's it, baby. You just lie there and take it.'

And, to his credit, he does. He takes every bit of what I'm saying and doing, without complaint – even if *without complaint* probably looks a little bit more like *being stabbed by pleasure*. His face is an absolute picture, and when I'm done spilling those ridiculous words all over him he can't hold in his shock any longer.

'Are you serious?' he asks. 'Are you serious? Come on, man, at least make it fair. You can't say stuff like that and expect me to keep it together.'

'Why not? Don't you like me using your cock like this?'

'I don't like it. I *love* it. Oh, God, I love it – especially when you use that word.'

'Which one?'

'"Use". Yeah, yeah. Use my cock to get yourself off.'

'Like this?'

'Ah, yeah, like that.'

'Mmmm, you feel so good. You're so thick and solid inside me. I barely have to do anything to get myself close.'

He's got his eyes shut again now, but in this really delicious way. It's like he's staring off to one side, sightlessly. Like he can see something that I can't, just hidden from view. And I think I know what it is too.

It's his orgasm. He's going to come, I think, and is using every bit of effort he has to stop that happening – though in truth he really doesn't have to any more. I almost pushed myself over with that last little speech, and seeing him straining like this just shoves me that last few inches. I rock against him once, twice, three more times, and that's all it takes.

'Oh, oh, I'm coming, oh, yeah, I'm coming,' I moan, but only because I can't manage any more. I really want to do justice to the sudden clenching burst of pleasure that goes through me, but all I can get out are those four simple words, stuttered and repeated in a rough sort of litany. The rest is all jammed up by the sheer tension of my orgasm, so fierce it feels like shoving more than anything else.

My pussy spasms around his cock, and I can feel how wet I'm making him. How hard I'm digging my nails into his sides, as I try to ride this out. I've never come so hard in my life, and it's an ordeal just to get through it. To feel all of it, and not turn away. To keep working myself on him, even though I desperately want to stop.

I have to stop, I think.

But I'm glad I don't. And I'm glad that I'm half-sane enough to see him, the second he gives in, too. Because giving in is really the term for it. He doesn't ease into his orgasm in a polite sort of way – he struggles and strains until the very last second, then simply abandons himself. He lets go of everything that holds him back, and pours all of his energy into surrender.

And it's a sight to see. His hands go to my hips, as though he can't bear to be apart from me a moment longer – and his body, oh, God, his body. It practically *ripples* with pleasure. I can almost see his orgasm happening beneath his skin, and I can definitely hear it in his voice.

He doesn't make a lowdown, bestial sort of noise, the way I expect. His cries go all breathless, and high, and sort of not like him at all. And yet this *is* like him. This is all of him, right down to the expression on his face.

It's one I don't recognise at first. I don't think he's ever quite given me one like it before. But once he has, I know it for what it is. I love it for being what it is:

Vulnerability.

Chapter Sixteen

I wake up just as dawn is creeping its way into his bedroom, to make its way over the folds of that ridiculous shower curtain. Only it doesn't look so ridiculous when it's bathed in that light. I can see the shapes and shadows of his furniture through the plastic, and each one is framed by golds and reds and other autumnal colours.

And when I turn toward his little narrow window, that light looks even lovelier. It winks like fireflies between the rooftops – the ones that stretch away from his apartment for ever and ever. I could almost believe I'm in some other city when I see it like this.

And I'm happy to see it like this for a long, long time. I don't even want to get out of his bed, despite the smell of sex all over the sheets, and the evidence of last night's meal hot on its heels. We had Chinese takeaway, and there's something that looks suspiciously like a spring roll just peeking out from underneath his pillow. A carton of chow mein is still on his bedside table, its contents spilling over the sides in a noodly waterfall.

We've made a mess. A really big mess.

But I couldn't care less. In fact, I can't keep the grin off my face when I see the havoc we wrought. I'm no longer Kit Connor, cautious librarian. I'm Kit Connor, destroyer of worlds. I raised my mighty fists and clobbered my own reality into smithereens, and now I have to live amongst the remains.

And I'm so, so happy about that. I've been given a second chance, I think. A second chance to be better, to be more daring, to take all the things I never thought I could have. I'm the me I always wanted to be, now, and for a second I'm so grateful for this that the impact of it blindsides me.

I lie in his rubbish-filled bed, breathless with it.

Then immediately want to thank him for this incredible bounty. It's largely down to him, after all. He didn't make my book more real – he made *me* more real. I was two-dimensional until I met him. I was a cliché of a librarian, frozen in my own fear for ever. And he actually held out a hand, and helped render all my facets. He filled in my form and popped out my corners, and let me run around on more planes than one.

He's a miracle worker, and I need to tell him that. I need to tell him that I'm no longer afraid to tell him anything, which is in itself an achievement. I've never not been afraid to tell someone anything in my entire life, but somehow I'm OK to do this with him. I even call out his name excitedly – like a kid who's just realised it's Christmas morning, and could you come down now and let me open my presents?

Only he's not there to answer. He's not in the kitchen and he's not in the bathroom, and when I suspect the wardrobe and quite suddenly wrench it open, he's not in there either. I'm actually contemplating looking under the bed or maybe in a kitchen cupboard – such is his reputation in tomfoolery – when he calls down to me.

Because naturally he's in the one place that's practically designed to give me a heart attack. I actually jolt to hear his voice coming out of the ceiling, and shoot a darting look at the corners of his apartment – as though he's going to be crouched up there, like Spiderman.

I wouldn't put it past him, to be honest. He's definitely the type to buy suckers for his fingers and toes off some dubious site on the internet, just so he can play an alarming game of sudden superhero with me.

And I can't fault him for that. In truth, I'm almost disappointed that this isn't the case. After a minute of nervous checking for webslingers, I find the source of him. There's a little sort of … attic slot in his ceiling just over his rickety bookcase, and he's on the other side of it. Only the other side of it isn't an attic at all. I can see that as soon as I stand beneath him, looking at the actual sky on either side of his shoulders.

Suddenly, the draught I felt while in bed makes a lot of sense.

Even if nothing else does.

'Are you allowed to be up there? I really don't think you should be going through holes in your ceiling to the outside. Unless that's the mystical portal to Narnia, in which case – give me a hand.'

'It's definitely not Narnia up here. I think a bird died inside this chimney.'

'There's a chimney?'

'It may not be a chimney. I dunno. It's some kind of steam-venting device.'

'So really it's more like *Bladerunner* up there.'

'It's definitely a lot like *Bladerunner*. Except … rubbish.'

'Stop doing my accent.'

'I'll stop doing it when you come up. Are you coming up?'

'Just answer me this one question before I do: are you sitting on something slanting or something flat?'

'It's like a cliff face up here. I've attached myself to the dead-bird chimney with a rope, otherwise I'd just glide right off.'

'You liar.'

'You're the one asking me if the roof is flat! Of course it's flat. You've seen my building from the outside, for God's sake. Get up here!'

He says that last bit while reaching a hand down to me, which suddenly seems a bit punier than it did before. Usually I think of him in beefy, burly sorts of terms, but of course that all changes once he's offering to haul me through a hole. I mean, he can't *really* think that he's going to get me up there like that. Not even after I've stood on the rickety bookshelf, and am a good deal closer to him and his minuscule arm.

I still can't see him doing it.

And then he totally goes and does it anyway. Of course he does. I don't even know why I doubted him. He could probably hurl me like a javelin if the need ever arose, so heaving me up through a hole poses no problems whatsoever. He just loops his arm around my waist and hoists me skyward, while I cling to him like a little monkey.

Though the most ridiculous thing about it is how much I enjoy being his little monkey. I like that he could possibly hurl me like a javelin. For a second I just sit where he's plonked me – on the edge of the hole – imagining a whole Olympics where he might get to exhibit this talent. He could wear those little Lycra shorts and powder his palms before he handled me, and then –

'Where've you wandered off to this time?'

I at least have the decency to look sheepish.

'You hurling me at a fantasy Olympics.'

'Interesting. Am I winning?'

'I'm pretty sure you get the gold.'

He does a little fist pump, the second I say it. A slow one, though, this time. A really considered and gracious one – as though he actually did just triumph at some imaginary sporting event. And I'll admit, I kind of love him more for that. I love him for having seventeen different types of fist pump, and for employing them so liberally that I'm kind of starting to understand them all now.

I can read him by his jockish gestures.

And by other things too.

He's got a beer, for a start – which probably isn't that good a sign, at six o'clock on a Saturday morning. It's probably not a good sign that he's even up here, or that he has a folding chair on this tiny expanse of roof for the express purpose of sitting and staring moodily off at the rising sun.

Because that's what it kind of looks like from where I'm sitting. And it doesn't look any different when I stand up, gingerly, and make my way over to him. I sit down next to him on the little ledge around the probably dead-pigeon-holding heating device, but once I'm up close he kind of ... bristles. He's not laughing any more and he's not fist pumping, and it'd be clear to just about anyone that he's unsettled.

Except for me, in all the places that I don't want it to be. I don't want him to be unsettled, because unsettled only means one thing. He regrets the 'I love you'. He's now deeply unsure about the time we're spending together. Last night we grew too close, and this is going to be his speech on how and why we should separate for a while.

It's about the vulnerability, I think, though the weird

thing is ... he looks even *more* vulnerable right now. He's sort of fiddling and peeling off the label on his bottle of beer, instead of drinking it. And he's not really talking. He's not even joking about the tent I make of his massive T-shirt around my knees – even though the move is designed to pull a comment out of him.

He should be saying something like *I can't wait to wear that thing again. You've given it a set of knee-boobs!* Only he doesn't. In fact, he doesn't talk for so long that I get nervous, and start making small talk about the most excruciating things.

'Did you see that thing on the news about monkeys?' I ask, even though there must be twenty different topics of more importance floating around between us. And I think I can say with some confidence that none of them are about monkeys. They're not even about his place of work – though that's what I try next.

'I bet the penguins never steal your shoes, huh?'

'Is that what the monkeys did?'

'Yeah.'

'And I'm guessing you like that.'

'You know I like anything to do with feet.'

'I do know that.'

'And animals grabbing things.'

'I knew that too. Sadly, however, penguins lack the opposable thumbs to complete the task.' He pauses to take a drink, which sounds like a casual sort of thing. In practice, however, it's much grimmer. It looks a lot like Dutch courage for the big gut punch, I reckon, so it's kind of an anticlimax when he just finishes it off with this: 'Plenty of dumb stuff happens, though.'

'Sounds like fun,' I tell him, though I swear I only do it

because it seems like the most casual, non-committal, encouraging sort of thing I could say. I really don't expect it to have the effect it does, which is to simply sink him further into this weirdly depressed mire.

'Yeah, it's fun all right. Stupid, useless fun.'

'Are you sure? Because working at Ocean World sounds awfully cool to me.'

'As cool as being a millionaire playboy?'

I'm kind of getting the drift of what he's driving at here, though he doesn't sound half as bitter as his words might suggest. There's something quite dark about them, but his tone remains almost light ... like he's half-amused by whatever predicament he imagines he's in, and half sort of despairing about it.

Either way, however, I'm not about to let him continue with this line of thought.

'Is that what you think I want?'

'That's what I know you want.'

'Yeah. Because millionaire playboys are so awesome in reality. They absolutely don't murder the nanny or gamble away their company's wealth or accidentally crash their yachts into someone's house.'

He laughs at that, but I can see he's still uncomfortable. He keeps making a weird circle with his left shoulder, like he's gearing up to punch something that isn't there. Some imaginary playboy perhaps, despite how little I actually care about that sort of thing.

He needs to know how little I care about that sort of thing.

'You know, when I came up here I was kind of worried you'd changed your mind about loving me. Not that you were stupidly worried about whether or not you're a millionaire playboy. So really, I've got to ask: when are you going to stop panicking about whether or not you're what I want? When are you going to realise that I'm just massively grateful that you're *you*? I don't care if you're rich or not, or don't want to be some perfect Master all the time.'

'It's not really about that. The Master thing doesn't bother me. The millionaire thing doesn't even bother me, really. I know I can be your fantasy, if that's what you need from me. It's just ...'

'What?'

He sighs, but I can tell he's going to say it. And he does, a second later, in yet another anticlimactic rush.

'I used to do something *worthwhile*.'

I mean, really. Why does he think any of this matters?

'You do something worthwhile *now*,' I say, though even as I'm doing so I'm getting this little lowdown frisson. This small, faintly unnerving feeling, about the direction this conversation is headed. In fact, I'm starting to suspect that his mildly interesting sexual proclivities are not the thing he was talking about when he said there was something I'd never want to know.

I think this is the thing I'd never want to know, even though I desperately want to know it. That frisson has turned into a kind of tingle, and I'm definitely holding my breath. And I hold it harder, when he finally says:

'Not like I used to.'

I have to hold it harder, in truth. I'm afraid of disturbing the air around him, in case it persuades him to stop talking. I can't even say the encouraging things I want to say, like *oh I'm sure it's not as bad as you think it is* or *maybe you'd feel better if you shared*. None of them seem adequate, which is probably why I end up going with 'mmmhmm'.

It's not even a word.

But luckily he accepts it anyway.

'You know what I used to be?' he says, and, though my insides are suddenly turning cartwheels and setting off fireworks, I think I do an admirable job of keeping it all hidden. Instead I nod sagely and make another deeply interested but totally casual sound.

I think it's sort of akin to a balloon rapidly expelling air.

And then he tells me, and it's all I can do to stop myself farting oxygen all over him.

'A firefighter.'

A firefighter. Is he serious? Did he wear the big pants and charge around on the back of one of those engines, like firefighters probably only do in my daydreams about heroic jut-jawed men from the 1940s? And if he did even one tenth of this stuff, I feel I really need to ask. What the hell does he think is wrong with that? Anyone who ever wrestled actual fire at any point in their lives is automatically awesome for ever.

I'm amazed that he doesn't know this.

But he really doesn't seem to.

'It's all I ever wanted to be, you know? And not just in that dumb kid way, when you think you're going to grow up and be so cool, in-between sliding down a big pole. I mean, I really wanted to fight fires. I really wanted to save people.'

He pauses then to gather himself, though I'm kind of glad he does. I need a moment, too, before he descends in a great and horrendous avalanche towards this next part. I can feel it coming before it's even here, but this moment of awareness doesn't really prepare me. It doesn't prepare him, either.

He looks like someone's planted a steel hook in his gut, and is slowly drawing all his insides out. His jaw has tensed into one straight, mean line, and he's staring off between the higgledy-piggledy rooftops at that rising sun, like his life depends on it.

'But the thing is, about saving people ... sometimes you don't. Sometimes you fuck it up.' He runs a hand over his face, over his hair. 'Nobody really tells you, before you get into it – though I guess it's kind of stupid that I didn't realise. Of *course* people die, in the real world. Of *course* you don't always get there in time. Life's not just this big fun fantasy, where everything turns out OK in the end. But I guess ... I guess I just thought it was, until the Hellerman building.'

I can't say I know exactly what he means, because I don't. But I do at least understand the concept he's driving at, in my own silly, probably very minor way. There's a moment in everyone's life when they have to face the crushing knowledge that nothing is quite as lovely as life seems in dreams.

Nothing is going to be awesome; nothing is going to be cool.

It's just this all the time:

'There was a wall, you see. And I could hear people screaming on the other side of it, even though everything was really loud by that point. You ever been near a burning building? It's so much fucking louder than you think it should be. Fire has this sound to it – this roaring, devouring sort of sound that you don't really appreciate when you're just, like, warming your hands on a bonfire. But when you're *inside* it ... it's huge. Plus, you've got all this shit coming down everywhere and stuff exploding and fuck, *fuck*.'

He spits out that last word the way most people would, if they'd just stapled their hand – or maybe forgot to file that report last Wednesday. In other words, he isn't the least bit dramatic about it. He doesn't rend his breast.

But somehow that only makes it worse.

'I just couldn't ... there wasn't anything I could do. I mean, later on I went over and over it, thinking there might have been something. Possibly I could have hit the wall in another place and broken through. Or maybe if I hadn't stepped on that exact spot I wouldn't have fallen. You know? But I didn't hit the right place, and I did step on that spot, and so that's just the way it goes. I fell two storeys and woke up with a broken arm, and that was that.' He even does a little dusting-off sort of gesture with his hands. As though none of this is a big deal at all. 'But of course it's never just that in my head. Because every time I imagine being that worthwhile person again, all I can think is: what if I can't save them a second time? What if I go back into it and the same thing happens, only worse? Maybe this time it'll be two hundred kids in a goddamn orphanage, trapped behind five miles of molten steel that's somehow turned to toffee, in my head. What if? And that "what if" never goes away. All the time I think: today is the day you'll be OK again. Today is the day, even though it never is.'

The tattoo, I think. Though of course I don't say it. I can't say anything. I've been rendered mute by all of this, and oh, God, there's still more to come. There's so much more to come. He's on a roll now, eyes all distant and faraway.

Words like knives in my heart.

'So I do this instead. I spend my days doing this ridiculous job, rather than being brave, and good, and all the things I always hoped I'd be. Because I'm selfish. That's the problem. I'm a selfish person, who worries more about feeling so helpless over the people I couldn't save than feeling like I helped because of the people I did.'

He gives me no warning that he's done and is about to turn and look at me. In fact, until he does it, I hadn't even realised that he's not looked at me since he started speaking. And then it's this weird, jolting shock, coupled with a kind of embarrassment to find that I'm absolutely sobbing my heart out. My face is soaked. His T-shirt is soaked. I don't even know how I managed to do this so silently that it's kind of crept up on me too, but there it is. I'm a crying fool.

And he thinks so too.

'What are you crying about?' he says, as though all of that was just nothing. He's even kind of half-laughing at my heartbroken state – or at least he's managed to put his face back into some semblance of OK.

But now he's the fool, because he honestly doesn't get it. He doesn't have any idea about the kind of person he is. I told him, but I don't think he listened – so I guess I have to tell him again. I have to really, really tell him again.

'Are you honestly asking me that?' I say, even though it's so hard to. It's hard to get words out, and hard to keep myself under enough control to express this. But I do it for him. I'd do anything for him. 'Do you really not know? Dillon, you're the least selfish person I've ever known. Even when you think you're being selfish, you're actually not. You've done more for me than any man I've ever known, and even after you've done it you don't think it's anything much. You don't even think this is anything much. Something *that* horrible happened to you, and you're more concerned about why you can't do it again. Do you even understand why you can't do it again? I'll give you a clue: it's not because you're selfish.'

I swipe at my face, but it's no good. It's like trying to stem the tide. And of course when he offers me the edge of his T-shirt, I blubber even harder. My voice sounds like it's been caught in a gravel grinder, and the effect only gets worse after he's said this:

'Are you sure?'

I mean, *how* is he like this? I don't understand how anyone can be like this. The urge to hold his face in my hands is so strong it's almost violent, so I simply do it.

'I'm so sure,' I tell him. 'You're just hurting, baby. You're walking around with a knife in your side, and you just don't know it.'

He puts his hands over mine in this wondering, half-dazed sort of way. Like he's surprised to find them there. He's surprised to find he's still sitting upright, I think, though I'm not sure why. Did he imagine he'd cave in on himself if he finally shared something so serious?

Or is it just such a shocking idea to hear that he's not to blame?

'You're right. You're right. I really didn't know,' he says, which suggests it's the latter. But then he ends it with this: 'Until you took it out.'

So I'm really not sure any more. I'm not sure of anything, apart from the need to do more than hold his face. I want to hold him, all of him, as tightly as I can.

'I thought I was the kind of person who couldn't say something like that, you know?' he says, but I can't say *yes, I understand* here. Because I don't. He's mad, I think, absolutely beyond bonkers, and I need to squeeze him really hard to get all of that crazy out. 'Like I'm supposed to be light and fun and it's such a relief to just …'

'Be you,' I finish, for him, and he answers in the middle of the sweetest sort of surrender – from the weight-bearing expanse of his shoulders, all the way on down.

'Yeah,' he says, as he allows himself relax. As he spreads one big hand over my back, and holds me against him like he's never going to let me go. 'Yeah.'

'You don't ever have to be anyone else with me,' I tell him. 'Because, God knows, I don't have to be anyone else with you.'

And it's true. I don't. I don't care if he sees me cry, or knows that I love him and love him and love him. I don't hesitate before I hold him in my arms, and when he spreads all of his weight on me, I bear it. I'd bear it in the middle of a burning building, thousands of miles from where we are now – in that place he still is sometimes. I'd carry him home, my one, my soulmate, my good, good guy.

I'd carry him home.

CPSIA information can be obtained
at www.ICGtesting.com
Printed in the USA
LVHW032113230620
658291LV00006B/73